ASSAULT WITH A
DEADLY ANIMAL

Realizing he was weaponless, Osbert hastily snatched up an oversized plastic frog, evidently designed to plant marigolds in, and concealed himself in the shadows.

There was enough light in the hallway for Osbert to notice that the evildoer carried a mean-looking switchblade knife. Osbert upended the frog, bated his breath until the would-be amputator came within arm's reach, and slammed the frog down over the miscreant's head. As the now frog-faced villain lunged blindly toward his assailant, Mrs. Phiffer cracked him smartly across the shin with her own chosen weapon, a plaster duck.

"Oh, well ducked, Mrs. Phiffer!" cried Clorinda from the other side of the room. "Jolly good show, Osbert! Chase him over this way so I can get a whack at him, too!"

Other Avon Books by
Charlotte MacLeod
Writing as
Alisa Craig

A DISMAL THING TO DO
THE GRUB-AND-STAKERS MOVE A MOUNTAIN
THE GRUB-AND-STAKERS PINCH A POKE
THE GRUB-AND-STAKERS QUILT A BEE
MURDER GOES MUMMING
A PINT OF MURDER
THE TERRIBLE TIDE
TROUBLE IN THE BRASSES

Other Avon Books by
Charlotte MacLeod

THE BILBAO LOOKING GLASS
THE CONVIVIAL CODFISH
THE CURSE OF THE GIANT HOGWEED
THE FAMILY VAULT
GRAB BAG
THE LUCK RUNS OUT
THE PALACE GUARD
THE PLAIN OLD MAN
REST YOU MERRY
SOMETHING THE CAT DRAGGED IN
THE WITHDRAWING ROOM
WRACK AND RUNE

Charlotte MacLeod
WRITING AS
Alisa Craig

THE GRUB-AND-STAKERS
SPIN A YARN

AVON BOOKS ◆ NEW YORK

AVON BOOKS
A division of
The Hearst Corporation
105 Madison Avenue
New York, New York 10016

Copyright © 1990 by Alisa Craig
Published by arrangement with the author
Library of Congress Catalog Card Number: 89-91928
ISBN: 0-380-75540-8

First Avon Books Printing: February 1990

AVON TRADEMARK REG. U.S. PAT. OFF. AND IN OTHER COUNTRIES, MARCA REGISTRADA, HECHO EN U.S.A.

Printed in the U.S.A.

RA   10   9   8   7   6   5   4   3   2   1

Good-Fortune is a giddy maid,
Fickle and restless as a fawn;
She smooths your hair, and then the jade
Kisses you quickly and is gone.

But Madam Sorrow scorns all this;
She shows no eagerness for flitting;
But with a long and fervent kiss
Sits by your bed—and brings her knitting.

—Heinrich Heine
"Das Glück ist eine leichte Dirne"

Chapter 1

Arethusa Monk, reigning queen of the roguish regency romance, writhed in the grip of ultimate tragedy. She'd just got her heroine, Lady Ermintrude, tied up with strips ruthlessly torn from her own silken petticoat, gagged with her own rich and delicate but not very tasty lace handkerchief, packed neatly inside the evil-smelling gunnysack, and tossed quite unfeelingly into the sinister black closed carriage drawn by four savage walleyed stallions. Burning with the fires of inspiration, Arethusa had reached for another sheet of paper and discovered there was not one single scrap left in the box.

After a moment's desperation and a fruitless effort to thread a roll of pink paper toweling with a design of frolicking hamsters on it into her typewriter before she forgot what she'd meant to write next, she bowed to the inevitable and started out to remedy her lack. Pausing on the doorstep to reassure herself that paper—plain white paper—was indeed what she needed, she happened to notice that she was wearing only bedroom slippers, a nightgown, and a bathrobe.

The bathrobe was, to be sure, a particularly thick, voluminous one that blanketed her from head to toes in the same deep pink fuzz with which her nephew Osbert deemed her brain to be stuffed. As far as modesty went, Arethusa

1

was more than decently covered. Still, she couldn't help feeling some slight hesitation as to whether a pink bathrobe was quite the thing for a woman of serious purpose to wear downtown to the stationery shop.

The right garb for the occasion was important to Arethusa. She prowled through her closets, summarily rejecting sequined evening gowns, flowing caftans, her billowing purple cloak, even her cartwheel hat with the night-blooming cereus on it. Somewhere among the depths, she came at last upon a tailored coat and skirt in sensible lilac tweed.

Arethusa supposed she must have bought the suit sometime or other. She couldn't recall when, where, why, or whether she'd ever worn it before; but there was nothing remarkable about that. Not remembering things was rather a specialty of hers. As she donned the skirt and buttoned the matching lilac silk blouse, she made a ferocious effort to concentrate on remembering the tiny jeweled dagger she'd secreted in Lady Ermintrude's garter before she'd sent her heroine alone on her parlous mission to the old mill at midnight. She also concentrated on that ream of plain white typing paper she must perforce obtain from Mr. Gumpert at Ye Village Stationer before she could do whatever she'd meant to be done with the dagger. What that was, Arethusa couldn't remember.

No matter, the action would come to her just so long as she didn't lose her mental grip on the dagger itself. Muttering over and over "A jeweled dagger and a ream of plain white paper," Arethusa exchanged her slippers for gray kid walking shoes, swirled her flowing mane of glossy black hair into a businesslike chignon, and crowned it with a severe helmet of dark green suede that had long gray goose quills shooting out in various directions. Granting her reflection in the mirror a purposeful nod while still chanting "A jeweled dagger and a ream of plain white paper," she set forth.

Arethusa didn't have far to go; it would have taken some ingenuity or a lot of walking in circles to go far in Lobelia Falls. From her ancestral dwelling to the town's main and indeed only thoroughfare was a matter of but thirty-seven brisk strides for a tall, vigorous woman in the prime of life. From her corner to Mr. Gumpert's shop called for rather more in the way of striding, however. Arethusa had to pass the public library, the local branch of the Royal Bank of Canada, and the police station which was also the residence of Sergeant Donald MacVicar and his wife, Margaret. She then crossed over and made a smart left turn at Miss Jane Fuzzywuzzy's Yarnery.

The yarn shop was a recent addition to Lobelia Falls's amenities. Miss Jane Fuzzywuzzy's lease having run out at the shopping mall in Scottsbeck, the proprietor had decided to flee the urban sprawl and emigrate to where the real knitters grew thickest. She was now getting nicely settled into a shop that had stood empty since Sergeant MacVicar had shipped the former occupant off to jail for malfeasance and a few other things.

Miss Jane, who was in fact Mrs. Prudence Derbyshire (though long widowed), was even now out sweeping her sidewalk as was her cleanly habit. She evinced no surprise when Arethusa hove into sight talking to herself. She did, however, exhibit a certain degree of perturbation when a smallish middle-aged man, wearing a trench coat with the collar turned up and a felt hat with the brim turned far down, pulled up to the curb in a bullet-riddled car of Japanese make, leaped past her, and rushed into the Yarnery through the door she'd left open to air the place out.

Wise in the ways of yarn buyers, however, Miss Jane did not rush after him. He might better be left to browse at will among the yarn bins while she remained to capture the last scarlet leaf from the huge maple tree that was shedding all over her share of the public walkway, for autumn had come to Ontario. She also wished to greet Miss Monk. She did this with some empressement, not because Miss Arethusa Monk was a particularly good customer, or indeed a customer at all; and not because Miss Monk was a celebrity. It was because Arethusa was the aunt of Osbert Monk, another celebrity better known to his vast reading public as Lex Laramie, but best known among natives of Lobelia Falls as husband to the former Dittany Henbit.

Let it not be thought that Miss Jane was a snob. Granted, Henbits had been among the first settlers of Lobelia Falls. Granted, Dittany's great-grandmother had been a founding member of the Grub-and-Stakers Gardening and Roving Club of which Dittany herself was now Honorable Secretary. Granted, Dittany was on the governing board of the Aralia Polyphema Architrave Memorial Museum. What counted with Miss Jane Fuzzywuzzy was that Dittany Henbit Monk was, and had been for the past several months, great with child.

Or so her friends and relatives had assumed when they'd started flocking to Miss Jane's for yarn to knit tiny garments. Once it had been definitely established that young Mrs. Monk was expecting not one but actually two bundles of joy, news of the impending double-header had sent the knitters stampeding back for the wherewithal to fashion duplicates. It was really young Mrs. Monk who'd got the Yarnery off to a rousing start in its new location. Therefore, whereas she had ignored the man, Miss Jane could hardly be faulted for feeling that a Monk in the hand was worth a good deal more than a stranger in a trench coat. She paused in her sweeping and made her manners to the lady.

"Lovely morning, Miss Monk."

"Hello, Miss Wuzzy. A jeweled dagger and a ream of plain white paper," Arethusa replied courteously.

Finding nothing remarkable in this reply, Miss Jane offered a comment on the weather to which Arethusa vouchsafed a gracious nod. To the passerby, had there been one at the moment, the two women would have offered an interesting contrast: the handsome, statuesque Arethusa in her businesslike tweeds and purposeful quills; the long-faced, rawboned Miss Jane in the frilly white apron and mobcap she affected during business hours.

Nobody had ever been mean enough to tell Miss Jane how ill these whimsies became her. It was perhaps not surprising, however, that when the man in the trench coat came stumbling out of the Yarnery in obvious distress of both mind and body and leaving a trail of little red splashes on the sidewalk, clearly visible now that Miss Jane had swept away the red leaves which might now be realized to have hidden the splashes he'd left on the way in, he turned not to the woman in the silly ruffled cap but to the one in the efficient green cloche.

Grabbing Arethusa frantically by her left arm, he gasped out, "The raveled sleeve!" Then his breath failed, his knees gave way, he crumpled into a pathetic heap of mackintosh at her gray-clad feet. Now that the two women had a clear view of his back, it was easy enough to spot the bullet hole with the dark red stain around it.

"Will you look at that?" said Miss Jane in understandable annoyance. "And to think I just finished washing my shop floor about two minutes ago!"

"Inconsiderate," Arethusa agreed absently. "What do you suppose he meant by 'the raveled sleeve'?"

"Must have been having trouble with his knitting," Miss Jane replied. "Lots of men knit, you know. Sergeant MacVicar tells me knitting used to be quite the thing among the Highland shepherds when he was a boy in Lochtrackenchie. Oh dear, what a way to start the day! My cousins from England are coming this afternoon and I did so want to have everything nice for them. Would you mind stepping across the street and giving the police station doorbell a punch?"

"Not at all. A jeweled dagger and a ream of plain white paper."

Arethusa was about to step off the curb when a second bullet-riddled automobile screeched to a halt in front of her. Two more men wearing trench coats with the collars turned up and felt hats with the brims turned down hurtled from the car, crouched beside the supine form on the sidewalk, and feverishly rifled its pockets while the two women watched in understandable bewilderment.

Their search appeared unavailing, for one of the men leaped to his feet, grabbed Arethusa by the same arm the first man had grabbed her by, and demanded savagely, "Where is it? What did he tell you?"

"A jeweled dagger and a ream of plain white paper," Arethusa replied automatically.

This was clearly not the reply the man had expected. "Are you sure that's what he—"

"Cheese it, the cops!" shouted the other.

True enough, the police station door had opened. Sergeant MacVicar was descending its front steps with as much haste as the dignity of his position would allow. Hastily grabbing their fallen colleague or adversary as the case might have been, one by the feet and one by the shoulders, the two dumped his body into their car. Just the way Lady Ermintrude's fell captors had bundled her into the coach, Arethusa noted. It was reassuring to see that she'd been accurate in her description.

She might have enjoyed and even benefited from a moment's professional chat with the dumpers, but this was not to be. One of them leaped into the car they'd both arrived in. The other leaped into the car which the dead man, for he was surely that, had been driving. By the time Sergeant MacVicar reached the spot where the red splashes lay thickest on the sidewalk, the two cars had roared off. The sergeant vouchsafed the two women a courteous nod and opened the investigation.

"Noo then, ladies, can you tell me what that was all about?"

"A jeweled dagger and a ream of plain white paper," said Arethusa.

"That wasn't it at all." Miss Jane was too exasperated by now to be diplomatic, even toward a Monk. "This first man—the one who bled all over everything—was knitting a sweater."

"Oh aye?"

"Well, it had to be a sweater, didn't it? Why else would he have had to unravel the sleeve? I didn't know the man was bleeding, of course, or I wouldn't have kept him waiting. Goodness knows what he's done to my nice clean floor. I can't imagine what my cousins are going to think. It's their first visit to Canada and I did so want them to carry a good impression back home. And I have to tell

you, Miss Monk, that if you say 'a jeweled dagger and a
ream of plain white paper' one more time, I really do
believe I'll take after you with this broomstick.''

"This is no time for hysterics," Arethusa replied severely. "Pull yourself together, Miss Wuzzy."

"My name is not Miss Wuzzy!"

"Noo, noo," said Sergeant MacVicar.

"Well, she keeps calling me Miss Monk," Arethusa
pouted. "I'm just trying to remember what it is I have to
buy at Mr. Gumpert's. I realize there's a worldwide con-
spiracy afoot to keep writers from getting any work done,
but I did think I might be allowed to accomplish a simple
errand without being subjected to threats of physical attack
by a woman dressed up as a sheep."

"I am not dressed up as a sheep," cried Miss Jane. "I
dress up like Miss Jane Fuzzywuzzy in order to advertise
my shop."

"Forsooth?" scoffed Arethusa. "Then you'd have done
better to name the place Uncle Wiggly's. Now if you two
will excuse me, I'll get on with my business."

"One moment, Miss Monk, if I may so address you
without giving offense," said Sergeant MacVicar. "Can
you give me further particulars concerning yon puzzling
incident?"

"What is there to tell? This international spy came
whizzing up and jumped out of his car—the one with the
most bullet holes in it—and ran into the Yarnery. Then he
came running out and grabbed me by the arm and started
to talk about the sleeve to which the lady at my right has
already alluded. He evidently inferred that I was the proprietor of the shop, though I cannot imagine why. Anyway, before I could correct his misapprehension, he dropped
dead. At least one may assume he was dead, since he
raised no protest when the other two spies came along and
took him away."

"Er—h'mph. How do you know the men were spies,
Miss Monk?"

"Because they were all wearing trench coats with the
collars turned up and felt hats with the brims turned down

over their eyes. They have to, it's in the international spy code. The first man may well have been a counterspy, which would explain his interest in Miss Wuzzy's shop. Or perhaps he was only confused. Judging from the memoirs one reads in the newspapers, assuming one does, spies customarily exist in a perpetual state of bewilderment as to whose side they're on at any given moment. It's possible, I suppose, that Miss Wuzzy here is a spy also, which would account for the sheep disguise. Would you care to confirm or deny the hypothesis, Miss Wuzzy?''

"I couldn't be bothered." Miss Jane did look a bit like Uncle Wiggly when she sniffed. "I'm merely a victim of circumstance and you're talking through that silly hat as usual. Those were no international spies, they were just a pack of hoodlums messing up my nice, clean sidewalk, not to mention the floor I'd just finished mopping."

Miss Jane shook her broom in total exasperation. "Sergeant MacVicar, you'll have to excuse me. I must see what's happened inside the Yarnery. It's tough enough getting established in a new location without the customers having to wade through puddles of gore to get to the yarn bins. Speaking of which, would you mind mentioning to Mrs. MacVicar that the blue shetland she wanted for your grandson's birthday cap and mittens came in late yesterday afternoon? I meant to pop over and tell her myself, but it slipped my mind. I was busy getting ready for my cousins, you know. Actually, they're putting up at the inn, but of course I'll have them over to the house for meals and—''

"Mrs. MacVicar will understand," said the sergeant. "Shall we go in together?"

They did. Arethusa remained outside, frowning down at the spots on the sidewalk and wondering why she wasn't at home writing. As she thus pondered, she heard herself being hailed by a familiar and well-loved voice.

"Whoo-hoo, Arethusa!"

"Clorinda!" Arethusa whirled to embrace the petite figure in the scarlet cartwheel hat and the elegant gold-and-silver eyeglasses who hurtled toward her on three-inch heels regardless of slippery fallen leaves and possible cracks in the sidewalk.

Back when she'd been first the wife, then the widow of Dittany's father, Clorinda Henbit had been not only the star of the Traveling Thespians and two-time winner of the Grand Free-for-All gold medal in archery but also the bosom friend of Arethusa Monk. Now married to Bert Pusey, a jovial salesman who traveled successfully in fashion eyewear, Clorinda was living a life far better suited to her ebullient personality and loving every minute of it. However, the lure of impending grandmotherhood and the chance of spending some time with her old friend had brought her flying back to Lobelia Falls.

Never one to tackle a situation by halves, Clorinda had been knitting up a storm ever since Dittany had managed to track her down at an optometrists' convention in Saskatoon and break the joyful tidings. Starting with booties, she'd worked her way up via bonnets and sacques to carriage robes and buntings. Even as she emoted her rapture at being able to walk down the street and bump into her favorite female in all the world, not counting her daughter and whichever twin turned out to be a girl, she was fishing in her pocketbook for a twist of yarn.

"Come on, Arethusa. I've got to see whether Miss Jane has any more of this pink left. I started a bed jacket for Dittany and ran out halfway up the left front."

"At last count, Dittany had been the increasingly less grateful recipient of seven knitted bed jackets: two pink, one blue, one white with pink and blue trimming, one yellow, one lilac, and one variegated," Arethusa pointed out. "Zilla Trott is knitting her a red one with fluffy pompons in case the weather turns cold. And if you're pondering the advisability of ripping out what you've done and starting another bunting, forget it. She's up to her armpits in tiny garments already. Egad, will this madness never cease?"

"Probably not," Clorinda admitted. "You know the old crowd. Once they get the bit between their teeth, there's no stopping them. But don't worry, dear, I've thought of something else.''

"Gadzooks, it needed only that!"

"Don't be negative, dear, it makes wrinkles. I just got the idea that now everyone's nicely started and the yarn shop's so handy, we might as well keep on and knit enough tiny garments for all the underprivileged wee ones in Canada.''

"What if the wee ones already have enough tiny garments?''

"Then we knit some for the States, and maybe Europe.''

"Thence to the Third World, I assume?''

"Well, dear, it would be good for détente. Do quit standing there darting those quills at me. I've got to get cracking. By the way, what are you doing out roaming the roads during your usual work time? Don't tell me inspiration has flagged.''

"Perish the thought! I'm roaming the roads because I have an important business appointment.''

"Really? I must say you do look awfully brisk and competent. I don't recall ever having seen you in that suit before. Where did you get it?''

"I can't remember.''

"Well, I don't suppose it matters. Whoever it was, they won't have one left in my size anyway. They never do. Where is your appointment?''

Arethusa shook her quills sadly and slowly from side to side. "I can't remember that either.''

Chapter 2

"Never mind, dear, I expect it will come to you." Clorinda expected no such thing, but one had to maintain a façade of optimism with Arethusa or be driven to desperation in consequence. "Let's get that pink yarn before I forget what I came for, too. I can always give the bed jacket to the Russians and call it *glasnost.*"

"We can't go in there," Arethusa protested. "The Yarnery's knee-deep in gore and Sergeant MacVicar is detecting."

"Darling, do save your tall tales for your vast army of—heavens to Betsy! What are those red spots all over the sidewalk?"

"Gore, of course. Spies are by nature copious bleeders."

"What spies?" demanded Clorinda. "Arethusa, have you any idea what you're talking about?"

"Certainly I have. I'm talking about those three international spies who dropped by here a few minutes ago. The first one had been shot and was dripping all over the place. Miss Wuzzy appeared to be somewhat miffed about the mess he was making."

"Do you mean Miss Jane?"

"Is that what she's calling herself now?"

"That seems to be what she prefers. I wish she wouldn't, it's so confusing with Jane Binkle living right next door to—Arethusa, what about those other two spies? Are they the ones who shot him?"

"I really couldn't say. He'd already been shot when he got here, his car was quite riddled with bullet holes. The other car was not so much riddled as pocked. I think I mean pocked."

"Pocked sounds all right to me. Were the two men pocked, too?"

"I saw no sign of pockment. Or is it pocation? At any rate they didn't appear to be bleeding, unless they were doing it in a civil and restrained manner."

"Where are they now? Did Sergeant MacVicar arrest them?"

Arethusa shook her hat decisively, causing considerable agitation among the quills. "He didn't get the chance. They were in the act of departing as he arrived. The two unpocked ones, if I'm using the term correctly, took the pocked one away."

"You're sure he was pocked and not riddled?" said Clorinda.

"Quite sure. All I saw was one bullet hole in the back of his trench coat, which is how I knew he was a spy like the other two."

"Because of one single hole? That would hardly seem definitive to me."

"Not because of the hole," Arethusa replied with quiet dignity. "Because of the trench coats and the felt hats with the brims pulled down over their eyes."

"Arethusa, dear, spies don't go around in trench coats riddling cars and pocking people. Spies wear long black overcoats and carry umbrellas with poisoned darts hidden in the shafts. I believe these men must in fact have been racketeers, also known as gangsters. They riddle the cars with their tommy guns, which they carry around in violin cases. Do you recall whether any of the three happened to have a violin case with him?"

"To the best of my recollection, no. They could have left them in their cars, I suppose. Are you quite sure about the trench coats, Clorinda?"

"Oh yes, positive. Trench coats and pulled-down felt hats are de rigueur in gangland circles. To hide those awful zoot suits, you know, and their slicked-down hair. I've watched them scads of times in the movies. Dear old Ditson never could pass up a George Raft or Edward G. Robinson rerun. I never understood why; Ditson was the sweetest, gentlest, most law-abiding man who ever lived. Hurry, Arethusa, never mind the gore. We've got to let Sergeant MacVicar know Lobelia Falls is being taken over by the mob."

To refuse such a call to civic duty would have been wholly graceless. Heedless of the splashes on the sidewalk, Arethusa turned toward the Yarnery. "Very well, Clorinda, if you say so. Perhaps I did get mixed up about the trench coats."

"One can't blame you, dear," her friend consoled her. "They're hardly in your period. If it had been a question of perukes and dueling swords, you'd have got it straight in no time flat. Ah, good morning, Miss Jane. Oh dear, he did bleed a lot, didn't he? Before I forget it, I wish you'd try to match this wool for me. After you've finished mopping up the blood, of course. Sergeant MacVicar, I do hope you have a few tommy guns over at the station."

Sergeant MacVicar was not a man to be easily disconcerted, particularly not by Clorinda, whom he knew of old. "I have not. You did not want one for yourself, surely?"

"Heavens to Betsy, no! I just want you to be prepared for the influx of gangsters. Or racketeers. I'm not quite sure whether the terms are synonymous, but I'm quite clear on the inadvisability of your letting Lobelia Falls be taken over by them. Ditson might have rather enjoyed having a few around because he used to think they were all like George Raft; but Bert, my current husband, as you of course know, takes an extremely dim view of mobsters. He's run into a few real ones during the course of his career, and is quite firm in his belief that there's not a heart of gold among them."

"An assumption in which I heartily concur," said the sergeant. "Do I deduce that your friend has been describing yon incident which led to the desecration of Mrs. Derbyshire's clean floor?"

"Derbyshire?" Arethusa, who had allowed her attention to slip back a century or two, perked to attention. "Is that another of her aliases, forsooth?"

The proprietress parked her mop in the bucket, drew herself up to her full height, and gave Arethusa a far from sheepish look. "My proper name, as Sergeant MacVicar can testify since it's on my vending license, is Prudence Elizabeth Derbyshire, or if you prefer, Mrs. Bentinck Derbyshire. Liberated woman though I am, I retained the name of my former husband. I should have thought the allusion to my shop name was obvious, especially to those in the literary profession, but I find that not all authors are as well up on the classics as one might expect. I've grown quite used to being called Miss Jane and don't mind a bit. Advertising my shop is how I look at it. I must say, however, that nobody has ever before called me Miss Wuzzy," she added with imperfectly concealed rancor.

In the bright lexicon of Clorinda Henbit Pusey there was no such grim word as rancor. "Then you've had a new experience," she cried gaily. "How delightful for you! I always count that day lost in which I haven't had at least one new experience."

Miss Jane, or Mrs. Prudence, retrieved her mop and went back to work. "I've had quite enough new experiences, thank you," she snapped as she scrubbed viciously at a gummy red spot. "Whatever that man's problems might have been, faulty coagulation sure wasn't one of them."

Comparing notes later on, Clorinda had to agree with Arethusa that the yarn lady did look a good deal like a lost sheep when she forgot to smile. Clorinda pointed out that Miss Jane probably resembled a happy sheep when she did smile. As neither of the friends had ever seen a sheep looking more than placidly content, they decided to give Miss Jane the benefit of the doubt and table the question for lack of data. At the moment, however, they, like the proprietor and Sergeant MacVicar, were more concerned with the dire tale told by the now partly erased bloodstains.

"What puzzles me," said Clorinda, "is why that gangster should have rushed in here and then rushed straight out again."

"He did not rush straight in and rush straight out." Sergeant MacVicar was, as well he should have been, a stickler for accuracy in observation. "Judging from the trail he left, he rushed in and circled around yon island display of baby yarn in the center of the room in a counterclockwise direction, passing the service counter on his way out."

"He was probably looking for me," said Miss Jane.

"He couldn't have been," said Arethusa. "He rushed right past you both coming and going."

"But that was most likely because he didn't realize who she was," Clorinda pointed out. "How could he, when he'd never been in the shop before? Had he, Miss Jane?"

"Never laid eyes on him in my life. And never will again, from the way he looked when they lugged him off."

"Yes, it's sad to think he never did know which was who. He must have thought you were in charge, Arethusa, since it was you he approached about his knitting problem. If in fact he had one," Clorinda sniffed. "That was no doubt a ruse or a hidden threat. What he must have meant, Miss Jane, was that he'd rip out all your sweaters if you didn't pay up. That's the sort of thing the mob would do."

"But he couldn't," cried Miss Jane. "The place was full of sweaters. Lots of customers bring me their pieces after they've done the knitting, you know, and I do the assembling and blocking for them. The true fit's in the blocking and it's an art to get it right, if I do say so. Why, I have half a dozen sitting on my work table right now. I'd better go make sure he hasn't gone and bled all over them just to assert his evil will."

"He'd have had to bleed backwards," Arethusa pointed out. "Considering his enfeebled condition, that would have presented no small problem in logistics." A writer of regency romances, in which heroes and villains were always fighting duels and odding each other's bodkins, naturally had to think of such things.

"Anyway, he didn't." Miss Jane was now at the work table behind the island display, sorting through a pile of knitted bits and pieces. "They're all right, thank goodness. Now let's see, Mrs. Pusey, you wanted the two-ply Babytoes Blush, didn't you? How many balls?"

"How clever of you to ask," said Clorinda. "Let's see, what did I want it for? Oh yes, to finish a bed jacket I started out of what I had left over from the bunting. Or was it the carriage robe? Anyway, it's for my daughter. Or somebody's daughter," she qualified, having to face the possibility that she might have got a wee bit carried away by an excess of zeal as far as Dittany's needs were concerned.

Clorinda and Miss Jane became involved in technical discussion. Sergeant MacVicar, having accomplished what little he could in the shop, went back to the station to put out a request for the apprehension of two bullet-riddled passenger cars last seen leaving Lobelia Falls, one with only a driver and one with a live driver and a what might or might not have been but probably was a dead passenger, all three of them wearing trench coats and felt hats.

Arethusa, left to herself beside the four-ply worsteds, was doing some earnest thinking. Why was she wearing this unfamiliar lilac tweed suit? What was the dark secret that gnawed at her very vitals? Who was the intense-looking woman standing in front of the mirror that Miss Jane kept hanging next to the work table so that customers could see how handsome they looked in their artistically blocked cardigans?

After a while, it dawned on Arethusa that the woman was herself. Others had often compared her to the Gainsborough portrait of Mrs. Siddons as Lady Macbeth. Now she too caught the likeness. Perhaps it was all those daggerlike goose feathers shooting out of her hat. "Is this a dagger that I see before me?" she murmured whimsically.

Zounds, that was it! "A jeweled dagger and a ream of plain white paper," she exclaimed, and bolted from the shop.

Naturally assuming the worst, Clorinda hastily completed her negotiations with Miss Jane and rushed after her friend. Instead of a semi-demented wanderer, she found a briskly competent Arethusa standing at the counter of Ye Village Stationer, asking Mr. Gumpert for a ream of plain white paper and selecting for herself a new purple pen and a box of typewriter ribbons as a special treat.

Greatly relieved, Clorinda picked out a funny card to send to Bert and two extra-long pencils with little clowns on the tops, one red and one blue. "They're for the twins' pencil boxes," she explained.

"A trifle premature, aren't you?" said Mr. Gumpert.

"I like to think ahead."

What Clorinda really liked was to buy things like foot-long pencils with little clowns on top, as Arethusa well knew. "What do you want to do now?" she asked indulgently.

"Don't you want to get back to your writing?" Clorinda replied.

"Not particularly. Lady Ermintrude can stay tucked up in her sack a while longer, she's used to being abducted. You, on the other hand, may have to rush off at a moment's notice to another optical convention. I tell you what, let's go over to your house and have a cup of tea."

In point of fact, the house now belonged to Dittany, and it was Dittany who'd refilled the kettle as soon as she'd heard the click of feminine heels and the sound of familiar voices coming down Applewood Avenue. Filling the kettle was no great chore; she'd been in the kitchen anyway, making hermits. During the earlier part of her wedded life Dittany would have been more apt to make molasses cookies with little crinkles around the edges, but those involved more bending, stretching, and juggling of cookie sheets than she found comfortable in her present condition. Hermits could be baked in one flat pan and cut up afterwards. Once she'd got her pan in the oven and the tea in the pot, she was glad enough to collapse into Gram Henbit's old rocking chair and visit a while.

"What's new downtown, Mum?"

Her mother's reply was hardly what she'd expected. "The mob is taking over Lobelia Falls."

Arethusa shook her quills. "Clorinda, I'm still not convinced it's the mob. I've thought it over carefully, and I'm quite sure there were no violin cases at the scene. You are quite positive international spies never wear trench coats?"

"But of course spies wear trench coats," said Dittany. "Ask anybody. Whatever are you talking about, Arethusa?"

"About the two men in the bullet-riddled car who—"

"Excuse me," said Clorinda firmly. "The car in which the two men arrived was not riddled, merely pocked. It was the first man who came in the bullet-riddled car, the one who bled all over Miss Jane Fuzzywuzzy's floor."

"Whoa!" said Dittany. "Don't say another word till I've checked the hermits and pried Osbert away from the ostriches."

"What for?" demanded Arethusa, sneaking a poke at the hermits and burning her finger slightly. "Can't you let sleeping Osberts lie, forsooth?"

Osbert Monk, nephew to Arethusa, husband to Dittany, son-in-law to Clorinda, and prospective father to the twins, was not sleeping, as the steady tap-tapping from the dining room attested. The house was not small, there was no special reason why Osbert had to work squashed into a little alcove off the dining room. However, that alcove was where Dittany had set up her secretarial service back when she was a self-supporting spinster. That was where she still typed up Osbert's final drafts and answered his fan mail; and where Dittany typed was where Osbert preferred to type also, for his was a love that transcended even the minor inconveniences which can be so much more testing than major calamities. The two in the kitchen were not at all surprised to hear glad cries and small sounds of the sort not usually made by Western writers interrupted in the midst of an ostrich stampede unless the interruptee is particularly fond of the interrupter.

Clorinda smiled the indulgent smile of a doting mother-in-law. Arethusa snorted. True to their respective daughter's and niece-in-law's admonition, however, neither said a word until Osbert and Dittany got stuck in the kitchen doorway.

"Oops!" said Dittany. "I keep forgetting there are four of us now. Back up a little, darling, and take your arm away from where my waist used to be. Only temporarily, of course. You can put it back as soon as we get clear."

"Aren't they sweet?" whispered Clorinda.

"I find them sickening," snarled Arethusa. "One might think the father of a growing family would have learned a little self-restraint by now."

"One might think a person who's written seventy-three amalgamations of ill-chosen verbiage which are loosely referred to as books would know how to spell words of one syllable by now," Osbert retorted. "What's all this about the mob muscling in on Miss Jane Fuzzywuzzy?"

"International spies," said Arethusa.

"They sound more like saboteurs if they were bleeding all over the mohair," said Dittany. "Maybe they were sent by a rival yarn shop to drive Miss Jane out of business. Start over again from the beginning, so Osbert can catch the nuances."

The witnesses were happy to oblige, pausing only to replenish their teacups from time to time and munch on hermits hot from the oven. Once Osbert found out Sergeant MacVicar was involved, he paid careful attention, breaking into the narrative only when it strayed too far from the point, which happened about one sentence out of three.

"Wait a minute, Aunt Arethusa. Go back to where the second man grabbed you by the arm. What did he say?"

"He said, 'What did he say?' "

"And what did you say?"

"Meseems I may have said, 'A jeweled dagger and a ream of plain white paper,' " his aunt replied somewhat sheepishly. "I was trying to remember what I wanted to write about the dagger till I'd got the paper to put it down on."

"Yes, of course." Far from greeting the remark with derision, Osbert understood perfectly. He'd had the same problem with a stray ostrich only the previous Thursday. "And what did the man say to that?"

"I forget. I have a vague idea he may have begun to request clarification when he was interrupted."

"By you?"

"No, by his confederate. The other spy who said, 'Cheese it, the cops.' They cheesed, which effectively terminated the conversation."

Osbert frowned. "Aunt Arethusa, are you quite sure he said 'Cheese it, the cops'?"

"What else would he have said?" Clorinda broke in. "The expression is standard among members of the underworld. I distinctly recall having heard gangsters say, 'Cheese it, the cops' any number of times on those reruns my darling Ditson used to watch. You wouldn't remember, Dittany. Daddy used to send you to bed before the gangster movies came on. He liked to think of you as a delicate bud of innocent maidenhood."

"As any doting father naturally would." Osbert had been giving the subject of fatherhood a good deal of thought lately, for reasons that were daily becoming more obvious. "But, Mother Clorinda, those movies were made back in the nineteen-thirties. 'Cheese it, the cops' would nowadays be considered hackneyed, trite, and dated."

"It did cross my mind at the time that the words sounded a trifle démodé," Arethusa conceded. "It struck me that these might have been elderly spies trying to pass themselves off as cousins of Al Capone. On the other hand,'' she added in deference to Clorinda, ''they may have been young gangsters on a nostalgia kick, if I employ the correct phraseology. Vintage clothes and swing music are back in fashion, why not vintage colloquialisms? You might perhaps inquire of Sergeant MacVicar as to the current status of 'Cheese it' in the underworld lexicon.''

''A splendid suggestion, Aunt Arethusa,'' cried Osbert. ''Feel like taking the kids for a walk, darling? Let's you and I go ask him right now.''

Chapter 3

"Perchance we ought to go, too," said Arethusa.

"I don't see why it should take a whole posse to ask one simple question," Dittany replied, knowing full well that Osbert was champing at the bit to get into harness as Lobelia Falls's one and only official unpaid deputy. "Surely you and Mum have more urgent and meaningful things to do."

Her mother was quick to take the hint. "Indeed we do, now that you remind us. What's the most urgent and meaningful duty on our agenda at the moment, Arethusa?"

"Hermits."

"You've had enough hermits. How about our going back to your house? You can fish Lady Ermintrude out of the sack while I try on all your hats. Then we'll have lunch at the inn. After that, we'll think of something."

Secure in the knowledge that her mother would in fact think of something, Dittany handed Arethusa the ream of plain white paper she'd been about to forget and shepherded them all out the door, not bothering to lock up because people usually didn't in Lobelia Falls. At the corner of Applewood and Chestnut they split up, the two senior members of the party skipping off like a pair of sixth-graders wearing each other's hats and the prospective parents making their decorous way toward the police station.

"I do love having your mother around," said Osbert. "She's so good at keeping Arethusa off our backs. Do you suppose any of that stuff they were talking about really happened?"

"Well, I find it hard to entertain the supposition that Miss Jane Fuzzywuzzy would scrub her shop floor twice in one morning if she weren't confronted with actual blood-stains," Dittany replied. "And I'm ready to believe Arethusa did tell that man 'A jeweled dagger and a ream of plain white paper.' That's precisely the sort of thing Arethusa would say if she found herself with a bullet-riddled corpse at her feet and an international spy or a superannuated mobster, as the case may have been, clutching her by the arm. Anyway, I expect the MacVicars themselves will have seen at least part of what went on. They're right across the street and never miss a thing, as you well know."

"Yes, dear, I know. You'd better let me lift you over that curbstone, it's an awfully high step for a fragile flower of femininity in your condition. Maybe I ought to run for Road Commissioner and get it lowered."

"Would you really do that for me, Osbert?"

"Sweetheart, you know there's nothing in this world I wouldn't do for you. Except of course to let Arethusa move in with us. Did I tell you she wants us to name the twins Flossie and Freddy?"

"No," said the fragile flower, "but I might have guessed. She still reads the entire Bobbsey Twins series straight through religiously once a year."

"It shows in her writing," snarled Osbert. "I wonder if Aunt Arethusa's the only best-selling author alive today who dedicates all her books to the Stratemeyer syndicate."

"Darling," Dittany protested, "I do wish you wouldn't tell fibs in front of the children. Arethusa's dedicated a book to me and one to Mum and even one to Ethel."

Osbert welcomed a chance to change the subject. "Speaking of Ethel, where's she been all morning?"

Ethel was the family friend, commonly referred to as a dog although her true lineage was anybody's guess.

"Up on the Enchanted Mountain watching the acorns drop, I expect. Don't try to evade the issue, Osbert. Arethusa even dedicated a book to you."

"Sure she did. 'To my renegade nephew, Osbert Reginald Monk, in the no doubt vain hope of reforming his literary tastes.' What's my son going to think of me as a role model when he reads that? Furthermore, I'd like to know what makes Aunt Arethusa think she's such an authority on taste. Hers is all in her mouth, which is generally full of our food. We may not have been able to reshape her taste, but we've sure as heck done plenty to reshape Aunt Arethusa."

"Yes, dear," said Dittany. "Shall we ring the bell or just walk in?"

Actually they did neither. By the time they got to the police station, Mrs. MacVicar was waiting for them at the open door. "Ah, there you are, Deputy Monk. Sergeant MacVicar was hoping you'd show up. Go straight into the office. Dittany, do you want to go with him or would you rather sit in the living room? I have some lovely photos of our grandson. He has a tooth."

"How nice! Perhaps he'll get another soon, then he can bite. But I do want to hear about the excitement over at Miss Jane Fuzzywuzzy's. I don't suppose it was half so wild as Mother's and Arethusa's descriptions."

"Perhaps not," Mrs. MacVicar conceded, "but it was wild enough, I can tell you! I wouldn't have believed such a thing could happen right here on Main Street myself; but there they were, two hoodlums in trench coats looking like something out of a George Raft movie, lugging that dead man off like a sack of meal. And there really were bullet holes in both cars. I saw them plainly enough with my own two eyes."

That settled the matter. Margaret MacVicar could no more take a liberty with the truth than she could have shown up at the Presbyterian Church on a Sunday morning in her bathing suit. The two women exchanged nods and followed Deputy Monk into the left front room that, with a large storage closet for the files and spare handcuffs, comprised the Lobelia Falls police station.

The interview didn't really tell the Monks a great deal. To their surprise, either the MacVicars' own or Miss Jane's testimony corroborated in virtually every detail what they'd already heard from Arethusa and Clorinda. Arethusa had in fact said 'A jeweled dagger and a ream of plain white paper' to the man who'd accosted her over the body of his fallen comrade or adversary, as the case might have been. Sergeant MacVicar divulged the fact that Miss Jane had been confident of Arethusa's exact words because Arethusa had already spoken them twice before apropos of nothing that made any sense to Miss Jane, and had called her Miss Wuzzy into the bargain.

Sergeant MacVicar himself had heard Arethusa deliver her enigmatic utterance yet again and had received an explanation which struck him as a sensible enough one by her standards. According to information received from Mr. Gumpert, she had subsequently entered Ye Village Stationer and purchased a ream of plain white paper. Dittany's assurance that Arethusa had actually carried the paper home and was perhaps even now at work on the jeweled dagger wrapped up that piece of the puzzle to everyone's satisfaction.

Pleased with the progress thus far, Sergeant MacVicar confided that Miss Jane had seemed more annoyed by the bloodstains on her clean floor than she had been over the sinister actions of the trench-coated interlopers. He and Osbert both found this attitude hard to credit and wondered whether Miss Jane might bear a spot of investigation. Dittany and Mrs. MacVicar insisted it was perfectly reasonable and men just didn't understand women.

They also saw no cause for suspicion in Miss Jane's having taken umbrage because the first man had grabbed Arethusa and not her. "I'd be slightly ticked off, myself, if I'd gone to the trouble of looking like a sheep in order to advertise the fact that I sold wool and he didn't even bother to notice," was Dittany's reaction.

"And I might be a trifle miffed, too, if I were a woman

not well-endowed with that comeliness of face and form which is alleged to attract members of the opposite gender and got passed over for a smasher like Arethusa,'' said Mrs. MacVicar, ''particularly if I was also the one who was stuck with having to re-scrub her floor. Don't you two bloodhounds go pestering that poor woman any more today. Miss Jane's had a ghastly morning so far, and I shouldn't be surprised if things got worse as the day rolls on. Just look out the window.''

A steady stream of people who might or might not be customers were going into the yarn shop, having to push their way through a crowd on the sidewalk pointing with ghoulish enthusiasm to various by now dark and trodden spatters on the pavement Miss Jane had tried so hard to keep clean. ''I must say I wish our telephone system always worked as well as the local grapevine,'' Mrs. MacVicar added with no little acerbity.

''Aye,'' said Sergeant MacVicar. ''The fiery cross has blazed across the back fences and the clans are gathering. Hoots toots, there's a new face in town. Who's yon dapper fellow with the natty umbrella?''

Well might the sergeant ask. From the well-polished uppers of his custom-made black shoes to the rolled brim on his square-set gray homburg, the middle-aged, good-looking, rather slightly built man walking toward them was a vision of sartorial elegance in the Savile Row manner. Not even Osbert's agent from Toronto, who visited Lobelia Falls fairly often now that he was in love with Arethusa, ever managed to look that urbane.

''Maybe he's from Scottsbeck,'' was the best Osbert could offer.

''He looks awfully respectable for Scottsbeck,'' Dittany demurred. ''Oh! Mum said the biggest reason Miss Jane was so upset about the bloodstains was that she's expecting her cousins from England and she was trying to get everything nice for them. I'll bet that's one of the cousins. The other must have stopped at the inn to get them registered or—what's so strange about his legs?''

As far as any of them could see, there really wasn't

anything strange about his legs. It was just that, as he drew closer and they could get a better look, he appeared to have more than the usual number. As he veered toward the curb, the onlookers noted an extra arm holding a duplicate umbrella, a second head wearing a second homburg. Altogether, they saw clearly as the figure turned to cross the street, there were two of him: one coming and one, as it were, going.

"Larruping locoweeds!" cried Osbert. "He's a them!"

"How fascinating," said Dittany. "I never realized Siamese twins were so aesthetically satisfying. It's like watching a ballet, the backward one in perfect step with the front one, only in reverse. I wonder if they ever turn around or if the backward one just becomes the forward one when they want to go in the opposite direction."

"What I'm wondering is whether they're going to stampede that mob over there," said Osbert.

Sergeant MacVicar was already buttoning his tunic and reaching for his cap. The appearance of Miss Jane's conjoined relatives, as they surely must be, was rapidly turning the assembled multitude, or what passed for a multitude in Lobelia Falls, into a veritable vortex of excitement. A spot of crowd control was clearly the most immediate concern in the sergeant's mind at the moment. As he hurried from the house and strode across the street, those inside and surely those outside could hear him uttering his most dreaded words: "Noo then, what's this all about?"

"Watching Donald in action is as good as a play," his wife remarked fondly, gazing out the window in the approved Lobelia Falls manner: i.e., standing to one side so the neighbors couldn't see her gawking. "Just look at that fresh little Poppy girl with her miniskirt practically up to her you-know-what, trying to give him some lip. Why isn't she in school, is what I'd like to know. Donald's ticking her off good and proper, and serves her right. There, she's going, and about time."

Gradually, the people were beginning to drift off, realizing that it was rude to stare and trying to give each other the impression that they hadn't actually been behaving in a fashion unworthy of responsible citizens. Of course this dispersement couldn't happen in a moment. While those inside were watching, the telephone rang. Osbert picked it up.

"Police station, Deputy Monk speaking. Oh, good morning, Sergeant Golightly. Both the cars, eh? That's quick work, I'm sure Sergeant MacVicar will be delighted. He's across the street breaking up a riot just now, but I'll tell him the minute he gets back. It's not much of a riot, more an unruly gathering, though he's got them fairly ruly by now. Just so long as those Siamese twins don't come out of the yarn shop too soon."

Evidently a question was raised at the other end of the line, for Osbert replied, "We have no information as yet. We believe them to be the English cousins of the lady who runs the yarn shop. That's right, the one who used to be in the mall over your way. She'd finding things quite a bit livelier over here. But tell me, was the body still in the first car? It was? But no identification as yet? Well, keep in touch, I'm sure you'll come up with something. Thanks for calling."

Osbert hung up the phone. "That was the Scottsbeck police, in case you hadn't guessed. They've found the two cars ditched in the big gully on that lonesome stretch of road going over to West Scottsbeck. The body of the man who bled on Miss Jane's floor was still in the car he came in, which is to say the one with the larger number of bullet holes in it. He had no identification of any sort on him and there's something peculiar about the license plates, but they've sent his fingerprints to the RCMP and put out inquiries and all that stuff. They're going to get back to us as soon as they have any further information. How do you feel, dear?"

"Hungry, oddly enough," Dittany replied. "Otherwise I'm fine. What time is it?"

"Heavens to goodness, it's after twelve and I haven't done a thing about Donald's lunch," cried Mrs. MacVicar. "And I'd promised him cullen skink. I expect your mother has a meal ready and waiting for you."

That was the polite way of saying she wished they'd get

out from under her feet so that she could go back to her kitchen. Dittany knew perfectly well her mother wouldn't have prepared a noon meal; Clorinda and Arethusa were going to the inn. However, she didn't say so because then Mrs. MacVicar would feel duty bound to invite them to stay and she was not at all sure how her stomach would react to cullen skink.

By now, the real excitement seemed to be over. People were still going in and out of the Yarnery but they were either on serious errands or making a decent pretense at being. Officers Bob and Ray must have got word on their radio that the cars had been found, for they drove up in the police car to take over the arm-waving and leave Sergeant MacVicar free to come home.

As he was about to cross back to his house, the Siamese twins emerged from the shop and walked briskly, one forward and one backward, in the direction of the inn. Miss Jane must be regretting that she couldn't take time out to serve them the elegant luncheon she'd no doubt had ready in her rooms over the shop. However, they would certainly have understood how impossible that was, considering the commotion they'd already witnessed and no doubt having got a hair-raising earful about what had happened at the Yarnery earlier on. Dittany and Osbert took their leave of Mrs. MacVicar, then lurked in the doorway so that they wouldn't seem to be tracking the twins in a spirit of vulgar curiosity.

"I could whiz home and bring the car around if you don't mind waiting another few minutes," Osbert offered. "Are you sure you feel like walking back, darling?"

"Yes," Dittany replied, "but I'm not sure I feel much like cooking lunch. Mum forgot the list I'd made out when she went grocery shopping yesterday and brought back mostly candied ginger and pickled mushrooms, neither of which I feel particularly in the mood for just now. I tell you what, why don't you and I stroll over to the inn ourselves? That is, if you'd care to invite a female blimp out in public?"

"Why, Miz Dittany, ma'am," Osbert replied enthusiastically, "how could I not want to be seen with a purty little lady like you? Shucks, if I'd o' knowed we was steppin' out on the town, I'd o' wore my Sunday socks."

"Now Deputy Monk, you know you look lovely in your mail-order shirt. That green-and-yellow plaid just matches my complexion," his bulging consort replied.

In fact Dittany was blooming. As soon as she'd found out she was going to be dressing for three, she'd gone on a spree at the Babyland Boutique in Scottsbeck. Today she was wearing an outfit of blue denim that must have been designed with the pregnant prairie princess in mind. It had ruffles around the skirt, the sleeves, the pockets, the yoke, and the neck, every ruffle edged in scarlet braid. Dittany rather wished she'd thought to borrow her mother's red cartwheel hat to set off her ensemble; but perhaps the ruffles were offsetting enough. She took Osbert's arm and let him escort her solicitously the short way to the inn.

The dining room was not yet crowded, but it was getting there. While most of the patrons were making a decent pretense of keeping their eyes on their plates, the uncouth few were sneaking furtive peeks over their menus at an interesting tableau over at the far end of the room. Two dapper Englishmen were sitting back to back on low stools that had been brought in from the cocktail lounge. Each had a small table drawn up in front of him, and each table had an attractive woman sitting across from the man in the middle. The one in the blue dress with the green-and-pink spots, wearing a borrowed green suede hat stuck full of gray goose quills, was Clorinda; the one in the lilac suit, wearing Clorinda's red cartwheel hat, was Arethusa.

Chapter 4

"Well, shuck me for a corncob!"

Dittany didn't say it loudly. As the lone bairn among two parents and two grandparents all living together, she'd been almost overwhelmingly well brought up. Both Osbert and the oldest Pitz girl, who was hostessing at the inn to lay up college money, heard her, however; and both concurred in the feeling thus conveyed.

"Maybe you'd like that table over by your mother," the Pitz girl offered demurely.

Osbert and Dittany said that would be fine; so she steered them to it, all three taking pains to look as if this were no big deal. Of course it would have been unthinkable for them not to stop and say hello to their respective mother and aunt, thus making it inevitable that they should get to meet the twins. Clorinda was delighted to make the introductions.

"This is my daughter, Dittany Monk, and her husband Osbert, whom you may already know as Lex Laramie."

The two men bobbed up in perfect unison, looking at the Monks over their respective right and left shoulders. "Not the Lex Laramie who writes those fabulous Westerns?" cried the one who'd been sitting with Arethusa. "I went absolutely ape over *Mayhem at the Mangled Mesquite*.

This is tremendous! Do you prefer to be called Mr. Monk or Mr. Laramie?''

"The boys around the bunkhouse mostly just call him Pard," said Dittany. She knew how Osbert hated to be gushed over. "And you're . . .''

"We're always referred to as the Bleinkinsop twins, for obvious reasons," said the one who happened to be facing her. "The different-colored ties are so you can tell us apart. I'm Glanville, the red." He and his brother made a smart quarter-wheel left so that Glanville could shake hands with the Monks.

"And I'm Ranville, the green." A further half-wheel gave Ranville a chance to shake hands, too. "But this is incredible!" he cried. "The two brightest stars in Canada's literary firmament, at one fell swoop."

They returned to their original position, facing the Monks again over their shoulders. "We recognized Miss Monk from her photographs, needless to say," said Glanville.

"And simply charged up and introduced ourselves like a couple of bobby-soxers," said Ranville.

"Miss Monk's a smash hit back home, as I'm sure I don't have to tell you," said Glanville.

"Everybody in London adores her madly," said Ranville.

"Ourselves included," said Glanville. "Hostess, can't we do something about these tables?"

"If that one over there were pulled over here," suggested Ranville.

"Then Mr. and Mrs. Monk could sit side by side facing us," added Glanville.

"And we'd both be able to see them at the same time," said Ranville.

"Sorry to put you to the bother," said Glanville.

"But we have to consider the logistics," said Ranville.

"We love being Siamese twins," said Glanville.

"It's quite fun working things out," said Ranville.

"And one's never at a loss for company," said Glanville.

"Yes, we never walk alone," said Ranville.

Dittany suspected that the quip was not new, but she laughed anyway because the twins did, and so did the rest of the party. Glanville and Ranville were not at all what she'd expected. They kept up a merry patter as Osbert and the eldest Pitz girl rearranged the seating arrangements to everybody's satisfaction.

By now, of course, the Monk-Pusey-Bleinkinsop party were the cynosure of all eyes and nobody was trying to pretend otherwise. Glanville and Ranville, as they insisted on being called since it would have been absurd to address them as Mr. Bleinkinsop and Mr. Bleinkinsop, must surely be used to being stared at. Both Clorinda, as the former ingenue, soubrette, and even occasional tragedienne of the Traveling Thespians, and Arethusa, as the reigning queen of regency romance, were quite accustomed to public notice. Dittany hadn't much minded playing to an audience back when she was playing tiny tot roles in her mother's company, but in her present condition she could have done with a trifle more obscurity.

Osbert, in the strong, silent tradition of the men of the West, plumb hated the spotlight. However, there wasn't much he could do about it now. Besides, he was too intrigued at the way Glanville and Ranville managed the amenities to feel self-conscious about his own situation. It was particularly fascinating to see them matter-of-factly get up and switch positions every so often so that Glanville got to face Clorinda and Ranville face Arethusa. The only difference this made to Osbert and Dittany was that Glanville looked at them sometimes over his right shoulder, and sometimes over his left, whereas Ranville had to turn his head sometimes left and sometimes right, depending.

As far as conversation was concerned, the twins had it pretty much their own way. Not even Clorinda, usually not the most silent member of any assemblage, managed to get more than the odd word in edgewise. Arethusa, who tended to withdraw into her own world of rakes, ruffles, and rapiers anyway, merely smiled her Lady Ermintrude smile and gazed at whichever twin happened to be her vis-à-vis at any given moment with those great, dark eyes which had been described variously as limpid pools of midnight and as fathomless depths of inscrutability. It was only a

matter of moments, Dittany realized, before both twins fell
in love with Arethusa.

Maybe they already had; the process didn't usually take
long. And maybe that wouldn't be so bad after all. In their
peculiar circumstances, being in love with the same woman
might be a good deal less of a strain on what in this case
could be referred to most accurately as the family tree.
Courtship could have become a real problem if they'd
fallen for two different women, especially if the women
didn't like each other. Or if Glanville didn't take kindly to
the object of Ranville's affections. Or, of course, vice
versa.

Had Clorinda still been Ditson Henbit's widow, Dittany
thought, there'd have been no problem at all. She and
Arethusa would have got along just fine as wives in a
singularly close-knit household. Naturally, though, no well-
bred British gentleman would be so crass as to make
advances to the spouse of a hotshot fashion eyewear salesman, even if Clorinda had not been so obviously and
enthusiastically about to become a grandmother.

"How long are you planning to stay in Lobelia Falls?"
Dittany asked the twins when she could get a word in.

"We're not quite sure," said Glanville.

"We want to see something of Cousin Prudence," said
Ranville.

"Since we've never met her before," said Glanville.

"But Prudence appears to be a busy lady," said Ranville.

"That shop of hers must do a whacking business," said
Glanville.

"Pru was busy as a one-armed juggler when we stopped
by," said Ranville.

"But she gave us to understand that the rush was a bit
unusual," said Glanville.

"Something about a man getting shot," said Ranville.

"I think you mean plugged, old boy," said Glanville.

"I stand corrected, old boy," said Ranville. "Plugged
he was. Out front, I believe."

"Right, old boy," said Glanville. "Cousin Pru apolo-
gized for the bloodstains on the sidewalk."

"Quite needlessly," said Ranville.

"We expected them," said Glanville.

"Been disappointed if we hadn't seen them," said Ranville.

"Out here in the wild west," said Glanville.

"Where men are men," said Ranville.

"Desperadoes and shoot-outs," said Glanville.

"All sorts of things," said Ranville.

"Part of the scene," said Glanville.

"Rather thrilling, actually," said Ranville.

"Makes us feel we've really arrived," said Glanville.

"Boring for you people, I suppose," said Ranville.

"Monotonous after a while, no doubt," said Glanville.

"Doesn't interfere with the social life, I hope?" said Ranville.

"Lively around here, is it?" said Glanville.

"Necktie parties and all that?" said Ranville.

"Oh yes," said Osbert. "Once a month or so we clean out the desperadoes and start over. Feel up to some dessert, darling? Or perhaps a shot of red-eye?"

"Just tea, please," said Dittany. "Darling, I think the joint's being raided."

Eyes that had been riveted on the Bleinkinsop twins suddenly were turning toward the doorway. Now that the inn had turned respectable, it had become an unusual occurrence to see a uniformed policeman on the premises; but there all at once stood Officer Bob, checking out the assemblage table by table. When he spied Osbert, he made a beeline, saluting smartly as he reached his goal.

"Sorry to bother you while you're eating your dinner, Deputy Monk, but the chief says could you report back to the station right away on a matter of urgent official business?"

"By George, Glan," cried Ranville, "did you hear that? Lex Laramie is a man behind the badge."

"By George, Ran, this is exciting," cried Glanville. "Just think, our first real genuine wild west deputy!"

"And here we've been sitting all this time," said Ranville.

"Not realizing," said Glanville.

"Without the slightest inkling," said Ranville.

"Totally unaware," said Glanville.

"Well, folks, I'd better mosey along," said Osbert, tossing money on the table lest the twins think he was trying to stick them with the check. "Do you want to stay and drink your tea, Dittany gal, or would you rather come with me?"

Dittany at once began struggling out of her chair. "I'll come with you and mooch a cup from Mrs. MacVicar at the public expense. She promised to show me the latest photographs of her newest grandson. He's got a tooth, you'll all be thrilled to know."

"Oh, jolly good," said Glanville.

"Snappish little blighter, is he?" said Ranville.

"We take our excitement where we can get it around here." Dittany was beginning to find Ranville and Glanville a trifle repetitious. "It's been lovely meeting you, and I do hope you enjoy your stay in Lobelia Falls. We'll be seeing you again, no doubt."

For tea in her own parlor this afternoon if Dittany knew her mother's penchant for hospitality, which she certainly did. Why couldn't those two—if in fact they counted as two, as she didn't see why they shouldn't since they obviously were—have stayed and helped Cousin Prudence in the shop instead of stravaging around picking up acquaintances among the local celebrities? That would have given them an interesting opportunity to work out a new set of operational logistics; whereas if they were planning to hang out with Arethusa and Clorinda, anything to do with logic in any form simply wouldn't enter in.

Dittany took Osbert's arm and resigned herself to running the gauntlet of wondering eyes as they left the dining room. "I wonder what Sergeant MacVicar wants you for in such a hurry?"

"Either he's got some new information on the shoot-out," Osbert guessed, "or else they're having another grand free-for-all over at the yarn shop and he needs me to answer the telephone again while he's out quelling."

"Mrs. MacVicar could perfectly well answer the phone,"
Dittany objected. "She does it all the time."

"Then it must be about the man who got shot."

Greatly to their puzzlement, though, they found Sergeant MacVicar with a visitor: a tall, comfortably padded
woman who seemed to exude a gentle aura of sugar and
spice and everything nice. She was wearing a smart, well-
cut ensemble of navy-blue piped in white but would have
looked more natural, thought Dittany, in a print housedress
and a checkered apron. Whoever she was, she showed
unfeigned delight at seeing Osbert and Dittany, particularly Dittany.

"Well now, I call this real progressive of you, Sergeant
MacVicar, having a woman on your staff, and a mother-
to-be in the bargain. I'm beginning to feel better about this
awful business already. Just so you don't go getting yourself shot, dear. Goodness knows what sort of traumatic
effect it would have on the baby."

"I never get shot," Dittany assured whomever the visitor might be. "My husband won't let me."

"Er—m'ph," said Sergeant MacVicar. "Mother Matilda, allow me to present Deputy Osbert Monk and—er—
Special Deputy Dittany Monk. Mother Matilda, as she
prefers to be known, is—"

"Not *the* Mother Matilda," Dittany broke in. Now,
here was a real celebrity!

"Yes, dearie," said the celebrity. "Mother Matilda's
Mincemeat, that's me. Which is what this awful business
is about, or else I wouldn't be here taking up your time
when you might be home knitting tiny garments."

"Don't worry about my time, Mother Matilda. I'm no
earthly good at tiny garments. Besides, we already have a
houseful."

"Dittany's a great cook, though," said Osbert loyally.

"And I always use Mother Matilda's Mincemeat, as did
my Grandmother Henbit before me. My mother, who's
now Mrs. Pusey, still does when she gets the chance,
which isn't often these days because she and my stepfather
travel in fashion eyewear."

Mother Matilda's strained features relaxed in a gratified smile, though only temporarily. "That's lovely, dear. I hear the same kind of story over and over again everywhere I go. Generation after generation, and to think it's come to this! I don't know what dear old Granny would say if she were alive today. She was the original Mother Matilda, you know. Mother took over when Granny's feet gave out, and now here's me carrying on the family tradition, as will my own daughter after me, if she ever gets the chance," Mother Matilda added dolefully. "It looks a bit iffy right now, I have to tell you. That's what comes of letting men into the business. They always want to organize things, then you get successful and look what happens. You wouldn't have a spare cup of tea lying around anywhere handy, Sergeant? I've been so kerflummoxed by this awful business that I plain forgot to eat. Haven't had a bite since last night's supper, if memory serves me correctly, as it generally does. What I wouldn't give for a nice, hot bowl of Granny's cullen skink right this minute! Nobody's ever been able to make cullen skink the way my grandmother did."

"Oh aye?" said Sergeant MacVicar. "Would you excuse me a wee moment, Mother Matilda?"

"Gladly, if you're planning to put the kettle on. While you're gone, Sergeant, I'll just fill in your deputies here on what this awful business is all about so's we won't be wasting your time. What you've got to understand, Dittany and Osbert, is that the man who died this morning over there by the yarn shop was a hero."

"Heavens to Betsy!" cried Dittany.

"And well you may say so," replied Mother Matilda. "He was also, I'm both proud and sad to say, my husband. And a finer man never drew breath, if I do say so. He was vice president in charge of nutmeg."

"Was he, indeed?"

"Yes, indeed. VP Nutmeg is the highest position in our organization, next to mine. Charles was our crown prince, as I used to call him, and a true prince he was. That was his name, Charles. Charles McCorquindale. We were distantly related, though we never managed to figure out just how. My granny was a McCorquindale before her marriage. But I'm digressing. I don't know how familiar you two are with the mincemeat business . . . ?''

"All we know is what it says on the jar," Dittany replied.

"Then you at least know that Mother Matilda's Mincemeat is a subtle blend of chopped beef, suet, apples, sugar, cider, raisins, currants, citron, dried orange peel, and a good many other things I needn't go into just now. Including a couple I wouldn't tell you about anyway. But what makes our mincemeat unique isn't so much the ingredients as the subtle blending. We don't just scoop up a jugful of this and a handful of that and bung 'em into the cauldrons the way some people seem to think. Every milligram of nutmeg, cinnamon, mace, and several more things I'm sworn to secrecy about is weighed, measured, and sniffed to ensure absolute consistency of taste and quality. Oh, we're sticklers, I can tell you that.''

"We believe you," Dittany replied politely.

Mother Matilda didn't seem to hear her. "Yes, it was stickling that got us where we are today, and stickling which I greatly fear has precipitated this awful business.''

"How's that?" said Osbert.

This time Mother Matilda heard. "Well, you see, Deputy, there's only one person alive in this world today who knows the whole secret recipe and that's yours truly right here. The paper it's written on in Granny's handwriting was handed to me by my mother on her deathbed. I took my oath then and there never to divulge the recipe to anybody until the time came for me to hand over my cap and apron, figuratively speaking, to Matilda the Fourth. Actually my daughter's Matilda the Fifth because it's really Great-Granny's recipe, but it was Granny who first developed the commercial possibilities, so we think of her instead of her mother as Matilda the First. You could argue it either way, though I don't suppose you'd particularly care to in the present circumstances.''

Osbert didn't suppose so, either. "So what that means is

that you have to go all over the factory every day telling everybody how much of which ingredient to use, right?''

Mother Matilda managed a wan smile. ''Lord bless you, sonny, how'd a high-powered executive like me have time for all that? Mother Matilda's Mincemeat is a multimillion dollar operation these days. If I told you what we spend in a year's time on orange peel alone, you'd think I was having a pipe dream. What we do is, we compartmentalize. That was poor Charles's word for it. We have a VP Cinnamon, as we call them for short, a VP Mace, a VP Cloves, and so on down through the list. They're all tried and true veterans, all sworn to secrecy. I'd have trusted any of them with my life. Though of course not with my recipe.''

The mincemeat magnate appeared for a moment close to tears, but she rallied bravely and went on with her explanation. ''I don't know how much you people here in Lobelia Falls know about the vicious internecine war raging in the mincemeat business today. We'd heard reports of spies infiltrating elsewhere, but never dreamed it could affect us until all of a sudden, things began to happen.''

''What sort of things?'' said Dittany.

''First it was VP Cider. The cider we use is sweet cider, fresh-squeezed in our own cider press, so naturally you wouldn't expect there to be anything wrong with it, right?''

''But there was?''

''I'll tell the world there was! You see, one of VP Cider's functions is to taste each batch of cider and make sure it conforms to our rigid standards. We can't always get the same variety and quality of apples, needless to say, so this tasting is another extremely important function. Well! VP Cider—Fred Perkins, his name is, Fred and I were in Sunday school together—was down in the cider store by himself, tasting a batch as usual, and he didn't send through the okay signal for the cider fetchers to come and get it. So the foreman decided after a while that he'd better go see what the story was because they needed the cider, you see. What the foreman found was Fred sprawled out on the storeroom floor in his shirtsleeves, drunk as a boiled owl, singing 'The Maple Leaf Forever.' "

"No!" cried Dittany.

"Yup," said Mother Matilda, "the jug he'd been testing turned out to be pure applejack. And there was Fred—a strict teetotaler, a thirty-third degree Mason, a Sunday school superintendent, and a high-ranking company official —the butt of opprobrium and coarse ribaldry. We naturally assumed the incident was meant as an extremely ill-conceived practical joke, but it certainly wasn't funny. Furthermore, we had to hold up production till Fred's mouth quit tasting like the bottom of a bird cage and he could get on with the job he's paid to do."

"And there were other incidents?" Osbert prompted.

"Too many. The most outrageous of all was VP Lemon Peel's getting debagged by masked marauders in his own office while his secretary was out collecting her afternoon tea. They just rushed in, pulled a typewriter cover over his head, hauled down his britches, lashed him to his swivel chair with his own suspenders, and dashed out again. Miss Flaubert dropped the tea and fainted when she came in and found him sitting there in a pair of lemon-colored boxer shorts. Another tasteless and pointless prank was the consensus, but then Charles began putting two and two together. And he saw!"

Chapter 5

"What was it he saw, Mother Matilda?" asked Dittany.

"Well, first I should explain that in our zeal for perfection, we at Mother Matilda's never trust to memory. Each of the VPs has his own segment of the mincemeat recipe on a separate card, which he's required to keep on his person at all times during working hours. I use 'his' in the impersonal sense, of course; several of our VPs are women. Right now I wish they all were, since the men seem so much more vulnerable to attack. But anyway, these cards are never taken off the premises except when the VPs carry them to the bank at night and pick them up again in the morning. Each card is kept in a separate safe deposit box, to which only the particular VP and I have keys."

"How far is the bank from the factory?" said Osbert.

"It's directly across the street. What our VPs generally do is drive up to the bank and park outside long enough to run in and get their cards, then swing across and drive into the parking lot, where our security guard lets them in through the side door, takes the car, and parks it. Then of course, the VPs are inside the factory and theoretically safe from molestation."

Osbert started to say something, but Mother Matilda held up an imperious hand. High-powered executives couldn't help it, Dittany supposed.

"Let me finish, Deputy. As I said, these disgusting incidents went on until it suddenly occurred to Charles that, while the formula cards were always found exactly where the VP had put them, they were always in a part of the clothing that had been vulnerable to search. Fred Perkins kept his card in his inside coat pocket, for instance, and when they found him he had his coat off. He was too befuddled, poor fellow, to remember whether or not he'd taken it off himself, but there it was."

"And VP Lemon Peel carried his card in his trousers?"

"Precisely. And while the entire recipe is quite lengthy, the information required for each individual ingredient doesn't amount to more than a few lines. You could copy it off in two shakes of a lamb's tail, slip the card back where you found it, and nobody would be the wiser. That's what Charles decided they must be doing. We'd been infiltrated! The recipe was being stolen under our very noses, one ingredient at a time."

"When did your husband come to that conclusion, Mother Matilda?" asked Osbert.

"Only last night. It hit Charles like a ton of brick. That was why he was a little late getting to work this morning. He'd stopped to see about having the formula recorded in that special ink you have to look at through an X-ray machine, or whatever it is that only shows up when you do whatever it is you do. I leave all that to the boffins."

Mother Matilda dismissed the world of science with an impatient wave of her hand. "Anyway, whoever's been doing these dastardly deeds must somehow have got wind of the fact that the jig was up. Or else the nutmeg formula simply happened to be next on their schedule, and this gangster act was another of their bright ideas. I have to tell you the police chief over in Lammergen doesn't believe me. He thinks it was a bona fide attempt at a bank holdup; but that hardly explains why the so-called bank robbers pursued Charles from there to here, shooting at him all the way, judging from the number of bullet holes Sergeant MacVicar says were found in his car."

"Why do you suppose your husband came to Lobelia Falls?"

"I think Charles was trying to decoy them away from the factory. He used to be a stock-car racer in his younger days, and may have thought he could easily shake them off on the Lobelia Falls road. Also, Charles had an extremely high opinion of Sergeant MacVicar's acumen and a very low one of Fridwell Slapp's. That's our police chief, I'm sad to say. It's my opinion that Charles was heading right here to the police station. By the time he got here, he'd been hit by one of the bullets and was, as you know, bleeding profusely."

Mother Matilda broke down for a moment, took a deep breath, dried her eyes, and fought gamely on. "Coming from Lammergen, he'd naturally have been on the wrong side of the road, and he must have known the other car was in hot pursuit. Whether Charles failed to make the U-turn for the station because somebody else happened to be in the way at the crucial moment or whether he thought it would be better to park and run across to the station, I couldn't say."

"Judging from the way he ran into Miss Jane's and ran straight out again," Dittany suggested, "do you think it's possible your husband simply got confused? Anybody might have, what with getting shot at all the way along and losing so much blood."

"So they might be," Mother Matilda agreed. "Charles was always inclined to be a trifle absentminded, anyway. Whatever happened, it's clear he meant to protect that nutmeg formula to the last. Though I suppose they must have got it off him when they . . ."

Mother Matilda's voice failed her. Dittany and Osbert sat silent, realizing how futile mere words of compassion would be in the face of so overwhelming a loss. It was Mrs. MacVicar who brought true consolation. In she bustled, carrying a tray on which sat three teacups and one steaming bowl filled with something that looked like fish chowder and exuded a seductive aroma of finnan haddie.

"Cullen skink!" cried Mother Matilda.

"Aye," said Sergeant MacVicar, who had followed his wife with the teapot. "And good as your granny's, I'll be bound."

"We'll see."

Mother Matilda was in command of herself again. She took the serviette Mrs. MacVicar had brought and spread it neatly over her navy-blue lap. She picked up the spoon, paused a moment to decide precisely where to dip, and essayed her first taste. To a high-powered food expert, this could be no trivial slurp. She sniffed, she sipped. She rolled the rich, creamy broth around on her tongue. Gradually the pain that had wracked her unbeautiful but by no means uncomely features subsided. She raised to her impromptu hostess eyes filled with tears of wonder and gratitude.

"Exactly the way Granny used to make it. To think that I should live to taste Granny's cullen skink again! Oh, Mrs. MacVicar, you've given me back my lost youth."

Mrs. MacVicar flushed and became very busy with the teapot. Canadian to the bone, she'd never quite got over the suspicion that praise to the face might really be open disgrace. "Here, Dittany, you'd better have extra milk in your tea. Did you get any lunch?"

"My husband took me out," Dittany replied demurely. "We wound up eating at the inn with Mum and Arethusa and the Bleinkinsop twins."

"The—you did say twins, Dittany?"

"That's right. Glanville and Ranville, their names are. They recognized Arethusa from her photographs, and it appears to have been the start of something relatively beautiful."

"But how?" It was not like Mrs. MacVicar to be incoherent. She simply knew that Dittany would know that she knew what twins were under discussion. Dittany, of course, did.

"Easily enough. They sat on a couple of stools placed, as I needn't say, back to back, with a table in front of each

twin. Arethusa sat across from one and Mum across from
the other. Osbert and I sat side by side at a third table so
they could look at us over their shoulders when they
weren't goggling at Arethusa and Mum.''

Refreshed by the cullen skink, Mother Matilda was
taking a keen interest in this unusual seating arrangement.
"My stars and garters," she observed, "you do paint a
curious picture. For one fleeting moment there, I thought
you must be describing a pair of Siamese twins joined at
the spine.''

"We didn't get into physiological details," Dittany replied, "but on the visual evidence, that's what they appear
to be. I have to say I was rather surprised at first to see all
those arms and legs on one person. But then when one
realizes he's actually two persons . . . unless they have a
jointly owned torso, which is quite possible since they
only wear one coat which has four sleeves and buttons
both fore and aft—or aft and fore, as the case may be—I
must say it gave me a fascinating new insight on the
possibilities of being twins. Glanville and Ranville seem to
have such a lovely time together.''

"Land's sakes!" exclaimed Mother Matilda. "Are you
by chance expecting twins yourself?''

"So Dr. Peagrim tells me, and he's never been wrong
yet," said Dittany. "At least he claims he never has, and I
expect he'd be the one to know if anybody does. He says
one's a boy and one's a girl, so I do in fact rather hope my
babies emerge one at a time with a decent interval between. You know how people talk.''

"Well, if you're not a caution!''

Mother Matilda set her spoon in the empty bowl with a
sigh that was partly of repletion and partly of regret that
there wasn't any more cullen skink to be had. "My gracious, that was good! Not to be nosy, Mrs. MacVicar, but
your granny didn't by any chance happen to be a McCorquindale?''

"Why, yes," the sergeant's wife replied. "That is to
say, she married a McCorquindale. That was my maiden
name, as a matter of fact.''

"Your folks were from around these parts, were they?"

"Oh yes. McCorquindales were among the early settlers of Scottsbeck, as you doubtless know. In fact they're one of the reasons it came to be called Scottsbeck. There were a lot that came over from Scotland in the early days: Frazers, MacDonalds, MacLeods of whom the McCorquindales are a sept, as I again don't suppose I have to tell you. They've spread out a lot, but some of the descendants are still around. I was born and grew up in Scottsbeck, but moved to Lobelia Falls as a bride and must say I've never wanted to leave here. So you think you and I may be related to one another?"

"How else would you have got hold of Granny's recipe?" said Mother Matilda.

"Frankly, I've never had a recipe," Mrs. MacVicar admitted. "I just make it the way my own grandmother did. She lived with us after Grandfather died, and did a good deal of the cooking. It seems to me I do recall her saying she'd learned from her mother-in-law, of whom she was very fond. My father was a doctor and my mother used to help him in the office quite a lot, so she was glad to let Granny take over the kitchen. Not that we didn't have a hired girl to wash the pots and pans," Mrs. MacVicar added, not out of vulgar ostentation, but because she knew what was expected of a doctor's daughter and a police chief's wife. "But how pleasant to meet you, Cousin Matilda, as I suppose I may as well call you. My own given name is Margaret."

"That doesn't surprise me a bit," said Mother Matilda. "Granny's middle name was Margaret. I declare, here I was feeling lorn and bereft, and it turns out I'm among family. You know, Margaret, I wonder whether you and I mightn't work out a written recipe and start considering the commercial possibilities of Granny's cullen skink? Not right now, of course. First we've got to get this awful business about the mincemeat recipe straightened out, then I've got to take a few days off so's I can sit around and feel awful about poor Charles. I'm going to bawl like a baby once I get the chance, but first things first, as Granny used to say.''

Mother Matilda laid her serviette back on the tray and straightened her spine. ''Margaret, what's your husband's first name?''

''It's Donald,'' Mrs. MacVicar replied with a slight hesitation and a sideward glance at the gentleman in question.

''Good. Now then, Cousin Donald, let's get down to business. I might as well tell you first as last that I have no more confidence in that fatuous old hairpin who calls himself Lammergen's police chief than I'd have in that doorpost over there. Less, in fact. The doorpost at least seems to be doing its job competently enough, which is a darn sight more than you can say about Fridwell Slapp. What I'm getting at is, I want you to be the one in charge of this awful business.''

''Umph,'' Sergeant MacVicar replied, ''that may not be possible, Cousin Matilda.''

''I declare, isn't that just like a man? Always wanting to make things complicated when a relative asks a perfectly simple favor.''

''The law is the law,'' Sergeant MacVicar sternly reminded his newly acquired cousin-in-law. ''I can and will investigate that portion of the ootrage which has been committed within the purlieus of Lobelia Falls, but I have no jurisdiction to enter yon mincemeat factory, wherein I misdoubt will be found the most vital clues to the identities of the perpetrators.''

''Then what am I supposed to do?'' snapped Mother Matilda. ''Sit on my hands and watch eighty-seven years' worth of dedication to the ultimate in gourmet mincemeat production trickle away down the drain? Not to mention letting the wicked assassination of the sweetest, dearest VP Nutmeg who ever trod this earth go unavenged?''

'' 'Vengeance is mine, saith the Lord,' '' Sergeant MacVicar reminded her.

''Aye, verily,'' she shot back. ''And the Lord helps

those who get down to work and help themselves find out who's helping themselves to my granny's mincemeat recipe. For Pete's sake, Donald, quit being so cussed Scotch and consider my position. Those crooks have already snaffled the cider, the lemon peel, the suet, the currants, and presumably the nutmeg. Mark my words, first thing you know, they'll be after the cloves and the cinnamon. By the time they get to the raisins, I'll be tottering on the brink of a hostile takeover."

"Yes, but—"

Sergeant MacVicar might as well have tried to stem Victoria Falls. "And they'll do it," Mother Matilda rushed on, "if there's nobody between them and me but that old poop Fridwell Slapp. Where's your Highland clan spirit, man? How can you refuse a simple favor to your own good wife's second cousin? Or maybe her third, but what's the difference? Do you want to go through the rest of your life choking on every spoonful of cullen skink that crosses your lips, remembering how you betrayed the blessed memory of that saintly woman who taught Margaret's grandmother how to make it?"

"Donald," pleaded his wife, "surely there's something you can do. Great-granny-in-law really must have been a lovely woman."

Much affected by this pathetic tableau, Dittany turned to Osbert. In turn, Osbert turned to Dittany. Both of them then turned to Sergeant MacVicar. It was Osbert who spoke.

"Not to be pushy or anything, Chief, but Dittany and I are wondering whether you might consider the fact that she and I aren't officially members of the Lobelia Falls police force. That means we're not bound by the same regulations as you and Bob and Ray and Ormerod, so I don't see any real reason why we couldn't do a little nosing around over in Lammergen and report back here to you. I might get myself taken on at the mincemeat factory as an apple corer or a salt shaker or something. Dittany could bring me my dinner pail at noontime and stop to chat in a friendly way with the choppers and peelers. Nobody's going to suspect a sweet young mother-to-be of being an infiltrator.''

"There now," cried Mother Matilda, "that's using your head for something besides a hat rack. The only trouble with your idea, Osbert, is that we have a cafeteria where all the employees eat. They don't go outside at all, so there's no way she'd get to meet any of them. It's not that we're mean to them, it's on account of sanitary regulations. You have to be real fussy around food, you know. Every employee has to get washed up soon as they come in, just like hospital workers, and put on a clean uniform which doesn't get taken off till they leave for the day.''

She turned to her cousin. "You'd like the uniforms, Margaret. The women have real pretty Mother Hubbards in different-colored ginghams depending on what department they work in: red for apples, yellow for lemon peel, purple for raisins, green for citron, and so forth. They wear elasticized mobcaps with cute little ruffles all around to cover their hair so's it won't get into the mincemeat. Hair in mincemeat was one thing Granny never stood for and neither will I.''

"But what about the men?" said Mrs. MacVicar.

"The men have plain cotton duck trousers—red or green or whatever, with checkered tops sort of like a loose jacket that buttons up to a high collar like a chef's uniform. They wear caps, too, only without ruffles. Not that they couldn't have ruffles if they took the notion, mind you. We don't practice sex discrimination unless we catch 'em out on top of the cinnamon bags doing what has no place in a well-run mincemeat factory, which I regret to say has been known to happen. But anyway, once they're dressed for work, we can't let 'em go roaming the roads and getting all unhygienic, as you must surely realize.''

"Oh yes," said Dittany, "we understand perfectly. And it's not as though there were much to go out for in Lammergen, anyway.''

"Oh, I don't know," said Mother Matilda a shade huffily. "We do have a dentist, and a real nice feed store.

If somebody's got an appointment or something we make an exception, but the general rule is once you're in, you're in for the day. So that lets you out, I'm afraid, Dittany. I couldn't possibly take you on as hired help because it wouldn't make sense to hire somebody in your present condition. The employees would get to wondering, which of course is what we want to avoid because there's talk enough already, and heaven only knows what they'll be saying once word about poor Charles gets around.''

She paused to dab her eyes, then ruthlessly dragged herself back to business. ''So it looks as though Osbert will just have to go it alone, if he's game to try and can get the time off from work. What do you do, sonny?''

''I'm a writer,'' Osbert replied modestly.

''I meant for a living.''

''That's what I do. I write Western stories.''

''And get paid for them?''

''Hoots, Cousin Matilda!'' Sergeant MacVicar had at last found something to amuse him on what had thus far been a day sadly lacking in light moments. ''E'en in Lammergen, surely folks have heard of Lex Laramie?''

''Well, of course, but—you mean that's him? This young squirt right here? Sorry, Osbert, but I've always pictured Lex Laramie as being seven feet tall, wearing wolf-hide chaps and riding a black stallion twenty-six hands high. And here you are, not one darn bit more leathery and hard-bitten than my nephew Harold, who's still taking bassoon lessons at the conservatory in Scottsbeck. I'll bet you don't even roll your own.''

''No, ma'am, I've never smoked at all. I tried once and it made me sick. I have been known to belly up to the bar for a shot of red-eye, though,'' Osbert offered lest Mother Matilda's illusions be completely shattered.

His only reward was a snort of disbelief. ''I'll bet you have! A shot of lime rickey would be more like it. Well, my stars, if that doesn't beat all! Anyway, I expect being a writer means you can take off whatever time you want. It's not as though you had any real work to do.''

"That's what you think," snarled Dittany. "Writing's about the hardest work there is. Try it yourself sometime if you don't believe me."

"Me?" Mother Matilda had the grace to blush for her misapprehension. "I wouldn't know where to begin, just as I don't know where to begin with this awful business. All right, Osbert, I apologize. I suppose you're also a famous detective in disguise. You wouldn't happen by any chance to be Sherlock Holmes, too?"

Chapter 6

Actually it was rather gallant of Mother Matilda to essay even this mild quip in so dire a situation; but Sergeant MacVicar did not consider the force he commanded a laughing matter under any circumstances. "When I introduced Osbert and Dittany Monk as my deputies, Cousin Matilda," he said rather coldly, "I spoke naught but the truth. Together, these two young folk have succeeded in clearing up three of the most baffling mysteries that e'er sullied the annals of law enforcement. Osbert Monk needs no fancy label, he is a host in himself. Whether he will be handicapped by the fact that his partner in criminology, as in life, will not be able to penetrate yon mincemeat factory, I much doubt. And I confess that I'd have been gravely apprehensive had she gone."

After Ditson Henbit's death, Sergeant MacVicar had got to thinking of Dittany as a wee, fatherless bairn. He was still finding the habit hard to break notwithstanding her present status as wife and incipient mother. He was giving her one of those benign looks of his, Dittany noted, and trying to think up something to say that wouldn't make her want to stamp her feet and flounce off in a huff.

"Howsomever," he concluded after a moment's cogitation, "I doubt not that Dittany will be assisting the investigation in her own inscrutable ways."

"Right now," said Mrs. MacVicar in no uncertain tone, "I think Dittany could use a bit of assistance herself. Take her home, Osbert, and make her put her feet up for a while. Can I offer you a fresh cup of tea, Cousin Matilda, or do you have to be getting back to the factory?"

"I'd better go back and call a directors' meeting, thank you, Cousin Margaret. Osbert, what you'd better do is present yourself tomorrow morning as an applicant for Director of In-House Security. We've never had such a position before, but Charles decided we needed one after poor old Fred got debagged. He'd actually made preliminary arrangements to hire somebody, so the staff won't consider it odd when you show up. In that position you'll have carte blanche to roam all over the place and question anybody you choose. Don't you think that's the best plan, Cousin Donald? You'll give Osbert a reference, won't you?"

Sergeant MacVicar stood up and bowed her toward the door. "Dinna fash yoursel' about the references, Cousin Matilda. Come, we'll go out together. I'll be nipping on over to Scottsbeck, Margaret, to inspect those two cars they've found ditched and to make sure the mortal coil which Cousin Charles so tragically shuffled off is being treated with due respect."

"Find out how soon Cousin Matilda can have him back, Donald," said Mrs. MacVicar. "I'm sure she'll want to get the funeral plans in order."

"I expect likely I will," Mother Matilda agreed, "once I've got this director's meeting over with. You can be sure of one thing, Cousin Margaret—dear old Charlie's going to get the rip-roaring send-off he deserves, bless his heart wherever he may be now. Osbert, your appointment's for tomorrow morning at eight-thirty sharp. We start early in the mincemeat business."

"Yes, Mother Matilda. I'll go straight home and write myself some red-hot references just as soon as I've put Dittany's feet up."

Up was precisely where Dittany wished her feet to be. Lugging a pair of twins around became increasingly hard on the pedal extremities, she was discovering. "I don't see why they can't have mother-to-be carriages as well as baby carriages," she fretted as they turned the corner onto Applewood Avenue.

"Want to play horsey?" Osbert suggested. "I'll get down on all fours and you can ride on my back."

"Thank you, dear, but you really ought to consider your dignity as Director of In-House Security," Dittany replied. "What name are you going to use?"

"I was thinking about something along the lines of Osbert Monk."

"But everybody from here to Halifax knows Osbert Monk is really Lex Laramie," Dittany objected. "Sorry, dear, I meant that Lex Laramie is Osbert Monk."

"That's all right, dear," Osbert comforted her. "I get confused sometimes myself. Then how about my being Reginald Monk, who happens to be staying in Lobelia Falls with his brother Osbert and Osbert's beautiful though bulgy wife. The one with the sore feet."

"Brilliant!" cried Dittany. "Then if people notice the resemblance, you can say you and Osbert are often mistaken for twins."

"Why can't I just say we *are* twins?"

"I suppose you could, now that you mention it, though it does seem to me there's almost a plethora of twins around here already. I wonder whether Mum and Arethusa went somewhere with Glanville and Ranville. Let's hope we don't find the answer in our front parlor."

"Not to mention in our kitchen, our dining room, or down cellar messing around with our new sump pump." This was the first sump pump with which Osbert had ever had occasion to become personally acquainted, and he tended to be rather fiercely protective of the relationship. "You know how fond of your mother I am, darling," he went on plaintively, "but doesn't she ever get tired of being sociable?"

Dittany heaved a fairly good-sized sigh. "She never has so far, at least not that I can recall. Is Mum beginning to wear on your nerves, dearest? We can always telephone

Bert and have him tell her she's needed right away in Moose Jaw or wherever he happens to be at the moment. I'm sure he misses her terribly. Reasonably sure, anyway.''

"It's all right, dear," said Osbert. "The situation's not that desperate. Anyway, it looks as though I may not be around much for a while myself, so I'd much rather have her with you while I'm off at the mincemeat factory. I do wish they had some kind of easy sit-down job you could do, though, like counting raisins.''

"I'm not sure how productively I'd be spending my time as a raisin counter, darling," Dittany demurred. "Furthermore, I have a slight hunch one of us ought to be looking for the solution right here in Lobelia Falls, because this is where everything always seems to end up sooner or later. Aha, I see the welcoming committee's right on time.''

Something large, black, fuzzy, and confusing was rushing toward them at what might best be described as a lollop. This was not a bear, a bison, or even a yak; it was Ethel, back from her nature walk and glad to be reunited with her family. Osbert stepped forward to intercept the charge before she could get too affectionate with Dittany, slapped her sides a few times, told her she was a good old mutt, and inquired whether she'd be interested in hanging around outside to practice her jumps in case Aunt Arethusa showed up.

Ethel signified that she wouldn't like this at all. The only things she wanted were her food dish before her and her loved ones around her. They therefore entered the house all three together, Dittany taking precedence because of her delicate condition and her aching feet. Once inside the kitchen, she collapsed on the cot that had stood since time more or less immemorial by the far wall behind the old iron stove with one of Gram Henbit's crocheted afghans thrown over it and another folded ready to hand at one end.

Osbert tucked her up tenderly between the two afghans, refilled Ethel's bowl, helped himself to a couple of hermits, and decided he'd better get in a few more licks on the ostrich ranch while he could, since production would inevitably fall off once Mother Matilda took him on as Director of In-House Security. Dittany wished him happy birding and shut her eyes. When she opened them, people were tiptoeing to and fro.

Strictly speaking, Clorinda, Arethusa, and Glanville were tiptoeing to. Only Ranville was tiptoeing fro, as needs he must if he and his brother were to reach their joint objective, which was obviously the front parlor. Dittany closed her eyes again so they wouldn't feel they'd tiptoed in vain or expect her to get up and make either conversation or tea, for neither of which she had any inclination at this time. She only hoped they wouldn't disturb Osbert en route, as he was sure to be preoccupied with Ralph and might say something hasty which he'd later regret.

Osbert had formed quite an attachment to Ralph, the seven-foot king ostrich who played a leading role in the work so soon to be temporarily preempted by Mother Matilda's awful business. Ralph was the name Osbert's parents had intended to bestow on him until Arethusa, who was his father's sister, had talked them out of that and into Osbert Reginald.

All through grammar and high school Osbert had hated his aunt with a hate that was worse than a hate for naming him Osbert. Once he got into college he hadn't minded so much because he'd already decided to become Lex Laramie and indeed sold his first short story to *Wild-Eyed Western* magazine while still a sophomore. Now he didn't mind at all because he knew Dittany would have loved him even if his name had been Shadrach, Meshach, or Abednego; but she could understand why he still retained a certain fondness for the name he'd never had.

Dittany was darned if she'd name the boy twin Ralph, though. No child of hers was going to play second fiddle to an ostrich. Once that was decided, she spent a minute or so wondering how her mother was coping with seating arrangements in the parlor. Then she thought, "Of course! The piano bench," and went back to sleep.

She probably hadn't been asleep very long before Clorinda

stopped at the cot long enough to ask, "Are you asleep, dear?" but seemed content to accept Dittany's "Yes, Mum," and let sleeping daughters lie.

Ethel thumped around a bit in hope of conning Dittany into filling her bowl yet again, but soon realized the tactic wasn't going to get her anywhere. She collapsed with a grunt and began to snore gently. To Dittany's half-listening ears came the tap-tap of Osbert's typewriter. It sounded like the patter of just-hatched ostrich feet.

Out from the front parlor rolled the strains of "Down Where the Wurtzbuger Flows." Clorinda had the happy faculty of being able to play by ear any song she'd heard often enough to remember how it went. She'd passed on the talent to her lone chick. Dittany was properly grateful and loved to play, but was not eager to usurp her mother's place at the piano just now; though it did occur to her to wonder what Mum was sitting on since the twins were presumably occupying the piano bench.

Dittany also wondered about supper. She knew she ought to get up and start fixing things, but didn't want to for fear the twins might take the activity as a hint that she wanted them to stay, which she most assuredly didn't. What they ought to do was get back to the yarn shop and take their cousin out to supper. Miss Jane must have had an utterly ghastly day, what with all that extra mopping and bodies on the sidewalk and those nosy hordes of customers pushing in on her.

The twins must have been thinking the same thing themselves, for soon she could hear them telling her mother and Arethusa that this had been absolutely super and they hadn't had so much fun in ages but they really must be getting back to Cousin Pru because surely the tumult and the shouting must have died away by now and she'd be wondering where they were; which their hostesses had to agree she almost certainly was. Mum was letting them out the front door, thank goodness. Dittany got up and began padding around in her stocking feet. She was scrubbing new potatoes at the sink when the two older women came out to join her.

"Well," cried her mother gaily, "the sleeping beauty has arisen. You ought to have something on your feet, dearie, that floor might be chilly. Did you and the twins have a good zizz? I remember when you were a dear little lump in my tum, I just wanted to rest and rest."

"Sometimes for as much as ten minutes at a time, if recollection serves me," said Arethusa. "You kept jumping up to change the trimming on the bassinet."

"Oh my stars, the bassinet!" cried Clorinda. "It's up in the attic still, I hope. Or did I lend it to somebody? But who? Dittany, what are we going to do about the bassinet?"

"Nothing, Mum. Osbert's parents have ordered us a lovely double crib from Eaton's."

"But when the babies are so teeny-tiny, a sweet little bassinet with ruffles and flounces and a dear little pink-and-blue blanket with teddy bears on it—or kittens, perhaps? Tom kittens and Tilly kittens? Maybe Miss Jane has a pattern. I could whip one up."

"Mum, you've already knit a lovely carriage robe, and so have Osbert's Aunt Lucy and Zilla Trott and Dot Coskoff and about six other people. Besides, two twins wouldn't fit into my bassinet even if you could remember what you did with it."

"We could get another, dear, and just put them side by side. Unless the twins turn out to be Siamese, but I don't suppose they would. We've never had Siamese twins in our family."

"Twins come in the paternal line," Arethusa pointed out, "so your family doesn't count. Or is it the other way around and our family doesn't count? But my father was a twin. And so," she added after a moment's thought, "was his brother."

"Not Siamese, though?" said Dittany.

"Oh no, Canadian to the bone. Were you planning to cook those potatoes or keep them for souvenirs?"

"Possess your soul in patience, Arethusa. You'll get fed. Why don't you and Mum have a little sherry? Maybe it will refresh your memory about . . ." Dittany was about to mention VP Nutmeg, but remembered just in time that this was a clandestine operation and she still wasn't supposed to know who the first grabber had been. ". . . about what that man with the bullet hole said to you before he died."

"But I've told you what he said," Arethusa protested.

"No, you haven't. You've told Mum, you've told Sergeant MacVicar, you've told Miss Jane Fuzzywuzzy, I expect you've told Glanville and Ranville and no doubt a few dozen more, but you've never said one single word to me. Think, Arethusa. Precisely what were the exact words he uttered?"

"Stap my garters!" Arethusa accepted the sherry Clorinda offered and helped herself to a considerable amount of cheese. "A fine time this is to expect me to think, ecod."

Any time was a fine time to expect Arethusa to think, as Osbert would surely have pointed out if he weren't still preoccupied with the ostriches. Dittany dumped the potatoes into the pan, thus demonstrating that there would be supper as a reward for cogitation, but refrained from putting the pan on the stove as a hint that potatoes might not get served to certain persons if they refused to exercise whatever it was they used for gray matter.

Where food was concerned, Arethusa could be a great one for catching a nuance. She knit her brows. She nibbled cheese, she sipped her sherry, she pondered deeply. A watcher might almost have been able to hear the gears clanking. At last, they meshed.

"Eureka!" Thus exclaiming, Arethusa choked on a crumb and had to be thumped on the back. Fortunately her recollection was not lost with the crumb. As soon as she was again able to articulate, she croaked, "His exact words were: 'The raveled sleeve.' "

Clorinda shook her head. "Not 'the raveled sleeve,' dear. It's 'the ravell'd sleave.' From that time when Macbeth murdered sleep, you know. Sleep that knits up the ravell'd etcetera. I could go on, but it's considered unlucky in theatrical circles to quote from Macbeth. Maybe that's why the man got shot."

"Are you intimating that his assassin was a disgruntled thespian, forsooth?" demanded Arethusa.

"It's a possibility that should definitely be explored," said Clorinda. "I expect he'll turn out to have been a member of some Shakespearean touring company. Leander Hellespont over in Scottsbeck would know, he's still in charge of the Shakespearean festivals, isn't he? Of course 'ravell'd sleave' is a redundancy because 'sleave' already means fibrous material that has been raveled or matted. This is very baffling, is all I can say. If you're looking for the chops, Dittany, they're in that plastic box marked 'eggs.' "

"And the applesauce is in the meat safe, no doubt," said her dutiful daughter. "Sit still, Mum. I'll manage."

Chapter 7

"The ravell'd sleave, eh?"

Supper was over. Clorinda and Arethusa had gone off to Scottsbeck in the Monks' station wagon to find out whether Leander Hellespont and his wife, Wilhedra, might have any information about traveling Shakespeareans. Osbert was alone with Dittany in the kitchen and intrigued by what she'd managed to worm out of Arethusa.

"And your mother claims a sleave is a—do you remember where we left the dictionary, pet? And what did I do with Mother Matilda's phone number? Ah, here it is."

Dittany brought the dictionary into the kitchen so she could eavesdrop while she checked her mother's definition, but Osbert's call was so short it was hardly worth the effort.

"Hello, Mother Matilda? This is Osbert Monk. I need to know whether your husband was given to reciting Shakespeare. He was? He did? Yes, he must have been. Thank you very much! I'll see you in the morning."

He hung up the phone and turned to Dittany, all agog. "Charles McCorquindale played Macbeth in his college dramatic society. I've got to see Sergeant MacVicar right away. Maybe you'd better come with me, if you feel up to it. I wouldn't know a sleave from a pocket. Was your mother right about that quotation, by the way?"

"Oh yes," Dittany assured him. "Mum's seldom wrong about anything to do with the theater. Darling, do you think Mr. McCorquindale was trying to tell Arethusa where he'd hidden the nutmeg formula?"

"If he wasn't, it seems odd he'd have been quoting Macbeth at a time like that. We know those other two men searched Mr. McCorquindale's clothes while he was either dead or dying on the sidewalk, then took him away in his own car. I can't think why they'd have bothered to lug him off if they'd found the formula then and there, can you?"

"No, dear. It can't have been because they wanted to conceal his identity, or they wouldn't have abandoned his body so close to Lammergen."

"So," Osbert continued, "it looks as though they had to take him and his car along for the simple reason that they hadn't completed their search, don't you think? And they ditched both the body and the car afterwards either because they'd found the formula or because they hadn't. Which, come to think of it, doesn't get us very far."

"But it was a brilliant piece of deduction, darling," Dittany consoled him. "You know, that end of the Lammergen Road does seem a lonely stretch because of the woods around it, but if you looked on the map you'd see that it runs quite near to the Scottsbeck shopping mall. I'll bet you a nickel what those men did was leave another car parked in the mall."

"Good thinking, pet," Osbert agreed. "Then after they'd got rid of the cars with the bullet holes in them, all they'd have had to do would be to run through the woods to the parking lot, pick up the other car, and drive away pretending they'd been doing the stores. Nobody would notice because there's always so much coming and going."

"Speaking of going," said Dittany, "why don't we? The MacVicars will have finished their supper by now. We can at least talk to the sergeant and see what he thinks."

"Right on, pardner. We'd better take the truck in case your feet give out again."

The Monks owned two vehicles. One was the big, newish station wagon which Clorinda had taken over to Scottsbeck; chosen by Osbert and Dittany not out of ostentation but so that Ethel could take her ease in the back. The other was a small, aged pickup truck in which Osbert had been wont during his bachelorhood to go camping; it was now used mostly for taking the trash to the dump. By happy coincidence, the truck also had room in the back for Ethel to spread out comfortably. Refreshed by all that supper and a pleasant snooze, she hopped up and unfurled her shaggy ears to the evening breeze as they cruised down to the police station.

The MacVicars were lingering over a postprandial cup of tea, watching a program about owls on their seldom-used television set. They appeared more pleased than not to be interrupted by Dittany and Osbert.

After the amenities had been dealt with, Mrs. MacVicar imparted the information that the Messrs. Bleinkinsop were dining with Miss Jane in her rooms. After the meal, they were scheduled to drive in Miss Jane's car to Scottsbeck, where various cousins in the second, third, and fourth degrees were gathering to eat dessert with their far-flung but closely connected relations. Miss Jane was quite excited about being the one to introduce the twins, albeit somewhat frazzled by the events of the day thus far.

"We'd like to search the shop while she's gone," said Osbert.

"Arethusa's remembered exactly what it was that VP Nutmeg said to her," Dittany amplified.

"Oh aye?" said Sergeant MacVicar. "And what was that?"

They told him and he nodded. "I see the force of your reasoning. We'd best get on with it, then, ere Miss Jane and guests depart."

Osbert hesitated. "I think, if you don't mind, Sergeant, it might be better if we didn't tell her precisely why we're making the search now. To the untrained mind, that sleave business might sound a trifle on the goofy side. Maybe you could just say you have to check up on things as a matter of routine but hadn't liked to interrupt while she was having such a rush of business."

"Belike I should have closed the shop," said the sergeant, "but it did not cross my mind that Cousin Charles would have hidden anything in so public a place. But needs must when the devil drives, though the idea does sound, as you so rightly remark, a trifle goofy. Come along then, lad. And lass, too," he added generously. "I cannot go in there without Mrs. Derbyshire's permission unless I swear out a warrant, which I could hardly justify doing on the basis of a quotation frae *Macbeth*."

Leaving Mrs. MacVicar to mind the phone, the other three crossed the street. As it happened, they had not a moment to lose. The twins were already stowed in Miss Jane's car, back to back on the rear seat with newspapers under their shoe soles to protect the upholstery, both happy as larks at the prospect of meeting a roomful of cousins. Miss Jane, dolled up in a fancy outfit crocheted of mohair and angora that made her look even more ovine than usual, was locking the side door that led up to her living quarters.

She didn't see why people had to come pestering her at a time like this and she wished to goodness people could get it through their heads that this plaguey business was no business of hers; but she supposed she'd have to let Sergeant MacVicar and Deputy Monk in if it was the law only would they please for pity's sake try not to make any worse mess than they could help because she and the twins had spent a whole solid hour putting the shop to rights after that mob had torn through it like a herd of wild elephants and if she'd known Lobelia Falls was going to be like this she'd have stayed in Scottsbeck.

Osbert, in one of those flashes of inspiration writers get at odd times, told Miss Jane not to worry as he'd brought along his wife to make sure he and the sergeant put everything back where it came from. His wife, he added, was downright persnickety about putting things where they were supposed to go.

Anybody who knew the former Dittany Henbit well would have greeted this assertion with a politely screened snicker. Miss Jane, being relatively new in town, took Osbert's word at face value and even went so far as to say it was nice of Mrs. Monk to help out. She then reminded the search party that, while she herself did not normally draw the blinds over the shop windows at night, blinds were there to be drawn when need arose, and they'd better draw them before they got started or they'd have another pack of gawkers out on the sidewalk rubbernecking in at them.

This was undoubtedly true. Word of the bizzare happening at the yarn shop must have been on the evening news, though none of those present had thought to listen. News in Lobelia Falls was never hard to come by, one way or another. Sergeant MacVicar took the spare key Miss Jane handed him and promised to lock up carefully when they left. She got into her car. They waved her and her passengers off, entered the shop, drew the blinds, and prepared to search.

Osbert looked around at the bin-lined walls, filled with yarns of many kinds and colors. "There's a heck of a lot to search through here. Mother Matilda told me the formula was written on a card that measures two by three inches and is sealed in plastic to keep it from wearing out. That means it's roughly the size of a calling card and fairly stiff on account of the plastic. If VP Nutmeg shoved it into a ball of yarn, I should think he'd have had to choose a big one, so we may as well not bother with the baby yarn."

"But he could have hidden something other than the formula," Dittany objected. "Something tiny, like a rolled-up slip of paper. Or maybe he grabbed Miss Jane's scissors off the counter there and cut the formula into little pieces."

"He was hardly here long enough for that, according to Mrs. Derbyshire's testimony," said Sergeant MacVicar, "but we must not ignore any possibility. I do think, howsomever, we can forget about the highest and lowest shelves. Cousin Charles was not a tall man, nor a young man, as I found out when I saw him this afternoon at the Scottsbeck morgue. With a bullet in his back it does not seem likely he'd have been able to do much in the way of stooping or stretching.''

''What if somebody accidentally bought the yarn he'd put whatever it was into?'' Dittany suggested.

''If VP Nutmeg was anywhere near as bright as Mother Matilda cracked him up to be,'' said Osbert, ''he'd have tried to guard against that chance as best he could. Suppose we begin by checking the bottoms of the bins in the middle rows. We can squeeze each ball of yarn as we put it back and see of anything crackles inside. Dittany, why don't you tackle that table of baby yarn in the middle of the floor, just in case you're right about the small object? Here, I'll pull this stool over to the table so you won't have to stay on your feet.''

''Thank you, dear.''

Dittany settled herself and began a tiresome routine of search and squeeze. By the time she'd finished her stint, she was as heartily sick of the way acrylic felt as the others must be of wool. They were all three sneezing from the fuzz, Sergeant MacVicar most impressively because he had the greatest expanse of nose to sneeze with. Furthermore, Dittany supposed, his ancestors must have been trained on snuff; perhaps the MacVicar sneeze had become hereditary.

Her back ached from perching so long on Miss Jane's stool; she got up and walked around the shop to work out the kinks. Not being a knitter herself, and certainly having no immediate need to learn, Dittany had hardly set foot in the place before except to attend the grand opening back in July. Miss Jane had done a good deal of fixing up since then. Dittany didn't remember having seen the cute little knitted animals and dolls which were now perched here and there with neat little cards beside them saying ''Not for sale . . . but I'll show you how to make your own.'' She quite lost her heart to the Raggedy Andy doll with his red knitted overalls and his blue-and-white-striped turtle-neck jersey. Too bad the sleeves weren't raveled, she thought absently. She took the doll down from the shelf and ran a finger up under the jersey, just in case. Raggedy Andy crackled.

"Osbert," she gasped, "I've found something!"

"What is it, dear?"

"A leaf from a memo pad that has 'From the desk of VP Nutmeg' printed on top, with two scribbled words and a bloody fingerprint."

"Tumultuous tumbleweeds!" He came racing over to her, Sergeant MacVicar right behind. "What does it say?"

"Just a second, let me see. Q something. Quimper, it looks like. Quimper Wardle. Could that be somebody's name?"

"Mother Matilda would probably know. I can show it to her in the morning," said Osbert. "Is it all right for us to keep this, Chief? She might be able to recognize the fingerprint."

Sergeant MacVicar was too big a man to take umbrage, but he did sound a wee bit more Scotch as he replied stiffly, "I myself have the ability to recognize yon fingerprint, Deputy Monk. As a matter of routine, prints were taken in Scottsbeck from the sad remains of Cousin Charles and I obtained a set, also as a matter of routine. That loop and whorl pattern with the small diagonal scar across it is unmistakable."

Osbert blushed. "Sorry, Chief, I meant to say handwriting."

"Oh aye. Cousin Matilda would indeed be the one to know about that."

"Why don't we phone her right now and find out whether the name Quimper Wardle means anything to her," Dittany urged. "Miss Jane won't mind if we use her telephone, Lammergen's not a toll call."

Sergeant MacVicar shook his head. "We'd best wait till morn, lass. The poor lady needs a wee bit of time to be alone with her grief."

"Or with her board of directors, as the case may be,"

said Osbert. ''Do you think we'd better complete the search, Chief, just in case VP Nutmeg left something else?''

''It would not hurt.'' Doggedly, Sergeant MacVicar pulled out an armload of four-ply worsted and went on squishing.

They kept on with the job until they'd covered every spot in the shop that the wounded VP Nutmeg might reasonably be supposed to have been able to reach in his valiant last-ditch attempt to save the mincemeat recipe. However, they unearthed nothing else except a couple of gum wrappers carelessly discarded and a blue button that looked to be off some woman's raincoat. At last they raised the blinds, turned out all but the night-lights, locked the door, and called it a night. Out on Queen Street all was serene now. It was time to go home.

Back on Applewood Avenue, Dittany and Osbert found Clorinda comfortably tucked up in bed with Ethel and a bag of gumdrops, reading *Macbeth*. She reported no progress in the matter of traveling Shakespeareans, which didn't surprise them a bit. She added that the station wagon had been making a funny little noise halfway between a squeak and a rattle, and what did they think it might be? Osbert suggested a rattlesnake singing soprano, and led his by now semiconscious wife along to bed.

Osbert and Dittany both slept soundly and arose betimes, but not so betimes as their nearest neighbors. Jane and Henry Binkle appeared on their doorstep spruce and wide-awake in their business clothes, carrying a fresh-baked pan of muffins, while the Monks were still bathrobed, unkempt, and wondering what had happened to the lid of the teakettle.

''Isn't it awful about what happened?'' was Jane's greeting. ''Who do you suppose did it?''

''Are we still talking about the episode at Miss Jane Fuzzywuzzy's yesterday morning?'' Dittany asked. Things could get awfully confusing if you didn't keep them straight from the beginning, as she knew from a lifetime's experience with Clorinda.

"Heck, no," said Henry Binkle. "That's stale news. We're talking about the robbery last night at Ed Gumpert's stationery store, though Ed's not even sure there was a robbery. More like vandalism, it sounds like to me—every darned ream of paper in stock torn open and scattered all over the floor. Ed's beside himself, I understand. Which would add up to quite a lot of Gumpert," he added reflectively. A life spent behind a counter with a box of biscuits and a cup of tea always ready to hand had not tended to make the stationer's shadow grow less.

"Oh, my stars and garters!" cried Dittany.

The ejaculation could have been interpreted as an appropriate reaction to the Binkles' shocking news or to her finally locating the teakettle lid behind the strawberry geranium plant on the kitchen windowsill. In fact, her outcry stemmed from a far different cause, one which she couldn't explain to the Binkles, dear old friends though they were, without breaking the vow of secrecy she'd made to Mother Matilda.

On the subject of the missing segments of the mince-meat recipe Dittany's lips must perforce be sealed, at least until Osbert had had a chance to get in some detecting over at the factory. She burned to know which color gingham Mother Matilda planned to dress him in. A houndstooth check, something along the color of Grimpen Mire, would really be more appropriate; but perhaps Mother Matilda wouldn't have been able to get any made up on such short notice.

That question, at least, would be cleared up when he got home tonight. She must be sure he put on his new underwear. Osbert was apt to be absentminded about sartorial details and it would hardly become his new office to get debagged in shorts that had seen their best days back when he was still a bachelor. Not that Deputy Monk would allow such an affront to happen as a general rule, but one couldn't be too careful the way things were going lately.

The Binkles said they couldn't stay for the kettle to boil, they had to get over to Scottsbeck and open their bookshop. They'd often wished there were enough customers in Lobelia Falls to have the shop nearer their home, but today they were grateful that it was safely tucked away in a quiet, peaceful shopping mall where nothing ever happened except burglaries, shoplifting, bomb threats, and the occasional riot during the markdown season. Dittany thanked them for the muffins and promised to give them a buzz if any Martians landed during the course of the day.

By the time she got through wishing Jane and Henry a happy day among the tomes and showing them to the door, the kettle was boiling and Osbert had the muffins toasting nicely. She made the tea while he got out the plates and mugs. They didn't bother setting a place for Clorinda. She'd be down when the spirit moved her, which wouldn't be for another hour or two and just as well under the circumstances. Ethel, needless to say, had already breakfasted and was off for her morning stroll around the neighborhood hedges and hydrants.

"I must say it's cozy with just the four of us," Dittany observed as she filled Osbert's mug. "Darling, do you realize what mornings are going to be like around here once the chicks get hatched?"

"Yes, dear." Osbert's reply was indistinct, not only because his mouth was full of muffin but because his mind was no doubt drifting off to the ostrich ranch, where he'd have spent another hair-raising morning among the feather rustlers had not Mother Matilda's need been more pressing. Dittany tried again a little harder.

"Darling, do you also realize why Mr. Gumpert's store got broken into last night?"

"Why, dear?"

"Because of what Arethusa said when that man grabbed her."

"What man, dear?"

"The one who shot VP Nutmeg. Or didn't but the other one did. He asked her 'What did he say?' and she said—"

"I know. A jeweled dagger and a ream of plain white paper." Osbert's attention was fully caught at last. "But Mr. Gumpert doesn't sell jeweled daggers, dear."

"He does so! Don't you remember those fancy paper

knives in the shape of jeweled daggers he got in for Christmas? We gave one to Arethusa and she gave us back a penny because it's supposed to be bad luck if you give somebody anything sharp. The penny's to pay you back so it isn't really a gift.''

"If it wasn't a gift, why did we give it to her?''

"Because it was there to be given, I suppose. Arethusa's not the easiest person in the world to buy a present for, you know. Anyway, Mr. Gumpert still had a few daggers left in his display case last time I was in the shop. I'll bet they're gone now, though. And while we're on the subject of going, hadn't you better go up and put on your best underwear? You're supposed to be in Lammergen by half past eight, aren't you?''

Chapter 8

Osbert was at the mincemeat factory right on the dot. So was Mother Matilda. Her eyes looked a bit red around the lids and she'd put on a black-and-white checkered gingham uniform with a black apron over it, but those were her only concessions to widowhood. She came out to the reception room to greet him, led him into her office, and shut the door.

The reception room had been folksy as all get-out with maple rocking chairs, rag rugs, red gingham curtains at the windows, and a large marmalade-colored cat serving as assistant receptionist. Osbert had expected more of the same here, but Mother Matilda didn't have so much as a potted geranium on her well-ordered desk. She plunked herself down in her swivel chair, nodded him into the less than sybaritic armchair opposite, and said briskly, "Now then, Osbert, what have you to tell me?"

"Reginald, please. I'm incognito. First I have something to ask you." Osbert pulled out his wallet and carefully fished out the slip of paper Dittany had found up Raggedy Andy's sleeve. "We conducted a thorough search of the yarn shop last night, and my wife found this. Sergeant MacVicar says the thumbprint is your husband's. Can you tell me whether that's also his handwriting?"

Mother Matilda slid her eyeglasses farther down on her

nose and held the paper out at arm's length. "Charles usually wrote a lovely neat hand. If he was scribbling the note in a moving car while getting shot at and with a bullet in his back, though, I expect this might be more or less the way it would have come out. There are points of similarity, that's the best I can say."

"I understand. And does the name Quimper Wardle mean anything to you?"

"Oh yes. Mr. Wardle works here, in peel procurement. At least I think he does. Mrs. Pettigrew, his department head, says he hasn't shown up for the last couple of days. Mrs. Pettigrew told me she'd telephoned Mr. Wardle's landlady to ask whether he was sick, and the landlady said she hadn't laid eyes on him since last Friday. If that man doesn't show up pretty darn soon, I can tell you, he won't be working for Mother Matilda any longer."

"How long has Mr. Wardle been with the firm?"

"A little over three months."

"And how long ago did the trouble with the VPs start?"

"Two months ago to the day."

"Um," said Osbert. "How did you happen to hire Mr. Wardle? He didn't come up through the ranks, obviously."

"No, he didn't, although it is our normal practice to promote from within if we possibly can. Not every employee will accept promotion if it's offered, you know. They get totally dedicated to a certain job and simply wouldn't be happy anywhere else. And of course peel buying isn't like mixing and stirring, for instance. There just isn't the same aesthetic thrill in it. That's why good peel buyers are so hard to find."

"Wardle's a good peel buyer, is he?"

"The fact of the matter is, he'd never bought a peel in his life before he came to us. He'd been buying anchovies for a well-known Worcestershire sauce manufacturer over in England. But he wanted desperately to get into peels because, as he explained, anchovies simply don't offer the same scope. That was understandable to us, naturally. Mr. Wardle's references were excellent, and we needed somebody in a hurry, so we decided we might as well give him a chance."

"Why did you need somebody in a hurry?"

"Because Miss Eagleton, who'd been with us for fifteen years, all of a sudden inherited ten thousand dollars from a distant cousin she never even knew she had, and decided to blow the money on a trip to Australia. She's going to spend a whole year with her brother who owns an emu ranch down there."

"Is she, by George?" cried Osbert. "Gosh, I never thought of emus."

"As why would you?" Mother Matilda rejoined somewhat haughtily. "I fail to see why emus are germane to the issue at hand."

"A detective has to keep an open mind, Mother Matilda. You did check Mr. Wardle's references, I assume?"

"Need you ask? We wrote to the factory—that is to say, our personnel director did—and they whizzed us back a reply that was even more glowing than the references he'd shown us in the first place. In fact, they begged us to let them know if we decided not to hire Mr. Wardle because the buyer who's taken his place just can't seem to get the hang of anchovies and they were hoping to wheedle him back. That's not precisely how they phrased it, but that's the gist. I can't say we've found Wardle any great ball of fire ourselves. However, we realize peels are a major readjustment and we've been willing to give him a fair trial."

"He hasn't been handling the job adequately?"

"Oh, he's adequate. Wardle's not a bad peel buyer but he's hardly what you'd call an inspired peel buyer. Miss Eagleton, now, there's a woman who knows how to buy peel! I'm just hoping—selfishly, I grant you—that Miss Eagleton doesn't meet her Mr. Right down under and fritter away her talents among the billabongs. Fred was saying just the other day—"

"By Fred you're referring to VP Cider?" Like his wife, Osbert felt it essential to keep the facts straight from the outset.

"That's right," Mother Matilda confirmed. "Fred was sitting in the cafeteria with Charles and myself after she left, having a midmorning cup of coffee and a mince tart. You must try our mince tarts, by the way. They're quite superb if I do say so. Anyway, Miss Eagleton's name came up and Fred said to Charles and me, 'I sincerely hope Miss Eagleton doesn't throw away the distinguished career that's ahead of her if she comes back. You mark my word, another few years' experience under her belt and that young woman could become one of the legendary names in peel procurement!' And Charles agreed with him. Charles was always quick to give credit where credit was due. Never was a VP Nutmeg more universally beloved.''

Mother Matilda permitted herself one brief sniffle before dragging herself ruthlessly back to the business at hand. ''Osbert—excuse me, Reginald—why do you think Charles wrote Quimper Wardle's name down like that?''

''Because he realized it was Wardle who'd shot him, is the best guess I can make right now.''

''But that's impossible! Quimper Wardle wouldn't say boo to a goose.''

''Did you ever try him? That is, get a goose and—''

Osbert thought perhaps he'd better drop geese as a subject for conversation. He could feel another plot beginning to simmer, and it never did to talk about a plot till one got it written down. And often not even then, because they always sounded so totally ridiculous when one tried to explain them to somebody that one got discouraged before one even started. Besides, Mother Matilda was doing something rather ominous with her upper lip.

''Let's abandon conjecture and look at the facts,'' he said briskly. ''Here we have a valued employee with a brother conveniently situated in Australia. This employee, namely Miss Eagleton the peel buyer, suddenly comes into a mysterious legacy from a relative she didn't even know, and is therefore able to indulge a no doubt long-held dream of going to visit her brother. She thus creates a vacancy into which a hitherto unknown Brit, allegedly with excellent experience in a related field—sort of related, anyway, or related enough for practical purposes—is, as I was working up to say, able to step on the strength of glowing references that purport to be from a well-known British manufacturer of Worcestershire sauce.''

''But of course the references were from the well-known British manufacturer of Worcestershire sauce,'' Mother Matilda retorted, angry that her acumen had been called into question, if only by inference. ''We checked them. I told you that.''

''And precisely how did you check them? You did not, for example, send your personnel director over to chat about Mr. Wardle with their personnel director?''

''That would have been contrary to company practice. We sent an airmail letter, as I mentioned before.''

''And where did you obtain the firm's address?''

''From their letterhead, naturally.''

Osbert nodded. ''Naturally. If you'd decided to telephone instead, you'd naturally have got the number off the letterhead too, wouldn't you?''

''Where else? We don't happen to have all that many British telephone directories lying around our offices. You could hardly expect us to, could you?''

''Of course not, that would be quite unreasonable. Mr. Wardle wouldn't have expected you to, either. The thing of it is, Mother Matilda, it's not at all difficult to filch a letterhead from a well-known company, and get some printer who's not too long on business ethics to run off some new letterheads using the same artwork with a different address and phone number. You then write your own references on the new letterhead, which means that the company you're applying to will write back to the wrong address. You've arranged for a confederate at that address to get hold of their letter, write a glowing reply signed with a forged name, and mail it back to the inquirer. If you'd telephoned instead of writing, they'd no doubt have been waiting for the call and have given you the same kind of snow job over the phone.''

''But how can we find out if we've been taken in?''

''Easily enough. Show me the letter. I'll telephone my

British agents and get them to check out the company address and the names of the alleged writers.''

Mother Matilda shook her head. "I do declare, that's one trick I'd never have thought of in a million years. I still can't believe Mr. Wardle would do such a thing, though.''

"I'm not saying he did," said Osbert. "I'm only pointing out the obvious possibilities for fraud. You say the attacks on personnel didn't start till a month after Wardle arrived. Is he your newest employee?''

"No, we've had two more changes since then. Dear old Willie Phee in Brooms and Buckets finally retired, and young Eppie Elias on the raisin belt left to have her baby. We had a lovely party for Willie and gave Eppie a baby shower. We'd been planning them for weeks.''

"And you've replaced both Willie and Eppie?''

"Oh yes, right away. We had to.''

"But those two were people you'd been expecting to lose, and they don't sound as if they were in positions where they'd have the same opportunity for access to the vice presidents as a peel buyer might.''

"No, I have to grant you that," Mother Matilda agreed. "Also, their places were taken by our own people. Willie's assistant was moved up to take his place. Edward, his name is. Then Edward's nephew Throgwold decided there wasn't much of a future for him at the Scottsbeck car wash, so he applied for Edward's former job, which we were to glad to give him. Throgwold's a lovely boy," she added in parenthesis.

"And Eppie's cousin Bern's wife Phillida, who worked for us before she was married, offered to hold Eppie's job on the raisin line till the baby's old enough to be left with Eppie's mother, who's a perfectly lovely woman and keeps a day nursery; so that worked out just fine. I'll grant you there might have been something fishy about that legacy of Miss Eagleton's, but who's going to start sniffing around to see what's wrong with ten thousand dollars? So you think Charles caught on to Quimper Wardle, eh, and went after him bullheaded, like the brave soul that he . . .''

The composure she'd been so rigidly maintaining broke at last. She fumbled wordlessly in her desk drawer for a box of paper handkerchiefs.

"I think Mr. Wardle will bear looking into, at any rate," Osbert replied gently after Mother Matilda had blown her nose and wiped bitter tears off her eyeglass lenses. "If you'll give me Wardle's letters and the address where he's been living, I'll see what I can find out and report back to you later in the day. By the way, here are my own references about the security job in case you want to show them to the personnel director. I faked up a couple of letterheads out of the Toronto telephone directory with the help of my home copier."

That was actually how it had occurred to him that the enigmatic Quimper Wardle might have pulled the same trick with the Worcestershire sauce company, but Mother Matilda didn't have to know that. She took the letters from him and put them inside a red morocco folder that lay on her desk.

"Thank you, Reginald. I'll just hang on to these till I see what you come up with at the boardinghouse. No sense going through the fuss and bother of putting you on the payroll if we can get this awful business wrapped up right away."

"The sooner the better, as far as I'm concerned."

Hearing about that emu ranch of Miss Eagleton's brother's had been raising the Old Ned with Osbert's sense of priorities. He loved being Deputy Monk, he sincerely craved to help Mrs. MacVicar's newfound cousin out of her dreadful predicament. He knew Dittany felt the same way, and he loved working in harmony with the wife of his bosom.

Yet there was the lure of the old Remington. It would not have been fair to say Osbert cared more for his typewriter than he did for his wife; he loved Dittany with a love that was greater than love, and the typewriter was only a machine. But the fact remained that he'd known the typewriter longer. And meanwhile, back at the ostrich farm . . .

Shaking off temptation, Osbert took Wardle's address and the probably spurious letter from the Worcestershire sauce manufacturer, told Mother Matilda again that he'd be in touch, and left the mincemeat factory.

Since Osbert was not yet and indeed might never become a bona fide member of Mother Matilda's staff, he hadn't ventured to approach the company lot but had simply left his car parked on the street in front of the main entrance. As he came out the door, he observed an elderly policeman in a uniform that had seen better days standing beside the big station wagon, stroking his grizzled chin in a thoughtful and deliberate manner. Nothing daunted, since there really wasn't anything here to be daunted about, Osbert walked straight over to him.

"Morning, Officer."

"Urf." The man thus addressed took his hand away from his chin and then didn't appear to know what else to do with it. "This your wagon?"

"Yes, it is. Or rather, no, it isn't." Osbert had forgotten for the moment that he was not himself today. "Actually it's my brother's. I'm staying with him and his wife until I find a job. That's what I've been doing at the factory, in case you're wondering. Applying, that is."

"Seen Mother Matilda, have you?"

"Yes, we had a constructive chat. At least I think we did. She's a lovely lady, isn't she? I thought it was awfully good of her to see me, my brother says she lost her husband only yesterday in tragic circumstances."

"Shot, so quick and clean an ending."

Osbert was not surprised to hear a Lammergen policeman quoting A. E. Housman. All policemen, at least all the policemen he knew, were poetically inclined. Sergeant MacVicar would recite "The Cotter's Saturday Night" at the drop of a helmet, officers Bob and Ray knew a lot of limericks, and Osbert himself was thoroughly conversant with the works of Robert W. Service. He did not, however, consider this particular snatch of Housman an apt one in view of the time it had taken the late VP Nutmeg to expire.

"I'm afraid the ending wasn't all that quick," he replied. "My—er—brother's wife's aunt-in-law happened to be talking with the proprietor of the yarn shop when Mr. McCorquindale drove up and went inside the shop and came out again. She says he left a trail of bloodstains all the way before dropping dead at her very feet. Hers and Miss Jane Fuzzywuzzy's, I should say. That's what the woman who keeps the yarn shop calls herself, for some unfathomable reason. Her real name, I believe is Derbyshire."

The policeman perked right up and looked official as anything. "Operating under an alias, eh? Has MacVicar arrested her yet?"

"Why, no. Now that you mention it, I don't believe he has."

"Huh! That's typical of MacVicar. Sitting on his hands looking pontifical while the citizens of Lammergen get gunned down in the streets of Lobelia Falls. Somebody ought to write a strong letter to the newspaper."

"Which paper would that be, Officer?" Osbert asked him politely.

The policeman slid his cap forward until the peak almost touched his nose, so that he could scratch the back of his head. Presumably the maneuver was calculated to stimulate thought, but it proved not to be efficacious.

"Darned if I know, now that you ask. I haven't read a newspaper since the time they ran that piece about my brother-in-law getting to be Head Hooter or whatever it was in the Loyal Order of Owls. Seems to me that was the Lobelia Falls paper, come to think of it. No use writing to them, they wouldn't print anything against MacVicar for fear he'd slap 'em in the jug. He can act fast enough when it's his own neck that's in the frying pan, you'd better believe. Well, nice talking to you, Mister. Drive careful and don't shoot anybody."

Chapter 9

Osbert promised to obey the local ordinances and started his engine. The address Mother Matilda had given him for Quimper Wardle was over in West Lammergen. He didn't anticipate any trouble finding his way since West Lammergen was mostly just the opposite end of the road that led from Lammergen proper, which happened by a cozy coincidence to be the road he was on at the moment. As for the house he'd been told to look for, that would have been hard to miss. Its entire front yard was filled with life-sized plastic flamingos, aligned in geometrically precise rows, spaced exactly one foot apart from beak to tail and from wing to wing.

Somebody had taken a great deal of trouble over those flamingos. Osbert wondered why. He didn't dare enter the driveway, which was guarded by a phalanx of mean-looking peach-colored plaster ducks with ferocious orange beaks, but left the car out by the curb and walked up to the door, half-expecting to be met by an emu. Instead, the woman who answered his knock reminded him of a tawny pipit. He couldn't think why this should be so, he didn't recall ever having been reminded of a tawny pipit before. Anyway, she greeted him pleasantly enough.

"Good morning. Did you bring my pinwheels?"

"Er—no, I didn't," Osbert replied, somewhat nonplussed. "I didn't know you wanted any."

"But I ordered them three weeks ago!" she wailed. "I'm desperate for those pinwheels. How do you expect me to finish my magnum opus without them?"

Happily, Osbert was in a position to offer assistance. "When I was in kindergarten, we used to make pinwheels out of colored paper. What you do is, you start with a square and make diagonal cuts at the corners, only you don't cut all the way to the middle. Then you bend every other corner in toward the middle and stick a pin through to twirl it by and Bob's your uncle. It's quite simple, really. If you'd supply a piece of paper, a pair of scissors, and a suitable pin, I could show you in about half a minute. Unless my hand has lost its ancient cunning, that is. I used to be a real whiz at pinwheels when I was five. In fact I was graduated from kindergarten magna cum laude, but my academic career was mostly downhill after that."

"Oh, I'm sure it wasn't! Come in, come in. Just thread your way between the frogs and don't trip over the toadstools. I have some lovely metallic foil with varicolored stripes that will be just the ticket for pinwheels. Better than bought ones, I'll bet, now that genuine celluloid is not to be had except at fantastic prices and in short supply. Oh, sorry, I should have warned you about the stegosaurus. Don't you adore his scales? I made them from the lids of cat-food cans."

The stegosaurus was roughly the size of a cabinet grand piano. Wardle's landlady must have a great many cats, Osbert thought. It occurred to him that he'd somehow got beguiled from his original purpose in coming to West Lammergen.

"Perhaps I should explain," he began as he seated himself at a professional-sized drafting table and measured a precise eight-inch square from a sheet of iridescent peacock-blue foil with squiggly trails of gold, silver, scarlet, and emerald running through it, "that I didn't come here about pinwheels. Though I have to say this one appears to be coming out quite nicely considering how long it's been since—the pin, please. Ah, thank you. See, that's how it's done. You can make them however big or small you want to. I just happen to believe eight inches is the optimum diameter for a paper pinwheel.''

He blew on his creation. It spun like anything. The landlady was jubilant.

"You've opened my eyes to a whole new avenue of self-expression. I can see myriads of pinwheels, galaxies of pinwheels, infinities of pinwheels! How can I ever thank you?''

"You might show me Quimper Wardle's room," Osbert replied at once.

"But Mr. Wardle's not in it.''

"So I've been informed. What I'm trying to find out is, where did he go? Perhaps I ought to explain that I'm here on behalf of Mr. Wardle's employer. Mother Matilda's getting quite worried about him.''

The landlady giggled. "What's a mother for? Come to think of it, though, I expect I ought to be worrying, too. Mr. Wardle's rent is due tomorrow and I need the money to pay for the bow ties.''

"Bow ties?" said Osbert. "I thought it was pinwheels.''

"Pinwheels too, but the bow ties are another of my top priorities. They're to put on the flamingos," she explained. "You know, the kind that come pre-tied and hook on with an elastic band. I'm making a statement about conformity.''

"For or against?''

"That's for the viewer to decide. I'm an artist, not a preacher.''

"And your medium is flamingos?" Osbert was still gamely trying to keep the facts in order.

"My medium," the landlady stated rather grandly, "is kitsch.''

"Kitsch? You mean like—well, big green frogs with holes in their backs?''

"Precisely. If it's tacky, if it's garish, if it's so cloyingly cute and whimsical it makes you long for a shot of insulin, then it sets my creative juices pumping ta-pocketa-

pocketa-pocketa like the mad scientist's chemistry tubes in the old horror movies. I can't help it, that's just the way I am. Actually, those flamingos by themselves are somewhat too tasteful and conservative for me, but using them in a massed arrangement does tend to lift them out of the prosaic and mundane, don't you think? And the bow ties will make all the difference. But you say you're anxious to get hold of Quimper Wardle. Whatever for?''

''He's needed back at the mincemeat factory,'' Osbert improvised. ''They're running out of orange peel. And since you've intimated that you're about to run out of rent money . . .''

''A point well taken. Come along then. I'm Mrs. Phiffer, by the way. Perhaps you've heard of me?''

''Oh yes.'' Osbert was too busy picking his way through a minefield of pots filled with plants made principally of scrubbing brushes and mousetraps to add that he'd first heard of her only a short while ago from Mother Matilda, which was probably just as well. ''My name is Monk. Reginald Monk, not to be confused with my brother Osbert. I'm sort of a temporary personnel assistant just now. These plants are quite—er—evocative.''

''Oh, do you think so?'' Mrs. Phiffer made a moue of disappointment. ''They're intended to induce a mood of utter boredom.''

''That's just what they evoke,'' Osbert hastened to reassure her. ''What I meant to say was they bore me stiff. Honestly, I've never been more bored by anything in my whole life. Even my—er—brother's mother-in-law would be bored by them, and she's not a person who bores easily, I'm here to tell you. Is this Mr. Wardle's room?''

''This is it. I had a lovely flibbertigibbet made out of old bathmats and toothpaste tubes hanging on the door, but Mr. Wardle didn't seem to think it was in keeping with the dignity of his position, so I had to take it down. I suppose what you want is to look around for clues and all that sort of thing. Letters from sinister foreigners saying 'Fly at once, all is discovered.' Or from his girlfriend saying 'Come at once or I'll elope with the undertaker's assistant.' ''

"Precisely," said Osbert. "It's not as if I were just trying to snoop, you know, it's for Wardle's own good. Mother Matilda's threatening to tie a can to him if he doesn't get back to work pretty darned soon."

"I'm none too keen on Mr. Wardle's missing his payday, myself," Mrs. Phiffer confessed, "nor do I care whether you snoop or not. We free spirits are above petty conventions. In fact, I used to do quite a lot of snooping myself, back when I was making the stegosaurus. What else was there to do? I kept running out of cat-food lids and had to hang around waiting for the neighbors' cats to get hungry again. That was a heartbreaker, I can tell you, walking down the street and having to watch all those inconsiderate felidae lolling around on their porch steps burping and washing their whiskers or else slinking around the fields after poor, innocent little cutesy-pootsy mice when they might have been scoffing up another round of pussy goo. I'll leave you to your snooping, then. I'm simply bursting to go make a pinwheel and see how it feels!"

Off she ran, merry as a pipit. Osbert supposed it was something to have been able to bring a ray of sunshine into this woman's kitsch-crammed life, though he didn't like to think what might come of the pinwheels. He put on the gloves he'd brought to avoid leaving fingerprints, although he felt awfully overdressed in them and they did make it awkward trying to rifle drawers and handle such correspondence as there was, which was not a great deal and most of that addressed only to Occupant.

In fact the scope for searching was far less than he could have wished. The room was not large and either Wardle had taken some of his possessions away with him or else he hadn't brought many in the first place.

The missing peel buyer's wardrobe was of good quality but hardly lavish: two suits—one gray worsted, one brown tweed—three sets of underwear, three shirts fresh from the laundry, two that needed to go, and a smallish pile of socks Osbert didn't bother to inventory. Wardle might of course have taken a packed suitcase with him, though an empty suitcase and a small carry-on bag were sitting in the closet.

If he'd gone away of his own volition, though, Osbert thought it rather odd that Quimper Wardle hadn't taken his razor, his toothbrush, or, most inscrutably, his bridge-work. A contraption of wire and steel with a bicuspid, a canine, and an incisor attached was lying on the nightstand beside the narrow bed, where a drowsy peel buyer might naturally park it before drifting off to dreamland. That Wardle had not resumed his portable dentition on rising suggested to Osbert that either Mrs. Phiffer's boarder was in a hurry, that he was awfully absentminded, or that he hadn't been planning to chew anything.

Perhaps he hadn't been able to take the time. Here were Wardle's pajamas, thrown down in a heap although he appeared to be neat in his habits by and large. Here was a small hole in the pajama coat where a button should have been, and here under the dresser was the button. The fragment of cloth still caught in the threads suggested that the button had not fallen but had been wrenched off, either by a frantically hurrying Wardle or by a ruder hand.

Here also was a section of broken-off brown shoelace approximately five inches long, but where was the brown shoe it came from? A pair of well-polished black shoes sat in the closet, a pair of calfskin slippers lay under the bed along with a great many dust kittens. Perhaps Mrs. Phiffer was saving them to do something creative with. But no-where could Osbert find a single brown oxford, much less a pair. Was it possible that a sober, respectable Englishman who wouldn't say boo to a goose had of his own volition put on a shoe that was incapable of being properly tied and walked out into the night? Where to, for Pete's sake?

Osbert pondered. If, for instance, Quimper Wardle had got up in the night, as a man no longer young might well have felt a need to do, and had not been able to find his slippers because they'd been kicked under the bed, there would have been nothing remarkable about his thrusting his feet into the shoes that happened to be lying ready on the mat and letting the laces dangle. But Wardle could hardly be still in the bathroom; surely Mrs. Phiffer would have noticed by now. And the bed was made up, so perhaps he hadn't been asleep at all.

And why would he have wrenched off his pajamas in such a hurry? Because Mrs. Phiffer had poured itching powder down the legs and back in a burst of creativity? But what would she have achieved by that unless she'd hung around to observe the effect when Wardle donned his pajamas? And if in fact she had hung around, and if she was so dad-blanged free a spirit as she cracked herself up to be, why hadn't she come straight out and told Osbert what happened then? He hoped she'd finished her pinwheel by now because it looked as if he'd better haul her up here posthaste to answer a few questions.

Osbert went out into the hall and stuck his head over the stairwell. "Mrs. Phiffer, could you come upstairs a minute, please?"

"Just a second while I—ouch! Oh, it's beautiful!"

Seconds later, Mrs. Phiffer came scampering up the stairs, holding her pinwheel by its pin. To Osbert's practiced eye, her maiden effort wasn't a patch on his own masterly achievement. She was happy with it, though; he supposed that was what counted. He made the polite noises she obviously expected, then got back to business.

"I wanted to check on a few details with you, Mrs. Phiffer. For one thing, did you make up Mr. Wardle's bed that same morning you last saw him?"

She blew on her pinwheel and shook her head. "I'm not sure it was the last morning, but I know I made the bed sometime because the bed's been made, as you can see for yourself, and it wasn't made by him because he never did."

"But you didn't straighten the room? I notice his pajamas are still on the floor."

"I noticed them, too," she replied coldly, "and they can stay there for all I care. I don't think it's quite respectable for a landlady to be picking up her lodger's pajamas. I'd have told him so, only the subject never came up before. Mr. Wardle's usually quite neat in his habits."

"So I gathered. What it looks like to me, Mrs. Phiffer, is that this time Mr. Wardle must have left here in a hurry. For one thing, he forgot his bridgework."

"So he did." Osbert was somewhat unnerved to catch the covetous glint in the landlady's narrowed eyes. "One could do something terribly exciting with those," she murmured.

"No doubt," Osbert replied, "but I shouldn't try it if I were you. Is Mr. Wardle generally in the habit of wearing all his teeth?"

"I assume he must be. I expect I'd have noticed the gap if he weren't. The artist's eye, you know. And Mr. Wardle's a smiley kind of man."

"What about his clothes?"

"Oh, he definitely wears those. I don't know what sort of place you think I'm running here, Mr. Monk, but—"

"All I meant was, could you tell me if any of his clothes are missing from the closet? There are two suits hanging here; has he taken any away?"

"No, he only brought the two with him. He told me he'd traveled light when he left England because he wasn't sure how things were going to work out at the mincemeat factory and he didn't want to pay for extra luggage. Once he was properly settled, he said, he was going to have his brother ship the rest of his things over to him. He does have a pair of flannel slacks and a green jersey he likes to wear on weekends."

"Then those must be what he had on when he left that last time." Now, Osbert felt, they were getting somewhere. "Does Mr. Wardle have a car?"

"No, he rides a bicycle to work. Mr. Wardle says that in England everybody rides a bicycle to work. He doesn't see why he shouldn't go on doing so here in Lammergen just because nobody else does. Do you?"

"Heck, no," said Osbert. "I think it's a great idea. Where's his bicycle now, I wonder?"

Mrs. Phiffer returned him a blank look. "To tell you the truth, I haven't given that bicycle a moment's thought. I try never to think about bicycles. There's so little one can do with a bicycle, except ride it. Or not ride it, of course.''

One could take the bicycle apart and hang the pieces in the garage, Osbert thought, but he decided not to suggest it. Mrs. Phiffer's garage was probably crammed full of artificial aardvarks, anyway. "Where does Mr. Wardle keep his bicycle when he's not riding it?'' seemed a safe enough question.

Moreover, this was one to which Mrs. Phiffer had a ready answer. "Out in the shed behind the kitchen. I had to move my duck mold to make room.''

"You mold your own ducks?''

"Naturally. Ducks offer a great deal of scope, you know.''

"I'm sure they do. You didn't actually see Mr. Wardle riding off on his bicycle the day he disappeared, by any chance? Was that last Saturday?''

"Yes, Saturday. Or was it Sunday? Or possibly Monday? Not later than Monday, I'm positive, because that was the day I made up his bed fresh for the week. I always change my boarder's bed on Monday. One simply must keep to a routine or nothing would ever get done. Don't you find that to be so?''

"Oh yes, unquestionably. But you honestly can't recall which day you last saw Mr. Wardle?''

"Perhaps it does seem a trifle dull of me, but you see Mr. Wardle's not exactly inspiring, either. He's like the bicycle, there's just nothing much one can do with him. Except change his bed on Mondays, and he gets dreadfully upset if one tries to be creative about that.''

"I guess what we'd better do,'' said Osbert, "is check out the shed and see whether the bicycle's still there. By the way, does Mr. Wardle own a pair of brown shoes?''

Mrs. Phiffer perked up. "Indeed he does! Lovely ones with wing tips and little holes poked into the leather. I could look at them for hours.''

"You haven't taken them somewhere to look at?''

"I'd never do that! I respect my lodger's privacy.''

"You don't remember throwing away part of a broken shoelace he may have left in the wastebasket or somewhere?"

"Heavens, no. Think of all the things one could do with a broken shoelace."

"What about the outside help? You don't have somebody who comes in to clean once a week, for instance?"

Osbert made the suggestion with no great degree of enthusiasm. Mopping and dusting did not appear to be part of Mrs. Phiffer's routine. In fairness to her, he didn't see how much cleaning would be possible in an establishment so rife with creativity. Mrs. Phiffer only gave him a pitying smile and shook her curls.

"Is that all, Mr. Monk? Not to hurry you off, but I'm simply itching to get back to my pinwheels."

"And I mustn't keep you," Osbert replied courteously. "I think we've done about as much as we can here. Just one more question: when you made up the bed, did you happen to notice anything that might be considered unusual about the bedding?"

She pondered a moment. "No, I don't recall a thing. Except, I suppose, for the suicide note on the pillow."

Chapter 10

"Suicide note?" cried Osbert. "Did you keep the note? Where is it now?"

"Still on the pillow, of course," the landlady replied. "I didn't want to disturb Mr. Wardle's arrangement any more than I could help. He'd done a positively superb job: the pillow askew, the pajamas thrown down in a dejected heap, the carefully disheveled bedclothes—all so dramatically understated. Grant you, I missed the fragment of broken shoelace. Subtle nuance just doesn't cut the mustard with me, I'm afraid. My predilection is for the bold, sweeping effect, as you may have gathered."

"I did have a feeling it might be, Mrs. Phiffer. Could you show me the note, please?"

"I'd love to. Shall I dishevel the bedclothes to give you the full effect?"

"But then you'd have to make up the bed again," Osbert pointed out. "Why don't you just skew the pillow a little, and let me visualize the rest?"

"Oh yes, that's a far more creative approach." Mrs. Phiffer drew down the spread and skewed the pillow a little. "Voilà!"

Osbert bent forward, careful not to touch the sheet of paper that lay—artistically, no doubt—on the clean pillowcase. Quimper Wardle had pinched a piece of Mother

Matilda's Mincemeat stationery, he noted with disapproval. Could this be a case of *falsus in uno?* Anyway, the note was simple and to the point, as might have been expected from a man of business.

"This has been a catastrophic debacle. I find myself unable to continue. Pray grant your forgiveness for the turpitude I have committed and for that which I am about to consummate. *Moriturus te saluto.* Yrs, Q.J.G.L. Wardle, B.A., P.T.O., Past Hon. Sec. R.S.A.B."

"I wonder what 'Past Hon. Sec. R.S.A.B.' means," said Osbert.

"Past Honorable Secretary, Royal Society of Anchovy Buyers,' " Mrs. Phiffer replied briskly. "That's perfectly obvious. What I'm wondering is what the rest of the note means."

"Offhand and pending further study, I'd say it means Mr. Wardle found himself in the soup because of some awful thing he'd been up to and can't go on doing whatever he did. He wants to be forgiven for that and for another crime he hasn't committed yet."

"But if he's planning further perfidy, why does he say he can't go on?"

"Good question. It's what we in the field of literature call a non sequitur."

"How cute. And what's this last bit all about?"

"It means that he who is about to die salutes you. 'You' in this case meaning, presumably, you."

"That was sweet of him. One does like being included."

Osbert gazed at her in wonder. "Mrs. Phiffer, it never occurred to you that this note might have been genuine?"

"Well, naturally I realized at once that this was a genuine note, insofar as it was written on real paper with what I should say on cursory examination was a poorly functioning ballpoint pen. As for the text—Mr. Monk, by 'genuine' do you mean that Mr. Wardle was trying to tell me he actually meant to go somewhere on his bicycle and kill himself?"

"The bicycle would be inferential, but the general tenor

of the note does indicate that what he had in mind was *felo de se,* also known as suicide.''

"You do have a marvelous eye for nuance, I must say, Mr. Monk. First the broken shoelace and now this! But my lodgers never commit suicide. They may throw tantrums and storm off in huffs—in fact, they always do, sooner or later—but they never kill themselves. Why should they? Why should he, if it comes to that? Can it be that Mr. Wardle's turpitude was only something like having bought the wrong kind of peel? Maybe it wasn't even his fault. He might have ordered the right peel and the peel people delivered the wrong kind. Cassava peel or manioc peel or something. These things happen all the time; he needn't have taken it so dreadfully to heart. Oh, why didn't he talk to me? I could have made cocoa and told him the race is not always to the swift.''

"That would have been kind of you.''

Osbert was touched by the landlady's obvious sincerity, though he couldn't help wondering what she might have put in the cocoa. "We'd better leave this note where you found it for the time being, and draw the covers back up the way you had them. I'd suggest you not show or even mention the note to anybody else until we find out what's happened to Mr. Wardle. He may have changed his mind, you know, and it could be awfully embarrassing for him if the story got around. It's quite likely he'd be so angry with you he'd go off in a huff without paying his rent.''

"Oh, say not so!" cried Mrs. Phiffer. "I'll simply die if I can't pay for those bow ties. What are we going to do?''

"I'd suggest we go downstairs and hunt for that bicycle. You say he generally leaves it in the shed?''

The shed was easily searched but unfruitful of result. The narrow niche reserved for Mr. Wardle's use was empty, and Mrs. Phiffer's penchant for mass arrangements left no other space where it could have been put. The backyard was full of multicolored plaster ducks. The garage contained only a great many crepe paper owls and a

1952 DeSoto painted in the MacDonald of Sleat hunting tartan and wearing a sporran on its radiator grille.

"So the logical assumption is that Mr. Wardle has in fact ridden off on his bicycle," Osbert conceded at last. "Mrs. Phiffer, if you were looking for a likely place to commit suicide, where would you go?"

"Over to the mincemeat factory and eat myself to death."

"But what if Mother Matilda wouldn't let you?"

"Then I wouldn't do it."

The landlady's reasoning was valid enough, Osbert supposed, but her reply was unhelpful. He tried another track. "What I mean is, do you know of any conveniently situated cliffs a distraught peel buyer could plunge from with a reasonable expectation of breaking his neck when he landed? Or perhaps a dark and dismal mere surrounded by weeping willows and suitable for self-induced drowning."

"Oh yes," cried Mrs. Phiffer, "I know the very mere. You can't get to it by car, but there's a footpath."

"Which would also be navigable on a bicycle?"

"Easily. Children ride their bikes over there in the summer to swim. It's rather far to walk."

"How far? Two miles? Three? Can you show me the path?"

Mrs. Phiffer didn't think it was much over four miles away. All Mr. Monk had to do was cut through the field across the way, continue on to the big water tower, and keep going until he found himself having to choose between stopping at the brink or falling into the water. She made no offer to accompany him; it was clear to see that she wanted to go back in the house and make some more pinwheels.

Osbert didn't want to walk all the way to the mere either, but what else could he do? He might perhaps go back to the factory and see if anybody had a bicycle to lend. No, that would be likely to set the employees wondering whether he was in fact the Reginald Monk he pretended to be. Walking was his only course.

He paused at his car long enough to take his camera out

of the glove compartment and sling it around his neck. This would indicate to watching neighbors, of whom there no doubt were several, that he was most likely some artistic friend of Mrs. Phiffer's in quest of the picturesque. The camera would also come in handy should he find any sign of Mr. Wardle, such as the odd hand or foot, scattered along the way. There was also, he realized, the chance that Wardle's alleged suicide might not have been self-induced.

Pausing to take a picture of the water tower just in case anybody was still watching, Osbert located the opening of the path to the mere with no difficulty since all he had to do was follow the bicycle tracks, of which he found a tasteful assortment. It would have been nice if he'd been able to pick out Quimper Wardle's tire prints, assuming Wardle had in fact come this way, but the fact that there were bicycle tracks at all encouraged him to proceed.

The day, now that he had time to consider the matter, was crisp and sunny, the breeze of exactly the right velocity to cool the overheated brow without ruffling the equanimity. The path was wide enough to follow easily, narrow enough to let the tall, yellowing grasses brush against his legs now and then in a friendly way. This would be good country for ostriches, Osbert couldn't help thinking, though he supposed they'd have to wear mufflers in the wintertime.

Thus musing, Osbert realized after a time that he was enjoying his walk. Like all clean-living, high-thinking Western writers, he was an outdoorsman at heart though not always in practice. The only trusty Remington he owned was that trusty old office-model typewriter, which performed well enough back in the dining room on Applewood Avenue but would have been an awkward piece of equipment to take on a hike.

After an hour or so among the beauties of nature, Osbert was almost disappointed to find himself confronting a line of weeping willow trees and hearing the quack of ducks not cast by Mrs. Phiffer. He'd reached the mere.

As meres went, Osbert didn't find this a particularly exciting specimen. Its main attraction must be that it was here where other meres were not.

"Merely a mere," he murmured aloud.

It gave him rather a jolt to hear a croaky, froggy voice reply, "Speak up, sonny. How'm I s'posed to hear if you mumble?"

"Oh," cried Osbert, "I beg your pardon. I thought you were a stump."

Osbert's had been an excusable misapprehension. The elderly person hunkered down on the bank of the mere did not actually have moss growing over him or her, as the case might have been. However, there was an overall effect of mossiness that might have deceived an even eaglier eye than Osbert's, particularly if that eye happened to be somewhat distracted by ducks. Evidently accustomed to being fed by the cyclists, a picked squadron of them were closing in on him, uttering loud demands for popcorn and sandwich crusts.

Osbert did happen to have a couple of hermits in his pocket which he'd brought along in case of emergency, but he was darned if he'd part with them to this rowdy lot. He was groping for words to convince them that they were quacking up the wrong pant leg when the elderly person took a hand in the matter.

"Garran! Gerrahahere! Cussed critters! Just like the rest of 'em these days, always looking to get something for nothing. Back in my day, a duck wasn't too proud to stick its head in the mud and grub up a few roots. Nowadays they want everything handed to 'em on a silver platter. Why shouldn't a duck do an honest day's work for its living, same as I had to back when I was its age? That's what I'd like to know. Eh, Bub? Answer me that, will you?"

"I—er—"

"How come you ain't working? Young sprout like you ought to have something better to do than lollygag around here bothering the ducks, getting 'em all riled up, start 'em quacking and stomping and making a nuisance o' theirselves worse'n them boom-boxes the kids bring with 'em. You got a boom-box with you?''

''No, I—er—''

''Huh! Then why ain't you out earning the money to buy one? I bought my own ukulele when I was ten years old, with money I earned turning the wringer for my Aunt Josephine. She used to do all the washing for the mince-meat factory, just herself and me to help when I wasn't in school. We was awful workers in them days! Had to be; Mother Matilda was one fussy woman, I can tell you. Was that how come she wouldn't hire you?''

''What makes you think she wouldn't hire me? I'm doing an errand for Mother Matilda right now.''

Perhaps this was indiscreet, but Osbert had decided he might as well tell the truth since this elderly person most likely wouldn't be listening anyway. As luck would have it, the elderly person was.

''What kind of errand?''

''One of her employees is missing. She sent me to find him.''

''That so? Wouldn't happen to be the fella who drowned himself last Friday night?''

''You—er—?''

''Yup, that's why I'm here. I'm guarding his clo'es. I don't like to take 'em away till I've made certain sure he ain't coming up. But if anybody gets 'em that ain't entitled to 'em, it's going to be yours truly.''

Looking to get something for nothing, then. This elderly person was a fine one to criticize the ducks, thought Osbert, refraining from saying so.

''I don't want the clothes myself,'' he explained, ''but I'd very much like to take a look at them, if you don't mind. Where are they?''

''I'm sitting on 'em.''

''Then would you mind—er—''

''Yup, I would.''

''How about if I pay you to get up?''

"How much?"

"What's your customary fee?"

"Four bucks if you touch, two if you look."

"Fair enough." Osbert dug in his pocket and pulled out two dollars. "I won't know whether I'll want to touch the clothes until after I've seen them."

"How do I know you won't grab 'em and run?" said the elderly person sneakily.

"Here, I'll put the other two dollars over on this big rock. No, I won't," Osbert contradicted himself as a couple of ducks started after the money with gleams in their eyes.

"Put another rock on top, so's they can't get at it," the elderly person suggested.

That made sense, so Osbert did. "All right, there's your money. Now would you mind standing up?"

"Nope, I wouldn't mind a bit. Question is, how'm I going to manage it?"

"Would you like me to give you a hand?"

"Now you're talking! Just let me get my feet under me."

That took some doing. Eventually, however, the elderly person managed to get satisfactorily adjusted for the maneuver and held out a hand that appeared to have been fashioned from the sort of roots a duck might drag up from the bottom of the mere. "Okay, Bub. Take 'er slow and easy."

Osbert tugged. This was harder than he'd expected—it felt like hauling a waterlogged stump. At last the elderly person stood more or less upright and tottered a step or two from his or her previous location, then settled down in the new spot with an air of being about to take root.

Osbert didn't care whether he or she rooted or not. The clothes were now exposed to view and must, he thought, have made for awfully damp sitting. Both the dark green jersey and the gray flannel slacks were soaking wet.

"Is this how you found them?" he asked.

"How I found 'em was, I tripped over 'em trying to get

away from them cussed panhandling ducks,'' the elderly person replied with no doubt justifiable acrimony.

"I meant is this where they were lying? Right in this very spot?''

"If that's what you want to know, why didn't you say so in the first place? Anyways, I ain't telling.''

"Why not?''

"Because you ain't given me them other two dollars yet. You're going to touch them clothes, I can tell from the grabby look in your eyes. Just like them ducks over there, trying to beak me out o' something for nothing.''

"All right,'' said Osbert. "Yes, I am going to touch these clothes and yes, I'm going to give you the other two dollars, but not till you quit playing games and answer my question. Were they where they are now and were they folded up like this, or did you fold them yourself so they'd be more comfortable to sit on?''

"They was where they are, but spread out like as if they was put to dry. Only they wasn't wet then, just sort of damp. They keep getting wetter on account of soaking up the dew or something. I ain't telling you whether I folded 'em till you give me them other two dollars. That's another question an' you said only one.''

"Fair enough. Here you are, then.'' Osbert removed the top stone and handed over the money. "Since you've already handled the clothes, I don't see any harm in my handling them again. I want you to watch and make sure I don't carry anything away.''

"Watching's extra,'' said the elderly person.

"Now who's being a duck?'' snapped Osbert. "Don't watch, then. See if I care.''

That settled the matter. The elderly person stared without flickering an eyelash while Osbert examined first the green jersey, which told him nothing of interest, then the gray flannels, which told him all he needed to know.

In the first pocket he tried, Osbert found a wallet containing forty-seven dollars and thirteen cents Canadian and five British pence, along with an expired membership card in the Royal Society of Anchovy Buyers bearing the signature of Quimper Wardle, Hon. Sec. In the other side pocket he found a sheet of paper that had been roughly torn off a memorandum pad, headed FROM THE DESK OF VP LEMON PEEL. On it were hastily scribbled figures and symbols which could only refer to the part played by that vital ingredient in the manufacture of Mother Matilda's Mincemeat.

Chapter 11

"Good show," cried Osbert. "Now we have to find the bicycle."

"You going to search the bicycle, too?" asked the elderly person.

"No, I'm going to ride it back to town and see the police chief about getting the mere dragged."

"Dragged to where?"

"What I meant was, I'm going to arrange for somebody to bring a boat and a kind of a scoop thing with long ropes on it that they can drag along the bottom."

"Won't work," said the elderly person.

"Why not?"

"Because this mere don't have no bottom."

Osbert permitted himself a little laugh. "I can't believe that. All meres have bottoms."

"Then how come they call this one Bottomless Mere, eh?"

"I wasn't aware they did."

"Well, they did and they do and it is," the elderly person retorted snappishly. "What do you want to drag the bottom for, anyway?"

"Because if Mr. Wardle has actually drowned himself, we've got to get him out."

"I don't see what for. He ain't going to be much good

to anybody if you do, far as I can see. Mother Matilda won't want him back all bloated an' slimy, will she?''

"No, I shouldn't think she would," Osbert had to admit, "but she does want to know what's become of him. If Mr. Wardle's not coming back to work, she'll have to hire somebody to take his place. Surely you can understand that?"

"I s'pose I could if I was o' mind to work on it for a while," the elderly person conceded. "So what it boils down to is, you're hoping to show her you've killed him off so's you can grab his job, eh. Is that it?"

"No, that's darned well not it," Osbert retorted irately. "I don't want his job. I wouldn't take his job if Mother Matilda offered it to me on a silver platter."

The elderly person was not impressed. "Huh, that figures. Them ducks don't want his job, neither. They just want to lollygag around looking for somebody to give 'em a—"

This seemed to be where Osbert had come in. He left the elderly person berating the ducks and went to hunt for the bicycle.

He couldn't see why Mr. Wardle would have bothered to hide his bike since the indications were that he hadn't been planning to use it any more. Why wasn't it right there with the clothes? If some thief had come along and stolen the bicycle, why hadn't he taken the money out of Mr. Wardle's wallet while he was about it? Perhaps there'd originally been more money than there was now and the thief had left some for the next thief, although that did suggest a remarkably forbearing attitude in a person of criminal tendencies.

Further exploration exploded the hypothesis of any thief at all, philanthropic or otherwise. Osbert found the bicycle leaning against a tree over on the other side of the mere. What was it doing here? Being a writer, Osbert could easily picture the distraught apprentice peel buyer riding aimlessly around the mere, wearying of the bike, parking it here and wandering back to the other side. Perhaps Wardle had sat and brooded for a while on the bank until at last he'd torn off his outer garments in despair and waded into the murky waters.

Perhaps the ducks had swum quacking after him in the hope that he might after all be good for a handout. They'd have been in for a sad letdown when the allegedly bottomless deeps closed over Wardle's head and the former Hon. Sec. of the Royal Society of Anchovy Buyers became one at last with the finny denizens of the mere.

After a moment's reflection, Osbert realized he might perhaps be overoptimistic in supplying the mere with even hypothetical finny denizens. The ducks could well have eaten them all, if there'd been any around in the first place. What difference did it make? He had more pressing things than fish to think about.

Even though Wardle's slacks and jersey had been lying relatively unmolested since Friday night, Osbert felt uneasy about leaving them here any longer. He took a photograph of the garments as they lay on the bank, and another of the elderly person as witness to the taking of the first picture. Then, to the loudly expressed chagrin of the elderly person, he strapped the soggy evidence down on the bicycle carrier and set off awheel to find Lammergen's police chief.

True to his reputation, Fridwell Slapp did his utmost to keep from being found. Little did he reckon with Deputy Monk, though. Barely fifteen minutes after Osbert had pedaled into town much in the manner of Young Lochinvar coming out of the west, he had Slapp cornered in the hindmost booth of the Du-Kum-Inn Café and Live Bait Shop.

Osbert's first thought on entering the café was "This is no place to order a sardine sandwich." Recollecting, however, that breakfast had been a long time ago and that any prospect of getting back to Dittany's home-cooking might be even farther in the offing, he did request a glass of milk and a mincemeat tart. As a goodwill gesture, Osbert also offered to buy a tart for the police chief, but Slapp said traitorously that he was fed to the eyeballs with mincemeat and would have two chocolate eclairs instead.

While they consumed their dainties, Osbert explained the need for a boat and a dragging device. Fridwell Slapp explained why he didn't see much sense in dragging the mere. Osbert then suggested they call in the Mounties. Slapp demurred that he didn't like to bother them. Osbert looked Slapp square in the eye and said, "In that case, I expect what I'd better do is go over to the mincemeat factory and ask Mother Matilda what she thinks."

Thereupon, Slapp said well, he guessed maybe what they'd better do was go out there with a boat and drag the mere. Osbert said that was a great idea, so he ordered another mincemeat tart while Chief Slapp and the waiter, who turned out to be VP Live Bait, held a lengthy technical discussion. Their talk eventually culminated in a decision to commandeer an aluminum rowboat belonging to one Zingbert Angelus and borrow a drag scoop from Zingbert's brother-in-law whose name Osbert failed to catch.

Such complex negotiations would naturally take time. Probably quite a lot of time, Osbert suspected, considering Fridwell Slapp's general modus operandi. Having by now finished his second tart and feeling no inclination toward a third, he suggested that he himself might fill in the waiting period by riding Wardle's bicycle over to Wardle's late place of residence and seeing whether Mrs. Phiffer could identify the vehicle and the clothing as her tenant's. Both Chief Slapp and VP Live Bait thought that was a great idea, so he went.

Mrs. Phiffer acted pleased enough to see him. However, Osbert found it not easy to capture her full and undivided attention. The bow ties had been delivered during his absence and she was absorbed in sorting them as to color and pattern before putting them around the flamingos' necks. In order to expedite the matter, Osbert took a hand in the sorting. He became so caught up in the creative process that he had to call himself sternly back to his original mission.

"Mrs. Phiffer, I want you to look carefully at these clothes and this bicycle, and see whether you can tell me whose they are."

"But naturally I can tell you whose they are. They're Mr. Wardle's. If they weren't, why would you bother asking me to identify them?"

"Mrs. Phiffer, this is now a police matter. You have to be absolutely certain. Are these exactly like the clothes you've seen before on Mr. Wardle?"

"No, of course they're not. Any time in the past when I've seen these clothes, they were clean, dry, and occupied by Mr. Wardle. Now they're wet, empty, and look as if they may have been sat on by some elderly person on a damp riverbank."

"But you have the eye of an artist," Osbert prompted. "Can't you visualize the clothes as being dry, clean, and on Mr. Wardle? As for the bicycle, I'd be glad to wheel it around back and put it in the shed where Mr. Wardle used to keep it, if that will help any."

"Oh yes, that will make all the difference," said Mrs. Phiffer. "Excuse me, I'll try the visualizing first. I have to shut my eyes. Do you want me to visualize Mr. Wardle in his underwear first and extrapolate from there?"

"Do whatever feels right to you, Mrs. Phiffer."

"Then if you don't mind, I'll visualize him taking off his overcoat to reveal the slacks and jersey beneath. I don't feel quite comfortable about confronting the eidetic image of a man I really didn't know all that well in his underwear."

"Understandably," Osbert replied since she apparently expected him to say something. After that, he waited in silence until she opened her eyes, all excited.

"It worked! I saw Mr. Wardle plain as plain. Unfortunately, however, he was wearing his brown tweed suit. I'll have to envision his coming from work and changing into the slacks and jersey."

"By all means, do," said Osbert.

"Yes! Yes, I have it now," cried Mrs. Phiffer after a short period of intensive visualizing. "I cannot for the life of me imagine why he ever bought that jersey. Green is definitely not Mr. Wardle's color."

"But that is definitely his jersey?"

"Why else would he be wearing it? Of course it's his."

"And the slacks?"

"Absolutely. No question. And if you ask me, I say it's high time he bought himself a new pair."

It might well be past time, but Osbert thought he wouldn't go into that. Mrs. Phiffer was urging him, "Now let's do the bicycle. This is fun! You get on and I'll try to visualize you as Mr. Wardle."

Osbert was not at all keen on being mentally pictured as Mr. Wardle. However, he got on the bicycle and rode it around to the shed while Mrs. Phiffer trotted gamely after him, visualizing for all she was worth. She never did manage to convince herself that Osbert was Mr. Wardle, to his secret relief. Once he'd got the bicycle stowed in its customary slot beside the plaster duck mold, though, she not only recognized the vehicle but produced a crayon rubbing of its tire tread that she'd done one morning in a spurt of creativity. The front tire had a nick in its tread that she'd caught to perfection. She did a second rubbing of the nick while he looked on, thus establishing the bicycle's provenance beyond question.

"These rubbings are really delightful," she remarked, holding them up side by side. "One could do something interesting with them, don't you think?"

"I certainly do," said Osbert, "and I have every intention of doing it. Would you mind signing your name at the bottom and, if possible, adding the date when you did that first one?"

Mrs. Phiffer couldn't quite remember but she thought it must have been sometime around the end of July. Osbert said that was close enough, so she put down "July 30 approx." and drew a little flamingo after it. Osbert thanked her profusely and folded the two rubbings carefully inside his wallet. He then requested use of the telephone to call his wife, while his new acquaintance went out to start putting the bow ties on her flamingos.

Dittany was at home by herself and sounded glad to be so. Clorinda, she told him, was attending a luncheon party at Arethusa's with the Bleinkinsop twins and Miss Jane, who'd sneaked a couple of hours off from the Yarnery to enjoy her cousins who in turn appeared to be enjoying her. All was peace and amity. Miss Jane must have decided to forgive Arethusa for calling her Miss Wuzzy, which was the only sensible thing to do. After Miss Jane went back to the Yarnery, the other four were planning to play cribbage, using two boards and changing partners every other hand.

Dittany had been invited to join the party, but had declined on the excuse that she had to stay home and count her bed jackets. She was fascinated to hear of Osbert's discoveries, and promised she'd pass them on to Sergeant MacVicar as soon as she could get hold of him. Osbert in turn promised to drive her over to see the flamingos as soon as Mrs. Phiffer got all their bow ties satisfactorily adjusted, and closed with many fond professions of a private and personal nature.

Before leaving, Osbert went up and got the note from the pillow. He'd decided he'd better add this to the rest of the evidence before Mrs. Phiffer thought of something more interesting to do with it. He got her to sign a receipt, locked the note with the wet clothing and the impounded bicycle in the back of his station wagon, and drove back to the Du-Kum-Inn to ascertain whether any progress had been made on the dragging.

To his amazement, he found the expedition ready to roll. A large yellow truck with a large yellow driver— which is to say a large man with yellow hair, a yellow beard, and yellow overalls—was sitting directly under the Live Bait sign. In the back of the truck were an aluminum rowboat, a great deal of rope, and a something or other that must be the dragger.

As Osbert soon learned, the large yellow man was none other than Zingbert Angelus. VP Live Bait, whose own name turned out to be Frank, took pleasure in introducing them. Zingbert said he was pleased to make Osbert's acquaintance, although of course he said Reginald's since Osbert was still maintaining his pseudonymity, and Osbert replied in all sincerity that he was happy to make Zingbert's.

On this harmonious note, they set out. Frank, who'd got his nephew to mind the shop for the afternoon, joined

Zingbert in the truck while Fridwell Slapp rode with Osbert in the station wagon. There was, Osbert learned, a road leading into Bottomless Mere from North Lammergen which was navigable by four-wheel vehicles most of the way; and this they took.

Before leaving the café, Osbert had thought to purchase a large bag of cheese popcorn. By scattering handfuls at strategic locations, he was able to divert the ducks' attention while the other three got the boat in the water and organized the dragger. This was essentially just a big scoop weighted with rocks to hold it on the bottom, or where the bottom would be if the mere had one. Osbert asked Chief Slapp about this.

"Heck, no," was the chief's reply. "Bottomless Mere ain't bottomless. If it was, we wouldn't let the kids swim there, would we? Answer me that."

Obediently, Osbert answered that no, he didn't suppose they would. He certainly wouldn't let any child of his own swim in any bottomless mere and Chief Slapp could bet his bottom dollar on that, assuming he had no moral scruples against gaming.

Chief Slapp asked Osbert how many kids he had, and Osbert, forgetting for the moment that he was supposed to be Reginald, said two, only he didn't quite have them yet. Chief Slapp said kids one didn't have yet were the best kind and wasn't it a shame they couldn't stay unhad. Osbert essayed a light laugh in the interest of diplomacy although he didn't think Slapp's remark the least bit funny, and asked how deep in fact Bottomless Mere really was. Slapp said not very except for here and there, which failed to clarify the matter. Then the conversation lapsed.

Dragging meres is a boring business, as Osbert was soon to find out. Only the ducks appeared to get much out of the proceedings and that was mainly on account of the cheese popcorn. Zingbert and Frank manned the drag ropes while Osbert rowed the boat. Chief Slapp hunkered down on the bank beside the elderly person to direct the operation. This was a euphemism for taking a nap, as the three men in the boat and no doubt the elderly person as well all realized.

"If this guy's been missing since Friday, you'd think he'd be coming to the top by now," Frank said after a while. "What usually happens is, after a period of immersion, they start to bloat. The noxious gases contained within the cadaver impart a buoyancy which causes it to rise, by which time it's a ghastly spectacle and generally has a few parts eaten off by the fish, of which there are quite a few in Bottomless Mere, the walleyed pike being particularly mean buggers, eh, in their pleasanter moods and even nastier at their worst."

Frank embroidered his theme at such length and with such enthusiasm that Osbert began hoping they wouldn't find Wardle after all; and in fact they did not. True, their dragging equipment was not of the best and their technique probably left something to be desired since, as Zingbert Angelus trenchantly expressed it, none of them had ever dragged anything before except their feet. They did bring up a number of ancient artifacts, including part of a 1926 Essex Super Six which Mrs. Phiffer might have been able to do something with if they could have figured out how to get it ashore without swamping the boat, but they found no evidence of the missing Wardle.

Zingbert Angelus suggested that this might be due to the erose nature of the bottom which, though not really bottomless, did have a few deep holes here and there either on account of being fed by springs or just out of general cussedness. Frank offered the further hypothesis that Wardle might have put some rocks in his socks or possibly encased himself in quick-hardening concrete before taking his final plunge, in which case it would take quite a while for him to disintegrate to the point where some portions might become salvageable.

None of the three expressed any inclination to wait around and find out. Osbert was particularly glad to get ashore. In accordance with protocol among cooperating law-enforcement bodies, even though he'd continued to present himself as merely an interested bystander doing a little favor for Mother Matilda, he turned over Wardle's clothes and bicycle to Chief Slapp. This took a bit of doing, as Chief Slapp didn't want either the clothes or the bicycle, thought Osbert was being unreasonably picky in wanting a receipt for them, and was still demanding petulantly to be told what anybody thought he was going to do with the plaguey things when Osbert bade an amiable good-bye to Zingbert Angelus and Frank the bait man and headed for home.

Chapter 12

It was by now far too late to stop at the mincemeat factory. Mother Matilda was probably over at the funeral parlor with her apron off, receiving the condolences of other mincemeat magnates. Osbert decided he might as well make his report to Sergeant MacVicar and leave the rest till morning. Right now, he wanted his Dittany and he wanted his supper. Those two mincemeat tarts hadn't stuck to his ribs the way he'd thought they would. In fact, about the time the draggers had hauled up that old Essex, he'd found himself churlishly begrudging that cheese popcorn he'd bestowed in such lavish handfuls on the ungrateful ducks. Had Mrs. Phiffer been present now, he thought, she wouldn't have had any trouble envisioning his stomach as an empty cavern.

That got him to thinking about some of VP Live Bait's more graphic anatomical observations. A person might have thought these would take away his appetite, but they only made him feel both hungry and depressed.

Even the longed-for homecoming was less delightful than Osbert had envisioned. Dittany's arms were as warm and her lips as sweet as a husband could wish, but they weren't all that easy to get at with the twins in the way. Furthermore, it was hard to put much brio into his embraces with Clorinda cheering him on from the sidelines and Arethusa snarling remarks that would surely have got her kicked out of the International Moonlight and Roses Writers' Organization did its members but reck how their reigning queen talked to her own nephew when she wasn't swishing around the convention hall in her pink velvet robes with the fake ermine trim.

Adding injury to insult, the women had gone ahead and eaten without him and Arethusa had snaffled all the little onions out of the mustard pickles as she always did if he wasn't around to beat her to the draw. Dittany had at least managed to save him a goodly portion of stew and some dumplings, not to mention salad, biscuits, cheese, and approximately seventy-five degrees of an apple pie she'd baked that afternoon because she thought he might want a change from Mother Matilda's mincemeat. Osbert ate as a man with a purpose, pausing only to bestow an occasional pat on the back or peck on the cheek of his beloved spouse, and trying not to listen to the ever-running stream of dialogue between his aunt and his mother-in-law.

Dittany, too, was trying not to listen. "I must say I'm getting a wee bit fed up with the Bleinkinsop twins," she confided to him sotto voce. "I thought Siamese twins would be fascinating to know, but they're just people, like anybody else. Anybody who's not fascinating, I mean."

"I understand, darling," he answered. "It's too bad you didn't get to meet Zingbert Angelus. There's kind of a subtle fascination about Zingbert. Nothing you can put your finger on, but it's there all right. Zingbert's one great guy to drag a mere with, I can tell you that. Mrs. Phiffer's pretty fascinating, too, in her own way. She wants you to drop over and see her flamingos as soon as she finishes putting their neckties on."

"My stars and garters, darling, you have had an interesting day!" murmured his wife. "What do you say we stick Mum with the dishes and go someplace where I'll be able to hear you tell me all about it?"

"Sure thing, pardner. How about the police station? I ought to report to Sergeant MacVicar anyway. You'd bet-

ter put on a few of those knitted bed jackets or something
before we go, though. It's getting a bit nippy out."

"I'll wear that big pink-and-purple shawl Zilla crocheted. She meant it for a carriage cover but her crochet
hook got the bit between its teeth and stampeded on her.
That's the only thing I've got that still meets in the middle." Dittany raised her voice to attract the chatters' attention. "Mum, may I wrench you away from the Bleinkinsop
twins for a moment?"

"Yes, dear, of course. I was just telling Arethusa that
Ranville—"

"Mum! Osbert and I are going down to see Sergeant
MacVicar. Will you be wanting the car tonight?"

"No, Arethusa and I thought we'd spend a quiet evening right here making peanut brittle. Assuming there are
any peanuts lying around that you have no other plans
for."

"Sorry, Mum, we're fresh out. I've got walnut meats in
the pantry, if you'd care to make fudge instead."

"Or penuche," Arethusa suggested.

"How about walnut brittle?" said Clorinda. "I've never
heard of anybody's making walnut brittle. That would
offer a new challenge."

"So it would," said Dittany. "We'll leave you to meet
the challenge, then. Ready, darling?"

Osbert said he was, so they went, taking Ethel with
them for the ride. Sergeant MacVicar and his wife were
pleased to receive all three and greatly intrigued by Osbert's
report.

"Then it's your belief, Deputy Monk," said the sergeant, "that Wardle was one of the two who effected the
demise of Cousin Charles, and has done away with himself
in a fit of remorse."

"I don't know whether it's my belief or whether it's just
the belief Wardle wants us to believe," Osbert replied.
"Dittany, did Archie ever call back this afternoon? I meant
to ask you back at the house, but what with all the static in
the background, I forgot."

"As who wouldn't, dear? And I meant to tell you but I

thought it might be better to wait till I could make myself heard. Besides, I wasn't too sure how you'd feel about letting Mum and Arethusa in on the doings. The gist according to Archie, and I'm quoting so you needn't waggle your eyebrows at me, Sergeant MacVicar, is that Wardle's story about the anchovy business is a lot of codswallop.''

"Aha!'' cried Osbert. "Then I was right about the forged references.''

Dittany nodded. "You couldn't have been righter, precious. The well-known manufacturers of Worcestershire sauce have never heard of Quimper Wardle, much less written gushy letters about him. The address on their alleged letterhead is actually that of a rather sinister tobacconist's shop which does a tidy business on the side as an accommodation address for persons of low repute.''

"And the Royal Society of Anchovy Buyers?''

"They do not list him as a member and wouldn't have made him Hon. Sec. in any case because that's a hereditary post which can only be held, one gathers, by somebody who's swum upstream from the primordial anchovy egg. Archie says the Society was pretty darned sniffy about the whole business. They're determined to sue Wardle if he ever floats to the surface. So, whoever he was or may still be, Quimper Wardle's a phoney as you suspected all along. I hope the twins inherit your brains, dear.''

"I hope the girl twin inherits your adorable little nose, sweetheart,'' Osbert replied with at least equal fervor.

"Arh'm,'' said Sergeant MacVicar. "Might we not get back to the subject at hand?''

"Sure, Chief,'' Osbert replied. "Er—what was it?''

"M'well, even assuming that yon Wardle, whatever his real identity, may in fact have hurled himself into Bottomless Mere in a fit of remorse over his ill-doings, we are still faced with the dilemma of who was his accomplice. We must e'en suppose that the raid on Mr. Gumpert's store was prompted by your aunt's cryptic remark about the ream of plain white paper and the jeweled dagger, must we not?''

"Actually, I think she mentioned the dagger first," said Osbert, "but yes, I believe we must. Which means the store was raided by the same two rustlers who shot Mother Matilda's husband. And if Wardle killed himself Friday night . . . wait a minute! If Wardle did kill himself Friday night or if somebody else killed him," Osbert added, thinking of that wrenched-off pajama button, "he couldn't have taken part in yesterday's episode at all. So those two sidewinders in the trench coats would have had to be two different sidewinders."

"The possibility had not escaped my notice, Deputy Monk. Nor had the possibility that Wardle's untimely demise, if in fact he is dead, was not self-induced. What we appear to have run into here is, in the words of the late Mr. Churchill, a riddle wrapped in a mystery inside an enigma."

"And we have nothing to offer but blood, toil, tears, and sweat," said Osbert. "I'll report to the mincemeat factory first thing in the morning."

"Stout lad! You're a credit to the force, Deputy. Noo then, that yon Wardle perpetrated the debagging of VP Lemon Peel would appear obvious in view of your having found what purports to be a copy of the mincemeat formula in the pocket of Wardle's discarded trousers. You turned the document over to Chief Slapp, did you not?"

"It wasn't much of a document, just a few words scrawled on a memo pad sheet with 'VP Lemon Peel' at the top. Yes, I gave the note to Slapp but I made myself a copy first. I'll show it to Mother Matilda when I see her; she'll know whether it's a bona fide copy of VP Lemon Peel's part of the recipe or another red herring like Wardle's letter of reference. I have a copy of the suicide note here, too. Someplace."

Like most writers, Osbert tended to accumulate oddments of paper with frequently indecipherable notes written on them. He fished out a handful from various pockets and sorted through them, pausing now and then to cock an interested eyebrow while Dittany and the sergeant waited with what patience they could muster. At last he found the one he was looking for.

"Here we are. What does that sound like to you, Chief?"

"It sounds like the pompous haverings of a silly loon," Sergeant MacVicar replied severely, "and shows a lamentable fecklessness of mind in one who purports himself to be anticipating the solemn hour. I dinna like it, Deputy Monk."

"I dinna like it, either," said Dittany, who had naturally been reading over the sergeant's shoulder. "If Wardle really planned to bump himself off, why should he have bothered to stick with his alias?"

"We can't be sure Wardle isn't his real name, dear," Osbert pointed out.

"But we do know he's not entitled to the R.S.A.B. That's an abbreviation for Royal Society of Anchovy Buyers, isn't it?"

"Unless he meant Rotten Society of Artful Burglars, sweetie."

"Psha," said Sergeant MacVicar, and the Monks could not but agree with him.

"So what do we do now?" said Dittany.

"Just keep in the picture and see what develops, I guess," Osbert replied. "Maybe I'll be able to collect some fresh leads at the factory tomorrow. What do you say, dear, shall we go buy Ethel an ice cream?"

Ethel seemed to think that was a great idea, so they bade the sergeant a friendly good night, asked to be remembered to Mrs. MacVicar, who had by now gone off to her yoga class, and set off in quest of pistachio.

This seemed to be a night for ice cream. The walnut brittle had not been a total success; for some reason the stuff had dug in its heels and refused to harden. Therefore, Arethusa and Clorinda were trying it out as a topping, as they explained when Dittany and Osbert entered to find them up to the eyebrows in French vanilla and sticky brown goo. They offered to share, but Dittany and Osbert said no thanks, they'd just had ice cream and Ethel mustn't have any either, since she was probably too fat though it

was impossible to tell under all that shaggy black fur.
Anyway, they were planning to turn in early because
Osbert was fatigued from a strenuous day and Dittany was
worn out just from hearing about it.

Both slept well and woke refreshed. Osbert took extra
pains with his showering and shaving.

"I hink I wea y oo hoot," he remarked as he was flossing
his teeth.

"Your blue suit?" said Dittany, rightly divining what
he was trying to say. "You only wear your blue suit when
you go to Toronto."

"But the only reason I go to Toronto is to see Archie,"
Osbert replied quite distinctly, having by now finished
flossing, "and I don't go there anymore. You know Archie prefers to come here so he can gawk at Aunt Arethusa
and heave deep, meaningful sighs which she doesn't hear
because that little pea brain of hers is off at Ranelagh
chasing a rake. I don't know why he keeps trying."

"Archie knows faint heart ne'er won fair lady, dear."

"But why should he want to win Aunt Arethusa? What
the heck does he think he'd do with her after he got her,
answer me that? I just wish he could have seen her last
night, slopping that stringy caramel stuff all over her chin.
It was enough to turn your stomach. Oh, sorry, dear. Shall
I bring you some orange juice?"

"No, I'm all right. I'll go down and put the kettle on
while you get titivated. You might as well make a good
impression on your first day, even if they do put you into
gingham rompers after you get there."

Dittany had the tea made and was sitting at the kitchen
table reading yesterday's paper, which she hadn't got around
to doing before what with one thing and another, and
Osbert was just bouncing into the room all dressed up in
his blue suit, when they had a caller. It was not the
Binkles this time, but Caroline Pitz. She was terribly
upset, which wasn't like Caroline at all.

"What's the matter?" asked Dittany. "The Architrave
hasn't burned down?"

Caroline lived directly across the street from the museum, so naturally she'd have been the first to know. She shook her head.

"Not burned. Robbed."

"You're kidding!" said Osbert.

"But what about Mr. Glunck?" cried Dittany. The curator lived in the museum where a previous curator had met an untimely demise, so Dittany's concern was natural. "They didn't—he wasn't—oh gosh! We're not short another curator, are we?"

"No, but Mr. Glunck's had an awfully uncomfortable night. They bopped him on the head with an artifact and tied him to the bedpost. Roger Munson just found him."

"Roger Munson? What was he doing at the museum?"

"Delivering a coffee cake," Caroline replied. "Mr. Glunck's been looking a bit peaked lately. Hazel thinks it's because he doesn't eat right, so she sent Roger with the cake and her key."

Hazel Munson, like Dittany and Arethusa, was a trustee of the Architrave Museum. Naturally she had her own key because one never knew. "Hazel told Roger just to go in and leave the coffee cake in the kitchen in case Mr. Glunck might be sleeping," Caroline amplified.

That would have been quite likely and nobody would have thought the less of the curator for doing so. The Architrave wasn't scheduled to open until ten o'clock and it was well-known that Mr. Glunck often sat far into the night authenticating artifacts.

"Roger arrived at precisely thirteen minutes past seven," Caroline went on. "He leaves for work at twenty-three minutes past, you know, and of course he didn't want to upset his schedule."

Dittany and Osbert both murmured, "Of course not." Roger Munson's schedule was as inviolate as a vestal virgin.

"When Roger went out to the kitchen, he heard funny noises from the bedroom. So he went in and there was Mr. Glunck all trussed up with bedsheets. Roger got him loose and came to get me because he couldn't wait any longer. So I went over and fixed Mr. Glunck some hot tea and cut him a piece of the coffee cake and then we looked around. As far as we could tell, the only thing missing's that jeweled dagger from the Thorbisher-Freep Collection of Theatrical Memorabilia that somebody or other played Macbeth with.''

Dittany nodded. She and Mr. Glunck both suspected the dagger to be an artifact the collector had picked up not from the estate of a distinguished actor but from some gimcrack souvenir shop. They only left it on display as a sop to the feelings of Wilhedra Hellespont, née Thorbisher-Freep.

''Maybe the burglars thought those were real jewels,'' she said, ''but the dagger's just a silly tin thing with hunks of colored glass set in the handle. Old Jenson Thorbisher-Freep tried to pretend they were—Osbert! A jeweled dagger! Caroline, did you see any plain white paper around?''

''Funny you should mention that, Dittany. Mr. Glunck had bought a ream of white duplicator paper that he was planning to use for running off lists of the Architrave's exhibits. He hadn't even got around to unwrapping the package, but the burglars had ripped it open and strewn the paper all over the office floor, just the way they did at Mr. Gumpert's. Sergeant MacVicar's over there now, rubbing his nose like anything.''

Chapter 13

Osbert was torn.

On the one hand, he ached to be with Sergeant MacVicar at the scene of the latest outrage, rooting through the artifacts for the essential clue. On the other hand, he'd committed himself to showing up at the mincemeat factory on the dot of half-past eight and time was getting on. Mindful of the way he'd got stuck yesterday envying the ducks their cheese popcorn, though, and not knowing where he might wind up today, he had no intention of leaving home without his breakfast.

Osbert therefore offered to fry Caroline Pitz an egg. She thanked him but refused on the grounds that she had to go tell the other trustees and besides she'd already had a muffin with her husband. Osbert wished her happy trails and began to fry eggs, one for Dittany and two for himself. Dittany decided she wasn't quite up to a fried egg this morning so he ate all three along with a few slices of toast and a good deal of marmalade. Thus fortified, he wiped a few crumbs off his mouth, took a tender farewell of his beloved, and went out to start the car.

As he drove over to Lammergen, Osbert could not but reflect again that this had been the route taken—only of course in the opposite direction—by the late VP Nutmeg in that ill-fated attempt to outrun his assassins. It wasn't all that much of a road: one lane either way and full of crooks and bends. This had really been an unlikely place to conduct a running gunfight at high speed. He wished he'd gone with Sergeant MacVicar to have a look at those two bullet-riddled cars. He could understand how the car Mother Matilda's husband drove had got so many holes in it, because there'd been one passenger to drive and one to shoot, but how had Charles McCorquindale managed to pock the other car all by himself?

Judging from what he'd seen of the Lammergen police force yesterday, Osbert didn't think he ran much risk of getting arrested if he tried a little experiment, so he speeded up as much as he dared. As he'd expected, he needed both hands and all his attention just to keep the car on the road. To have stuck his head out the window and taken potshots at a pursuing vehicle would have been futile at best and suicidal at worst. And worst was what would most likely have happened.

If Charles had waited for his attackers to draw along-side, which in itself would have been awfully perilous on this narrow road, he might have got in a few shots, but the odds were that they'd have potted him first. So many holes in his car and only that one bullet hole in his back suggested he must have managed to keep fairly well ahead of them all the way.

It was very puzzling. Reviewing the bizarre events of the past two days, Osbert writhed with impatience to the extent that a person could safely writhe while driving the Lammergen road. He supposed they'd made some progress yesterday, but he didn't feel any sense of achievement because he still didn't know whether Quimper Wardle was alive or dead.

If it had been the done thing for Mother Matilda's employees to go out of the factory for their noonday meal, he might have taken a swing over around Bottomless Mere to see whether anybody had floated to the top since yesterday. As Reginald Monk, Director of In-House Security, though, he could hardly go galumphing off in defiance of company rules and setting a bad example to the rest of the staff. Jumping jackrabbits, why did everything have to be so dad-blanged inscrutable?

Osbert had to park on the street again because he'd forgotten to ask Mother Matilda for a pass to the parking lot, but that was all right. He wasn't yet officially on the payroll anyway. Again he went in through the main door, gave his name to the girl at the desk, and was again ushered into Mother Matilda's office by the mincemeat magnate in person.

She was looking pretty wan and that black apron wasn't helping any, but she straightened her spine, thrust out her manly chin, and looked straight at him over the tops of her granny glasses.

"Well, Mr. Monk, what have you to report?"

"I have conclusive evidence that Quimper Wardle was not what he represented himself as being," Osbert replied. "As I suggested yesterday, his letters of recommendation were faked. He never worked for the well-known manufacturer of Worcestershire sauce. He was never Honorable Secretary or even a member of the Royal Society of Anchovy Buyers. In fact, it's entirely possible he was never an anchovy buyer at all."

"What? Why, that unprincipled scoundrel!" Mother Matilda's cheeks, which a moment ago had been virtually ashen, were now suffused with a not very becoming shade of purple. "I cannot believe I was so badly taken in."

"Oh, Wardle was a wily one," Osbert replied. "Not being accustomed to perfidy among your peel buyers, you naturally wouldn't have been apt to see through his malicious machinations."

"No, come to think of it, I don't suppose I would," Mother Matilda admitted, beginning to fade a little. "I was brought up to think of mincemeat making as an honorable profession, followed by honest people. I suppose Wardle deliberately traded on my innocence. My sainted granny must be turning over in her grave! These are terrible times, Mr. Monk."

"But in your granny's day, she'd have had to worry

about the grocer's putting sand in the sugar and trouts in the milk,'' Osbert pointed out.

"Oh, I know! I know! And stones in the raisins and the butcher weighing his thumb along with the lambchops. I suppose there's no more chicanery around than there's ever been. It's just that I'm minding it more because—I'm sorry, Mr. Monk. I'm trying to be brave, but—"

"I think you're being brave as anything, Mother Matilda,'' Osbert put in before she could get herself all worked up. "Now, before I get into details about what happened yesterday, would you mind taking a look at this? I should explain that it's a copy of a note I found in Wardle's pocket. The original was scribbled in pencil on a sheet of yellow paper torn from a memo pad that had 'VP Lemon Peel' printed on the top.''

Mother Matilda adjusted her granny glasses and studied the scrap Osbert handed her. "Why, this is Lemon's share of the mincemeat recipe! You say you found it in Wardle's pocket?''

"I said I found the note of which this is a copy in Wardle's pocket. His trousers were discovered, along with a green jersey his landlady has identified as one he often wore in his off-hours, lying on the bank out at Bottomless Mere. We may surmise that this means Wardle was the one who debagged your VP Lemon Peel and was swift enough to extract the formula card, copy down what it said, put back the card, and make his escape while VP Lemon Peel was still struggling to get the typewriter cover off his head and pull his pants up. On the other hand, that may be what we're meant to surmise, but that's not what really happened. You see, Mother Matilda, there's so much we don't know yet.''

"Then we'd better find out pretty darned quick.'' Mother Matilda flipped the switch on her intercom. "Imogene, get all the VPs into the conference room. I'm calling a meeting.''

"How soon, Mother Matilda?'' asked Imogene, who-ever she might be.

"In three minutes, and don't let them give you any excuses."

"Yes, Mother Matilda."

Mother Matilda stood up and straightened her apron. "Come along then, Mr. Monk. You're Reginald today, right?"

"Right," said Osbert.

"Here's the folder with those references you wrote. Do you need to brush up on what you said about yourself before we go into the meeting?"

"No, I can remember."

"Good. This way, then."

Mother Matilda ran a taut ship, no question about that. VPs of various descriptions were already flocking into the conference room, a spacious yet cozy apartment with portraits of four Mothers Matilda on the walls and gingham cushions on the chairs. They all looked at Osbert with ill-feigned curiosity but refrained from asking who he was. Mother Matilda clearly intended to tell them in her own good time and wouldn't thank them for trying to hustle her.

She took her place in the big rocking chair at the head of the table and motioned Osbert to the seat at her right. It struck him that this must have been where Charles McCorquindale used to sit and he felt a qualm, but only a momentary one because his attention was suddenly demanded elsewhere.

"Demanded" was the operative word. VP Citron would have been an impossible sight for any red-blooded man or even a fairly anemic one to overlook. She wouldn't have let them.

It was not that the tall, curvaceous, satin-cheeked, emerald-eyed redhead came straight out and shouted, "Hey, you new chap with the cowlick! Over here!" VP Citron wasn't fastening those Persian pussycat eyes on his blue ones with intent to lure, she was merely emitting some kind of invisible rays that bent his entire quotient of ions and positrons in her direction.

Osbert supposed a person could build up an immunity

sooner or later. Some of the older male VPs weren't even reeling in their seats. He himself, as a writer, was naturally intrigued by this phenomenon, and able to analyze his own reactions quite dispassionately. For the first time he was gaining an insight into the modus operandi of the genuine, natural-born femme fatale.

This must be how Aunt Arethusa was able quite involuntarily to enslave men so diverse as Archie, the intellectual aesthete and agent extraordinaire, and Andrew McNaster, the former crooked contractor and cobra fancier who was now in the movies, starring as the Sultan of Sneer. Being her nephew, Osbert of course had a built-in immune system that worked fine on Aunt Arethusa. Apparently it didn't function so well where vice presidents of mincemeat factories were concerned. He must discuss the phenomenon with Dittany when he got home. On second thought, he mustn't.

The mere thought of his lawfully wedded wife, however, was the charm that unwound the spell. Osbert was now able to view VP Citron objectively as just another gorgeous woman with a somewhat excessive amount of sex appeal and no doubt a superior talent for buying citron or Mother Matilda wouldn't keep her on the payroll. When she was introduced as Nissa Eveready and acknowledged his acquaintance with a three-hundred-watt smile, he didn't so much as blink.

And VP Citron didn't like that a bit. The emerald eyes narrowed, the ruby lips tightened. The curvaceous hips twitched, the luscious bosom heaved. The very checks of her green gingham wraparound seemed to murmur, "Grab on to my hook, you poor fish!" Osbert gave her a polite, impersonal nod and turned his attention to VP Cider.

This was Mother Matilda's pillar of rectitude, the Sunday school superintendent who'd got zonked in the storeroom doing a quality check. VP Cider was sitting next to VP Citron but he didn't seem to have his receiving apparatus turned on, either. His eyes were steadfastly on Mother Matilda and his regard showed, in Osbert's private opinion, something more than the customary chaste and tepid respect of a VP for a P. Osbert wished to heck Dittany or even Aunt Arethusa could be here to evaluate the gaze; Western writers couldn't be expected to know much about unrequited passion.

But was VP Cider's passion, if this was indeed passion and not just gas pains from too much quality testing, altogether unrequited? Osbert would be gum-swizzled if Mother Matilda wasn't returning Cider's gaze and if the expression on her strong, manly countenance was not, for one fleeting moment, that of a hooked fish.

The hairs in Osbert's cowlick prickled the way they often did on occasions when he'd thought of a particularly interesting new dilemma to throw the king ostrich into, or when he'd caught hold of the business end of a tangled skein he'd been trying to unravel in his capacity as Deputy Monk. Was VP Cider a business end? Had Mother Matilda's professions of grief for her late husband been mere sand in the sugar of deception? Was the allegedly dreadful business of the stolen formula nothing more than an elaborate ruse to rid her of VP Nutmeg so that she could put a new kind of spice into her private life?

Then who in fact were Mother Matilda's accomplices? Was VP Cider in on the doings? Had Wardle been her hit man or her dupe, or both? Had she been a party all along to his deceptions? Had she set Wardle up to be exposed once Charles McCorquindale had been got out of the way, and had she then disposed of her henchman as ruthlessly as he, or whoever had been with him, had gunned down VP Nutmeg?

That was an ugly thought, but Mother Matilda was by no means a pretty woman. Button her into a trench coat with the collar turned up, slap a felt hat on her head with the brim turned down, take off that silly apron and cover her lower extremities with a man's pants and a man's shoes, and who'd be able to tell the difference?

Osbert realized that he was goggling worse than VP Cider. He wrenched his eyes away from Mother Matilda and glanced around the table. VP Cloves had just come in and taken her seat. She must be the last of the lot, Osbert assumed from the fact that all the chairs were now full. In size, though, she was by no means the least.

Osbert thought VP Cloves must be a relative of Mother Matilda. She had that same granite chin, the same big-boned physique, the same large hands and probably the same oversized feet, though he hadn't noticed them when she'd entered the conference room and he didn't suppose it would be according to protocol for him to stick his head under the table and look. It was too late anyway, Mother Matilda was calling the meeting to order.

"I expect you're all mad at me for disrupting your morning's work," she began abruptly, "but you'll just have to lump it. I needn't tell you that we've had some pretty outrageous things happening around here lately."

She glanced down at her black apron, then faced the room again. "What's done can't be helped, but I've had all I'm going to take, and I'm putting a stop to it here and now. I want you to meet our new Director of In-House Security, Reginald Monk. Stand up, Mr. Monk."

Osbert felt this was laying it on a bit thick because he'd already been getting a thorough looking-over from the assembled VPs. Anyway, he stood as she bade him, glad that he'd worn his blue suit and trying to look formidable.

He must not be succeeding any too well because Mother Matilda went on, "I know he doesn't look like much but that's part of his strategy. Mr. Monk comes highly recom-mended. In fact, he's already done some important work for us. Tell them what you've found out about Quimper Wardle, Mr. Monk."

By now, Osbert was quite used to talking about Quimper Wardle. He gave a crisp, businesslike report, dwelling on the forged credentials and the lemon peel formula and leaving out the really interesting stuff like Mrs. Phiffer's pinwheels and the popcorn-eating ducks. It was gratifying to see their somewhat contemptuous smiles change to re-spectful concern.

He'd rather expected a babble of questions when he'd finished speaking, but none of the VPs said a word. It was Mother Matilda who retook the floor.

"Now that you've heard Mr. Monk, you must surely all realize how handicapped we are around here by our wholesome, uncomplicated dedication to mincemeat-making. We can't plug the security leaks ourselves because we don't even know how to go about looking for them. We need somebody around the factory who's got a real handle on perfidy, somebody who's able to plumb the cesspools of rottenness that lurk in the hearts of evildoers. Is that right, Mr. Monk?"

"I guess so," Osbert mumbled. He'd never thought of himself as a plumber of cesspools before, and he hoped to heck his Aunt Arethusa never found out he'd been called one in front of a whole roomful of vice presidents. Not that getting a handle on perfidy wasn't an honorable calling in its way, he supposed. After all, somebody had to dig out the rottenness. He lifted his head, stuck out his chin, and turned his eyes steadfastly from one to another VP all around the table. "Anyway," he said clearly and distinctly, "that's what I do and I'm here to do it."

Chapter 14

"You get a leak, you call the plumber."

That was VP Citron being flip, no doubt because Osbert was refusing to succumb to her wiles. He composed his features into an expression of semi-amused hauteur.

"Mother Matilda might have added that I anticipate everybody's wholehearted cooperation in getting this matter straightened out as quickly as possible. Now I'd like to get down to business, if you don't mind."

He left them no time to say whether they minded or not, but plunged right into the midst. "Can we in fact establish at least a strong likelihood that Quimper Wardle was the sole perpetrator of the outrages committed against certain people here present, as evidence found in his discarded clothing—namely and to wit: a copy of the lemon peel formula written on a leaf from VP Lemon Peel's personal memo pad—would lead us to believe? Was there, in short, any one of these incidents in which Wardle could definitely not have participated?"

Everybody looked blankly at everybody else. It was VP Currants who finally answered. This was a brawny giant of a man whose abundant gray hair suggested a powdered wig and whose fair-skinned, rosy-cheeked face was relatively unlined despite the weight of years he surely carried.

Osbert would have expected somebody smaller, darker, and more wrinkled.

"That's hard for us to answer, Mr. Monk. You see, we're busy people. We have our own concerns to attend to, yet we're used to a good deal of interaction. We're all over the place, as you might say. In this profession you can't just sit in your office and trust some computer to tell you how many currants you've got on hand at any given moment, or how many currants the third currant adder on the left is dumping into a particular batch of mincemeat. I have to be right out there among the currants: in the store-room sampling the sacks to make sure each currant is up to standard quality-wise, keeping the currant sorters eternally vigilant lest a substandard currant slip through our stringent quality checks, making sure the currant adders are maintaining their exact measurements. . . . I'm here, I'm there, I'm everywhere. Like the Scarlet Pimpernel," he added to clarify matters. "Right, everybody?"

Everybody nodded.

"Naturally I'm in daily conference with our currant buyer," VP Currant went on, "but I don't keep tabs on currant markets around the world or have the prices in, say, the latest Andalusian currant auction at my fingertips. That's the buyer's job. She knows what's expected of her and she does it. If she's out in the warehouse checking a delivery, I'm not there standing over her. She knows what she's doing and I don't have to."

VP Currants refreshed himself with a sip of water but held up a hand to show he wasn't through talking. "Right, everybody?"

Everybody nodded.

"So likewise, let's say I happen to run into Wardle heading for VP Lemon Peel's office. He's a peel buyer, right? I figure he's on legitimate business with my distinguished colleague, so I put him straight out of my mind because my job is currants and I can't let myself be distracted from performing to the utmost of my ability. And it's the same with all of us. Right, everybody?"

Everybody nodded again.

"But let's say you'd happened to observe Wardle in the act of hauling your colleague's er—garments down over his—er—person?" said Osbert.

"I suppose I might assume that my colleague had sat on a splinter or something and Wardle was about to administer first aid."

"But suppose he'd put a typewriter cover over your colleague's head?"

VP Currant shrugged. "If I happened to notice, I expect I'd surmise that my colleague suffered from an iodine phobia and Wardle was kindly attempting to spare him from having to look at the bottle. Since I'm none too keen on iodine myself, and since splinters aren't my department, I'd leave Wardle to cope and go on about my own business. Right, everybody?"

The unanimity quotient around the conference table was truly amazing.

"So what all this boils down to," said Osbert, "is that I'd better not expect any cooperation from any of you. Is that what you're trying to tell me?"

"It certainly is not," snapped Mother Matilda. "I'm sure personnel so well-trained in eternal vigilance during the pursuit of duty can't help having made acute observations of certain matters perhaps not strictly germane to their particular spheres of influence but vital to the welfare of the business as a whole. Right, everybody?"

She glared around the table. After a moment's startled hesitation, everybody nodded.

"So," she went on, "how many of you saw Wardle in the vicinity of VP Lemon Peel's office at the fateful moment? Don't try to make believe you don't know which moment I'm talking about and don't give me any more iodine phobias. VP Citron, your office is next to VP Lemon Peel's. Would it, in your opinion, have been physically possible for any male person bent on debagging to have passed your door without at least peeking in?"

"I shouldn't have thought so," VP Citron replied with a nasty glance at Osbert, "but one never knows. Now that you ask me, Mother Matilda, I do have a vague recollection of having heard Mr. Wardle's footsteps approaching my office and pausing briefly by the door before proceeding on past.''

''You're sure those were Wardle's footsteps you heard?'' Osbert asked her.

''Quite sure, Mr. Monk. I never make mistakes, as anybody here can tell you. It's one of my less attractive traits. Besides, he did a little heavy breathing when he paused. Mr. Wardle has—or should I say had?—a very English way of breathing. Right, everybody?''

''Oh, definitely,'' said VP Currants. It was a change from all those nods, anyway.

''And this was at the time of the—er—incident?'' said Osbert.

''I believe so. Wasn't that when Miss Flaubert fainted? I remember somebody—I believe it was you, VP Cinnamon— yelling 'Cut her corset strings.' I wondered what on earth you were talking about.''

''I'm not quite sure myself,'' confessed VP Cinnamon, who was a young man as VPs went. ''I'd happened to run against the expression in an old novel I read once and always thought it would be a rather marvelous thing to yell if one ever happened to find a suitable occasion. You know how odd bits of information stick in one's mind.''

''Does it stick in your mind whether Mr. Wardle was in the area where Miss Flaubert was fainting?'' said Osbert.

''I'm inclined to think he wasn't, or he'd have been dashing over to cut her corset strings,'' VP Cinnamon replied. ''Wardle's one of those Johnny-on-the-spot types. New broom, you know, trying to sweep all before him and make us Canadians feel like amateurs. Some Brits are like that.''

''Nonsense,'' said Mother Matilda. ''Naturally the reason Miss Flaubert fainted was that she came upon VP Lemon Peel in a state of—well, I don't want to embarrass him any more than he's been humiliated already. And naturally Wardle wouldn't have stuck around to get caught once he'd done the uncouth deed, so his absence after the fact is more indicative of guilt than his presence would have been. Right, everybody?''

Even Osbert nodded. There were indubitably no flies on Mother Matilda.

"As for the hard cider incident," he went on, "am I right in supposing just about anybody at all could have gained access to the cider storeroom?''

"Not just anybody," said VP Cider, "but Wardle certainly could have. As a peel buyer, he had legitimate reasons to visit the storeroom area, checking on deliveries and inventory in the performance of his duties. For a new buyer to wander into the cider store either because he'd lost his bearings or just out of curiosity wouldn't be at all unusual. The sweet cider we use in our manufacturing process would no doubt have been a novelty to him, since British cider is generally fermented.''

"Would it be possible for some of the cider in the storeroom to be fermented without your knowledge?" Osbert asked him.

VP Cider had to think that one over. "It might be possible," he conceded at last, "but it would involve technical know-how and some pretty complicated flummoxing of the inventory. More to the point, fermentation takes time. Wardle hadn't been with us long enough to have known the ropes or to have completed the process. My personal interpretation of the incident is that my all-too-literal downfall was brought about by the addition of some compatible alcoholic substance such as apple brandy to the cider I was to sample on that particular day.''

"How would that have been done, sir?''

"Easy as pie. All he'd have had to do was walk past and dump a slug of joy juice into the pitcher of fresh-pressed cider which the cider squeezers would have left on a small table near the entrance to the cider room, as they do every morning, and make himself scarce before I came along to drink it.''

"I thought tasters only tasted," said Osbert.

VP Cider shook his head. "Not me. I swig. It's my invariable custom to drink at least one full glass of sweet cider every morning, not only because I find this the best way to do a thorough quality check but also because the cider keeps my rheumatics from acting up on me. It's the malic acid that does the trick. Cider's absolutely crawling with malic acid.''

"You don't say."

"Ask your doctor. Malic acid's just the ticket for sloshing out the kidneys so you don't get gout. Look it up in the Encyclopaedia Britannica. And look at me, spry as a cat despite my hereditary affliction.'' VP Cider left his chair and cut a brief caper to demonstrate his agility, then resumed his place at the conference table and went back to being dignified.

"Very impressive, VP Cider," said Osbert. "Then you think Mr. Wardle could have known of your commendable habit?''

"He'd have had to be deaf and blind not to," growled VP Suet, a curmudgeonly-looking old fatty who was wearing his checkered cap pulled down over his forehead. "We get the therapeutic benefits of sweet cider drummed into us morning, noon, and teatime. VP Cider's even stuck up a poster in the cafeteria that says 'Drink More Cider.' You don't hear me going around telling people to eat more suet.''

Osbert glanced sharply at the speaker. Here, his detectival instinct told him, was an embittered VP. It must be the current fad against cholesterol, he thought. VP Suet could well be walking in daily fear that he'd be declared redundant and replaced by some upstart VP Soybean Derivative. A bleak prospect indeed for a VP to learn in late middle age that he'd devoted his life to clogging people's arteries, though Osbert couldn't imagine there was enough suet in Mother Matilda's Mincemeat to do the eater any harm. Probably the malic acid in the cider sloshed away the fat before it could settle down to its sinister work. Nevertheless, he had a hunch VP Suet would bear watching.

Further exploration revealed that Wardle could indeed not be eliminated from suspicion as the perpetrator of all incidents, whereas every other one of the VPs had alibis up to the eyeballs, or claimed to have. Osbert would have to check them out as a matter of routine, but he thought it more likely than not that so competent a group of executives would either have had sense enough to stay out of trouble or have had guile enough to cover their tracks.

Time was getting on. The VPs were casting anxious glances at their watches. Still, Osbert had one more question that must be asked. "Not to harrow Mother Matilda's feelings, but as you all know, your late colleague VP Nutmeg had his demise effected as the result of what must have been a pretty spectacular gunfight running all the way from here to Lobelia Falls. Did any of you happen to witness the start of that incident?"

Nobody nodded.

"Did anybody hear any shots?"

Nobody had.

"Did any of you happen to be inside the bank when VP Nutmeg went to get his part of the mincemeat recipe out of his safe deposit box?"

"You must remember, Mr. Monk, that VP Nutmeg enjoyed certain privileges not available to the rest of us," VP Suet drawled oleaginously. "We here had all been hard at work since half-past eight. According to my information, VP Nutmeg didn't reach the bank until around ten o'clock. By that time, I myself would have been out back in the cafeteria drinking a cup of tea. A well-earned cup I think I may say," he added with a malignant scowl around the table.

"Nobody doubts your tea was well-earned, Suet old man," said VP Apples, who until now had taken little part in the discussion. "I was having one with you, I expect. I generally do, as do we all. We VPs," Apples explained to Osbert, "tend to gravitate to the cafeteria in the middle of the morning and hold what we call our round-table discussion. We just push a few tables together and sit down as a group for an informal chat about various matters pertaining to our joint functions. We find this a pleasant and useful way of keeping our fingers on the pulse of the business.

We're so busy otherwise that we don't get much chance to communicate.''

"Do you participate in these daily meetings, Mother Matilda?'' Osbert asked her.

"Not I. I prefer my tea at my desk. Anyway, I'm quite aware that my presence could be an inhibiting factor in a free-for-all discussion. Please continue, VP Apples.''

"Well, I was just going to add that at noontime we join up with people who work in our own departments for discussion at a more specific level, and by teatime we're so pooped that we don't want to talk to anybody. Anyway, I expect that's why none of us happened to be at the front of the building where we might have heard some commotion from the street.''

"I see,'' said Osbert, although he wasn't at all sure he did. "And what about yesterday? Did you have your customary noontime get-together with the lower echelons?''

"We don't think of our fellow employees as lower echelons,'' VP Raisins reproved. "The way we look at it, we're all in the mincemeat together. Right, everybody?''

This had to be Mother Matilda's daughter, Matilda the Fourth or Fifth, depending on how you looked at her. She was a lot easier to look at than Matilda the Third; she must favor her father's side of the McCorquindales. She had her mother's innate sense of authority, though. With perfect grace, Daughter Matilda took the reins into her own slender hands.

"You've all got lots to do; why don't you buzz along to your departments? I believe I can tell Mr. Monk what he wants to know. You needn't stay, Mother, Mr. Throckmorton of Redundant Relishes is waiting for you to call back.''

"Thank you for reminding me, dear. I'll be in my office if you need me for anything, Mr. Monk.''

Mother Matilda led the procession out of the conference room. The rest of the VPs followed. VP Raisins moved up to sit beside Osbert. "I didn't want to harrow my mother's feelings any more than I had to either, Mr. Monk. This dreadful business is wearing her down terribly. I don't know how much longer she'll be able to maintain her stiff upper lip.''

"What about yourself?''

"Oh, I fell apart the minute I found out Daddy'd been shot. By yesterday morning I'd finished bawling my eyes out and decided I might as well get moving, so I went down and questioned our security guard and the people over at the bank about what had happened. You'll want to talk to them yourself, I suppose, but I can give you the gist right now if you like.''

"That would help a lot—er—should I address you as VP Raisins or Daughter Matilda?''

"You know, that's an interesting question. VP Raisins is more businesslike, but Daughter Matilda has a nice, dynastic ring to it. Most people just call me Tilly. Anyway, here's what happened as best I could piece it together.''

Daughter Matilda, like her mother, was wearing a black apron although the uniform beneath it was purple. She fished a hankie out of the pocket in case she felt a sniffle coming on, and began her report.

"Gerald—that's the security guard—told me he saw Daddy drive up to the bank at two minutes before ten. Daddy stopped the car out front, but left the motor running while he ran into the bank so that he wouldn't have to waste time starting it again. Daddy never liked to waste a second, regardless of what that old oink-oink VP Suet was intimating just now.''

"Your mother explained yesterday that your father had been out on company business,'' Osbert reassured her.

"Darling Daddy. He just lived and breathed mincemeat.'' Daughter Matilda sighed, then pulled herself together. "Anyway, Marie at the bank said Daddy was in his usual good spirits when he opened the box. He said good morning and she said he was running late, wasn't he, and he said yes, he'd been over to Scottsbeck on business. All perfectly normal and natural, you see. Then he took out his card. That's what we call them because that's what they are, just little cards covered in plastic. I have mine with me but I'd rather not show it because I've got it hidden in my—my personal effects. Now that we've been infiltrated, we're all so security-conscious it's pathetic.''

"That's okay, Daughter Matilda," said Osbert. "Your mother explained about the cards, too. So your father obviously wasn't expecting any trouble.''

"Not till he came out of the bank. According to Gerald, another car with two men in it had come up the street just behind Daddy's. After he pulled up to the curb, the other car had gone on a little way, then turned back and sort of dawdled along till Daddy opened the bank door and stepped on to the sidewalk. Then the driver put on a spurt, came up to the company parking lot, and stopped directly in front of the gate so that Daddy wouldn't be able to get in.''

"For Pete's sake! Real gangland tactics.''

"You bet it was. Gerald was right there ready to open the gate for Daddy, so of course he yelled at the men to move on out of the way. Next thing he knew, the man in the passenger seat was poking a gun at him. So Gerald ducked back into his little sentry box and got his own gun.''

"How come?" said Osbert. "Isn't that rather unusual? For him to have one, I mean?''

"I know. Because of the gun laws, you don't think of Canadians having pistols, or whatever they're called. Yes, it was unusual. In fact, Gerald had only had the gun since the previous afternoon when Daddy suddenly realized what was behind those rotten tricks Mr. Wardle had been pulling on the VPs.''

"We still don't know for sure Mr. Wardle was pulling them," Osbert reminded her.

"Well, of course it must have been Mr. Wardle. Nobody else is mean enough except VP Suet, and he wouldn't have the gumption. Anyway, Daddy said we had to tighten up on security and Gerald had better have a firearm, so he went and got him one. Daddy would, you know. I don't think Gerald had ever fired a gun in his life. Neither had Daddy, but that wouldn't have stopped either of them from doing it if they had to. We can't depend much on the police around here, as you may have heard.''

''I got to meet Chief Slapp yesterday.'' There was no need for Osbert to say more.

''Well, then. So these two men—Gerald says they were both wearing trenchcoats with—''

''Their collars turned up and felt hats pulled down over their eyes,'' Osbert finished for her. ''So was your father. Was that unusual for him?''

''No, not specially. Daddy was an awful ham, the old darling. He'd done some acting and he loved dressing up. That George Raft outfit was one of his more conservative turns. You should have seen him in his Inverness cape and deerstalker cap. Or his tartan trews and t-t-tam o' sh-sh-shanter.''

Daughter Matilda plied her hankie, then went bravely on with her tale. ''Gerald thinks Daddy must have realized right away that the men were after him. Daddy's mind worked like lightning, you know. Or maybe you don't, but it did. Anyway, Daddy leaped back into his own car and was most likely going to gun the motor and rush on the same way he was heading—by this time, of course, the bad guys' car was pointing back in the opposite direction—when a tiny tot in a fuzzy pink coat toddled out into the street with a wee doggie on a leash.''

''A wee doggie?'' exclaimed Osbert.

''A little woolly white one. Like a baby lamb, Gerald says.'' Daughter Matilda sniffled again. ''That was Daddy's pet name for me. When I was a wee tot myself, he'd tuck me in at night and say, 'Now go to sheep, my little lamb.' That was our f-favorite joke. He always said sh-sheep.''

She wiped away some more tears, took a sip of the water that still stood on the conference room table, and rushed grittily on. ''So Daddy gunned the car in reverse about twenty feet, made a fast U-turn right under the bad guys' noses, and was off down the road before they could get started. So they began shooting at him!''

"My gosh!" cried Osbert, although of course he'd seen it coming.

"Gerald says he just stood there with his mouth hanging open. Then all of a sudden he realized what was really happening and decided he'd better shoot, too. By that time, the men were starting to move. He tried to hit their tires but he didn't know how to aim the gun right and hit the body of the car instead."

"So that's how they got pocked," said Osbert. "I'd wondered."

"Gerald says he only hit them a few times and it didn't seem to do any good because the bad guys just kept going after Daddy. Then he couldn't see them anymore and the gun wouldn't fire because he'd used up all the bullets. So he called the police station, but Fridwell Slapp couldn't seem to get it through his head what had happened. He didn't show up till about twenty minutes later, and then he didn't do anything except poke around and ask stupid questions. And that's my story, Mr. Monk, for whatever it's worth to you."

Chapter 15

"And the parking lot man couldn't describe the two men at all?"

Dittany's voice sounded somewhat muffled since she was speaking from the depths of Osbert's "I'm an Old Cowhand" sweatshirt. A whole day apart had been hard on both of them. Now they were enjoying a conjugal cuddle on the kitchen couch with Ethel snoring gently at their feet, Clorinda doing something innovative to a panful of chicken and rice at the stove, and Arethusa sitting in Gram Henbit's old rocking chair with her eyes closed.

"Nope," said Osbert. "He said all he could see was the nozzle of that gun pointed straight at his collar button. I suppose that's understandable."

"Perhaps if you'd hypnotized him, he'd have remembered everything," Clorinda suggested. "One does, I've been told. Couldn't you have tried waving a pendulum in front of his nose?"

"I suppose I could have, now that you mention it," Osbert conceded. "The possibility didn't occur to me at the time. You weren't really meaning to put that vanilla extract you're holding into the chicken, were you?"

"Eh? Oh, so that's what this is. Actually I think what I had in mind was a dash of lemon juice, only I couldn't find a lemon so I thought perhaps lemon extract—though vanilla might be—''

"No, it mightn't!" Arethusa's eyes were wide open now, and brimming with horror. "Listen to me, Clorinda. Look straight into my eyes, Clorinda. Deeper, deeper. Keep looking, Clorinda. You are growing sleepy, sleepier, sleepiest. You are in my power, Clorinda. You must obey my every word. Go, Clorinda. Put that vanilla back in the pantry. This instant, Clorinda. Get with it, Clorinda."

"With what, Arethusa? Wake up, Arethusa. Oh dear, she's hypnotized herself. Now what shall we do?"

"Leave her alone," said Osbert. "Maybe she'll stay hypnotized and we'll be able to eat a meal in peace for a change. That chicken smells great just as it is, Clorinda, don't do another thing to it. If you burn to make yourself useful, why don't you pour yourself a little sherry and relax for a while?"

"But Osbert, that's not making myself useful. And I do so want to be a good mother-in-law to you."

"On the contrary, Clorinda, relaxing is the most useful thing you can do. Once you've quit waving that vanilla bottle around, Dittany will stop twitching. Then I can relax, too, and you'll have brought peace and tranquillity to our happy home. How much more useful could you get?"

"Well, of course. I hadn't thought of it that way. Would you like me to pour you some sherry, too?"

"I would," said Arethusa.

"Oh, goody, you're awake!" Clorinda flew into the pantry.

"Whatever is she talking about?" said Arethusa. "Osbert, what was that balderdash you were spouting about a tiny tot with a sheep on a leash?"

"I believe what I actually referred to was a tiny tot with a small white dog that resembled a lamb. Where the sheep came in was that Daughter Matilda told me her father used to call her his little lamb and tell her to go to sheep when he tucked her in."

"Are you sure he didn't say 'grow to sheep,' meaning to hasten the process of maturing so that he wouldn't have to bother tucking her in anymore?"

"No such thing," Osbert replied crossly. "He was merely making a play on words to amuse his infant child. Daughter Matilda says he always said 'sheep' when he meant sleep."

"As in 'Sheepytime Gal'?" said Dittany. "Or, 'sheep my little one, sheep my pretty one, sheep, sheep, sheep?"

"Or 'sheep that knits up the ravell'd sleave of—' "

Clorinda got no further. Osbert started from the couch like a panther from a crouch, leaving Dittany agape and Ethel somewhat annoyed.

"That's it!" he cried. "When VP Nutmeg mentioned 'the ravell'd sleave,' he was really talking about a sheep."

"What sheep, forsooth?" Arethusa demanded crossly. "I grant you knitting wool comes from sheep, but purveyors thereof don't keep sheep on their premises as a rule. You ought to know that, you've rustled enough of the critters in your so-called literary pursuits. First you remove the wool from the sheep by a process known, I believe, as shearing. Then you have to wash the fleece because sheep have no concept of personal hygiene, then you get a teazel and tease it."

"I'm not sure whether the teazel comes before or after the washing," Clorinda objected. "Though I grant you a teazel comes into the process somewhere," she conceded, for she was really devoted to Arethusa.

"The teazel is irrelevant," Dittany broke in. "The question before the house is, what sheep was VP Nutmeg talking about? Miss Jane may somewhat resemble a sheep, but she does not in point of fact own a sheep."

"Oh yes, she does," Clorinda insisted. "Miss Jane has a perfectly beautiful sheep. She made it herself."

Osbert stared. Dittany merely nodded. "You mean like those knitted doggies and kitties she has sitting around the shop?" she asked. "But we didn't see any sheep when we searched the place night before last."

"Oh my!" exclaimed Clorinda. "You don't suppose those gangsters rustled it?"

"You don't rustle sheep," Osbert replied somewhat crossly. "You just steal them. Miss Jane didn't report having a sheep stolen. The alleged gangsters never entered the Yarnery, and VP Nutmeg can't have been carrying a sheep when he came out or Sergeant MacVicar would surely have said so. Was this a tiny little sheep such as might easily have been dropped into a trench-coat pocket in passing?"

"No," said Clorinda. "Miss Jane's is quite a large sheep, almost the size of a real baby lamb. It's wearing argyle plaid socks and a blue Glengarry bonnet with a bright red toorie on top."

Osbert wrinkled his nose. "What's a toorie?"

"It's Scotch for a little ball of fuzz."

"I thought they were pom-poms."

"By pom-poms I assume you mean pompons," said Arethusa, "unless you happen to be referring to the Maxim automatic quick-firing rifle, which is hyphenated. Or used to be. I don't know whether they hyphenate them any more. Go look it up."

"I have more important things to do," snarled Osbert. "Come on, pardner, we'd better go find that sheep."

"Who am I, Little Bo-Peep?" Dittany replied firmly. "Wherever that sheep may have strayed to, I expect it can stay there till after we've eaten our supper. Ready, everyone?"

"Yes," said Arethusa.

They were all eating chicken and rice, which was excellent as Clorinda's concoctions usually were when she didn't get too carried away, when they heard a diffident knock at the door. "I'll go," said Clorinda, who was always ready to go anywhere. "Oh. Good evening, Miss—or Mrs.—er —Ms.—"

"I'm Matilda McCorquindale," said a voice from the doorstep. "Mother Matilda's daughter. Is this by any chance the house where Mr. Reginald Monk is staying?"

"Yes, it is," cried Osbert before Clorinda could blow the gaff. "Come in, Daughter Matilda. Meet my—er—brother Osbert's mother-in-law."

"Whose what?" demanded Clorinda.

Daughter Matilda smiled wanly. "You needn't maintain your incognito with me, Mr. Monk. I suspected from the outset that your Reginald persona was a ruse. Then this is in fact your own mother-in-law?"

By now Dittany had joined the group in the doorway. "That's right. She's Mrs. Bert Pusey, and I'm Osbert's wife, Dittany. And you're the Matilda McCorquindale who whanged me across the shins with your hockey stick twelve years ago this very day when the Lobelia Falls' girls' field hockey team beat Lammergen High six to three. The lady at the table is my husband's aunt Arethusa Monk, whom you may know as the reigning queen of roguish regency romance. My stars and garters!"

"What, dear?" said Osbert.

"Don't you see? Daughter Matilda has eyes like fathomless pools of inscrutability, too."

"Coruscating cactus, so she does!"

"I do?" said Daughter Matilda in understandable confusion.

"You certainly do." Clorinda clinched the matter once and for all. "The resemblance is quite remarkable. There's probably a family connection somewhere. The Monks are an old Lobelia Falls family, even though Osbert's father grew up in Toronto and steadfastly refuses to return to the land of his ancestors. Were there any Monks in your family tree, Daughter Matilda?"

The heiress presumptive to the mincemeat magnate giggled faintly. "I shouldn't be at all surprised. I'll have to ask my mother. Do you really think I look like Miss Monk? I'd be so honored."

"Of course you would, egad," said Arethusa. "The one drawback in being related to me, I regret to point out, is that you'd also be related to Osbert. However, one must take the tares with the tulips. If this were my house, I'd invite you to sit down and have some chicken."

"And if anybody would let me get a word in edgewise, I'd ask her myself," said Dittany. "Please join us, Daughter Matilda."

"But I can't simply barge in on you!"

"You're no relative of Aunt Arethusa if you don't," said Osbert. "Come on, Cousin Matilda, a hot supper will do you good. Won't it, darling?"

"Certainly it will," said Dittany. "She's got to keep up her strength. Sit over there next to Arethusa, Matilda, so we can admire the likeness."

The resemblance between the two was indeed remarkable, but the inscrutability was in fact present only in one of them. Whether a crooked lawyer, an honest literary agent, or a sexily sneering cobra fancier would ever fall instant victim to Daughter Matilda's fatal attraction was open to serious doubt; the younger woman was about as subtly alluring as one of her mother's mincemeat tarts.

To be sure, this was no denigration of her charms. A well-baked mince pie has its own wholesome appeal, and is surely a great deal easier to cope with. The big difference between the two, Osbert decided after serious cogitation, was that Daughter Matilda had looked perfectly natural sitting at the conference table in her gingham cap and wraparound, whereas Arethusa would have stuck out like a pomegranate in a scoopful of raisins. Conversely, there would be no incongruity in Arethusa's settling down in a pair of gauzy green harem pants for a quiet rest on a tiger skin rug, should she take the notion; in which situation Daughter Matilda would without doubt appear woefully out of place.

At the moment, however, sitting there at the kitchen table under the green-shaded hanging light, wearing a plain dark purple frock, with circles under her eyes from strain and weeping, and with her cap off to reveal long black hair done up in a knot much as Arethusa was wearing hers, Daughter Matilda could easily have passed for Arethusa's twin sister.

After a nip of sherry and a helping of Clorinda's chicken, the unexpected visitor began to perk up a little. "I mustn't stay long, I really should get back to help Mother be nice to people at the funeral parlor. The reason I came is that I'd like to get a look at that note you found in the yarn shop, the one that put you onto Mr. Wardle. I'm much more familiar with Daddy's handwriting than Mother is. He used to write me letters when I'd be away at summer camp or college, whereas he never had much occasion to write her because they were together most of the time. You wouldn't happen to have the note here, I don't suppose?"

"No, but we can get it easily enough," Osbert told her. "Why don't I phone Sergeant MacVicar and ask if he'd mind bringing it over here, since you're in a hurry? He'll have finished his supper by now, I expect."

"I wonder if he had cullen skink?" Daughter Matilda actually managed a feeble attempt at a laugh. "Mother is really excited about having met Cousin Margaret. It's been the one bright spot since Daddy was—yes, please do ask him."

Once he'd learned the circumstances, the sergeant said he'd come right over. "Oh, good," said Daughter Matilda. "Perhaps I'd better give Mother a ring so she won't be worried if I'm a few minutes late."

"You'll have to use this phone," said Osbert. "It's the only one we have."

"That's quite all right. Do I have to turn the little crank?"

"Not anymore, we only keep it for auld lang syne," Dittany explained. "Just dial the number."

"I see. Hello, Mother? I'm having supper with the Monks, and Sergeant MacVicar—yes, Cousin Donald—is bringing that note for me to see. I'll be along as soon as I've checked it out. Shall I go straight to the—oh, they have? Uncle Cadwallader, too? My gosh, where are you going to put them all? Cousin Penelope had better have my room. I suppose I could sleep on the—

oh, he is? Well, I'll just have to take a sleeping bag down cellar.''

"Nonsense," boomed Arethusa. "Come and stay with me."

"Oh, may I? Mother, Cousin Arethusa's invited me to spend the night at her house. Yes, isn't it lovely? Everybody says we look just alike only she's absolutely gorgeous and I'm just me. Yes, I'll tell them. See you in a while, then."

She hung up the receiver and turned to the others. "Mother says to thank you very much. We've got such a flock of out-of-town relatives over there that they're practically hanging from the eaves troughs. How do I find your house, Cousin Arethusa? I'm terrible at directions."

"Then why don't you come back here when you're finished at the funeral parlor, since you already know the way, and we'll pilot you over," Clorinda suggested. "Arethusa will probably be here anyway. We were planning to brush up on our tango in case Ranville and Glanville ask us to go dancing. They're a pair of Siamese twins whom we're helping Miss Jane Fuzzywuzzy entertain during their stay in Lobelia Falls."

"How kind of you," said Daughter Matilda. "I had no idea Lobelia Falls was such a cosmopolitan community."

"Stick around," said Dittany. "Oops, here comes Sergeant MacVicar with the note."

Here, indeed, he came, and there was the scrap of paper Dittany had fished out of Raggedy Andy's sleeve. Daughter Matilda examined the scribbles, then shook her head.

"Daddy never wrote this—never! He's written me letters on airplanes, sailboats, even once going downhill on a bobsled when he fell off in mid-sentence, and the writing's just not the same. I've saved them all, from the time I was a little girl. You can compare for yourselves if you like."

"Umpha," said Sergeant MacVicar. "This opens up new territory for investigation, does it not, Deputy Monk?"

"I'll say it does, Chief. One of the crooks must have

sneaked back to the shop in a different disguise during that hubbub later on and planted the note to turn us on to Wardle, don't you think? But was that because they knew Wardle had either killed himself or been murdered, and would provide a convenient dead end to the investigation, or because one of the two actually was Wardle and the other one was trying to frame him for the whole operation? Or," Osbert added for he was nothing if not fair-minded, "was it for some other reason?"

"We'll find out," said Dittany. "Come on, darling, we'd better go frisk that lamb. Sorry to run off, Cousin Matilda, but duty calls."

"I quite understand, Cousin Dittany. I must get back to Lammergen myself, Mother sounded awfully fraught. I do wish Uncle Cadwallader had stayed home, though I suppose it's unkind of me to say so. I'll see you all later, then. Does it matter what time I come?"

"Not to me, fair coz," replied Arethusa. "I never know what time it is, anyway."

"Except when it's mealtime," Osbert muttered. "I'll get your shawl, Dittany. What about you, Cousin Matilda? Don't you have a coat or something?"

"No, I forgot to bring one. It was still fairly warm when I left Lammergen and I wasn't intending to stay. I'll be all right," the younger Matilda added in the unconvincing tone people use when they're hoping someone will come to the rescue.

"Don't be silly, you'll catch cold and then where will you be?" said Clorinda. "I'll be glad to lend you my Mexican serape. It's the only thing I have that will fit you." Daughter Matilda was fully as tall as Arethusa and at least ten pounds heavier, no doubt from a lifetime's exposure to mincemeat.

"That serape seems hardly the thing to wear to a funeral parlor when it's your own father who's the guest of honor, as one might say," Dittany objected. "Can't we find something a trifle less ethnic? Arethusa, you wore your purple cape over here, why don't you let Matilda take that? It will go nicely with the dress she's wearing."

"So it will, ecod."

Arethusa even bestirred herself to go over to the coat rack, fetch the handsome garment, and show Daughter Matilda how to fasten the elaborately braided frogs. Swathed in its voluminous folds and looking more like Arethusa than ever, she tripped off a good deal less woeful than when she'd come. Sergeant MacVicar listened to the tale of the sheep and agreed to join Dittany and Osbert in going to look for it. That left Clorinda and Arethusa stuck with the dishes again. Things were working out just fine.

Chapter 16

"Are you sure Miss Jane's at home, Sergeant MacVicar?" Dittany asked him as they rounded the corner.

"Quite sure, lass. She is entertaining her twin cousins at a buffet supper in her flat, along with six other cousins who didn't get to meet them at the previous gathering."

"The Bleinkinsops seem to be as abundantly blessed with unknown cousins as the McCorquindales," Dittany was saying, when Osbert grabbed her arm.

"Hist!"

"Certainly I'll hist if you want me to, darling," she whispered. "But why?"

"See those two men looking in the yarn shop window?" he whispered back. "The skinny one with the cigar is VP Lemon Peel and the little fat one's VP Suet. How come they're not over in Lammergen paying their respects? You two slide on ahead to Miss Jane's, I'm going to lurk."

"Happy lurking, dear."

As Osbert melted into the shadows, Dittany took Sergeant MacVicar's arm and forged forth, though not very forcibly. Two cars were pulled up in front of the Yarnery, presumably they were the ones the cousins had come in. Another was parked down by Mr. Gumpert's; that must be the two VPs. Dittany and Sergeant MacVicar pretended not to notice them but stopped at Miss Jane's side door and rang the bell.

Miss Jane herself came downstairs to answer their ring, wearing a handsome blouse and skirt she'd crocheted out of blue ribbon, looking not at all sheeplike and even less pleased to see them. Dittany's involuntary exclamation of "Miss Jane, what a becoming outfit!" plus the fact that she herself was wearing a good deal of Miss Jane's yarn did a little to break the ice, but nowhere near enough. Sergeant MacVicar set himself to inducing the thaw.

"We apologize for intruding on your supper party, Miss Jane, but new information has come to hand which makes it imperative that we inspect your sheep."

"The one with the Glengarry bonnet and argyle socks," Dittany amplified. "It wasn't in the shop when we searched for clues."

"Why, so he wasn't," said Miss Jane after a moment's thought. "I'd quite forgotten. I'd taken Lammikin—that's what I call him—upstairs because I wanted everything nice for my cousins."

"When did you take him?" asked Sergeant MacVicar. "Was this before Mr. McCorquindale, as we now know him to have been, entered your shop?"

"No, it was after, when I went to remop the floor. Lammikin had got knocked over and there he was, lying in the middle of the floor. Not in one of the spots where Mr. McCorquindale had dripped, fortunately. But I couldn't know that at the time and I hadn't time to give the poor sweetie a good looking-over because everything was in such a flurry. So I rushed him upstairs and stuck him out of sight in my bedroom. And there he's still sitting, what with all the fuss and bother over Mr. McCorquindale and trying to have everything nice for my cousins. And now I've got a roomful of company upstairs and they'll be wanting their coffee, so I'm afraid you've come at an awfully bad time. Though if Mrs. Monk wouldn't mind just slipping quietly into my bedroom—I'd really rather you didn't come with her, Sergeant MacVicar, because if my cousins ever caught sight of the police chief going into my—a woman living alone can't be too—''

''We understand perfectly, Miss Jane,'' said Dittany. ''We can make believe my mother dropped her mitten when she came in to buy baby yarn, and I dropped by to pick it up and had to ask to use your bathroom. You needn't say bathroom if it embarrasses you, just tell them I have to pee a lot because of my delicate condition, which they can see plainly enough for themselves. I'll try to blush if anybody notices me. Sergeant MacVicar won't mind a bit waiting down here in the entryway. I shouldn't be long.''

''Oh yes, that will do nicely,'' said Miss Jane, ''only I'll say scarf if you don't mind. It's still a bit early for mittens. This way, please.''

Fortunately Dittany didn't have to go through the living room. She caught only a glimpse of the party: Ranville and Glanville in the midst, laughing and joking, people taking food from a side table, a good time being had by all. Quite in contrast to the scene that had taken place downstairs while the sheep was still in the shop, she thought ironically, as she turned away from the festive scene and followed Miss Jane into the bedroom.

Dittany could see why Miss Jane hadn't wanted Sergeant MacVicar in here and it had nothing to do with morals. It was just that this was the room where the shopkeeper had been dumping all the odds and ends she hadn't yet been able to make a place for elsewhere. Men didn't understand these things, but any other woman would naturally sympathize because she'd have a room in her own house that she didn't want anybody else to see for the same reason. Miss Jane fluttered her hands in a ''What can I do?'' gesture and gave Dittany a nervous little smile. Dittany gave her back an understanding nod and a ''What else could you have done?'' shrug. Reassured, Miss Jane reached behind a couple of boxes and hauled out Lammikin. Dittany took to him at once.

''Oh, isn't he adorable! How did you get him so fleecy? Look at all those millions of yarn loops and that cute little pink knitted nose. Maybe you can show Mum how to make one for the nursery. Now slide back to your cousins, Miss Jane. I can let myself out. This is just a formality, you know.''

Dittany already knew where she'd find what she was looking for. It would have been too stiff to go into Lammikin's socks, too big to hide among his loops. But the Glengarry bonnet had been stiffened with cardboard to hold its perky shape. As she'd expected, the cardboard had an extra bit of stiffening tucked in behind: a buff-colored rectangle covered in plastic. There wasn't much written on it, just a few measurements and abbreviations and one clear word: NUTMEG. In death as in life, Charles McCorquindale had been faithful to his trust.

Soberly she put the card in her skirt pocket and made her careful way downstairs, pausing to flush the loo in passing, lest any of Miss Jane's guests begin to wonder what that very pregnant young woman was really up to. Sergeant MacVicar, also faithful to his trust, was waiting for her at the bottom of the stairwell, willing her feet not to slip. Dittany landed safely and handed him the card. He glanced at it, made a Hibernian noise in his throat, and held the door for her to go out.

"Aye, lass," he said when he'd got her safely out on the sidewalk and away from Miss Jane's open window, "Charles McCorquindale was a leal man and true. I'm minded to take Margaret over to Lammergen the noo. We can pay our respects to her dead kinsman and give Mother Matilda the nutmeg formula."

"I'm sure that's what Mr. McCorquindale would have wanted," Dittany replied. "Those gangsters must be pretty sick at not having found his part of the recipe. I wonder how they're going to manage now that Wardle seems to be out of the picture. Osbert said there were about fifteen VPs at the conference this morning, and the crooks have only managed to pinch half a dozen ingredients so far."

"Well may they wonder, lass. It will require a bold stroke, I misdoubt. The question that preys on my mind is, was Wardle the only fly in the mincemeat?"

"It does make you wonder, doesn't it? But the question that's preying on my mind is what's happened to my husband? The VPs' car is gone, if that one down by Mr. Gumpert's was in fact theirs. You don't suppose they forced Osbert into it at gunpoint?"

"Noo, noo, dinna fash yoursel', it's bad for the bairns. I cannot see Deputy Monk allowing himself to fall into so dire a picklement. Belike he'll be waiting for us at the station. Mind the curb."

To Dittany's relief, when the sergeant had mother-henned her across the street and into the police station, they did find Osbert whiling away the wait by chatting with Officer Bob, whose turn it was this evening to man the desk. "Ah, there you are," Osbert said. "Are you all right, darling? Did you find the formula?"

"No problem—the card was inside the sheep's Glengarry. Sergeant MacVicar's going to deliver it to Mother Matilda as soon as he gets Margaret organized. Did the VPs catch you lurking?"

"Them catch him?" Officer Bob emitted a snort of derision, caught his chief's eye upon him, and got extremely busy with unfiled reports.

Osbert shrugged. "There wasn't much to lurk about, they didn't hang around long. It was rather interesting though, they were talking about Daughter Matilda staying with Aunt Arethusa."

"My stars! How in heck did they know?"

"They'd met her coming and going, which is to say that she was going as they were coming. I gather they'd all stopped to ask each other what they were doing here, and they'd said they were investigating for whatever good that might do, and she'd said she'd been having supper with Aunt Arethusa and was coming back to spend the night with her. I got the impression she'd been bragging to them about being related, though I can't imagine why."

Dittany laughed and straightened his collar. "Because Arethusa's reigning queen of the roguish regency romance, silly. I'm sure Daughter Matilda would have bragged about you too, if she hadn't had to respect your incognito."

"I bet she wouldn't. The way she went swishing off in that stupid purple cape—"

"It's a gorgeous cape. You just think it's stupid because Arethusa wears it."

"Well, naturally. Wouldn't anyone? Now that Lemon Peel and Suet know about Aunt Arethusa, I might as well quit trying to be Reginald."

"I don't see where that follows at all. Besides, how can you? You are."

"What I mean dear, is that since a family connection between the Monks and the McCorquindales has been established—"

"It hasn't, actually," Dittany pointed out.

"Well, I expect it will be as soon as somebody gets around to digging up the roots. Anyway, they'll think Mother Matilda took me on account of nepotism."

"What if they do? From what I've been able to make out, the mincemeat factory's rife with nepotism."

"Yes, but this is different," said Osbert. "VP Suet was sneering about me being Mother Matilda's pet nephew."

"He's just a jealous old goop. Darling, I think I'd better go home now, those stairs at Miss Jane's rather did me in."

"Oh, gosh! Here, sit down. I'll run over to Roger Munson's and borrow his stretcher."

"Osbert Monk, don't you dare! First thing you know, Roger'd be giving me mouth-to-mouth resuscitation. Sergeant MacVicar can drop me off at the house if you want to do some more lurking. Have there been any leads in the break-ins at Mr. Gumpert's and the museum, Bob?"

Bob said they hadn't been able to find a single clue and it looked to him like professionals, only he couldn't figure out what the heck they thought they were going to accomplish by pinching imitation jeweled daggers and strewing paper around and he wished to heck Charles McCorquindale had picked some other place to bleed in, though he supposed it wasn't very nice of him to say so about one of Mrs. MacVicar's relatives, and where was Osbert planning to lurk this time?

Osbert said he didn't want to lurk anywhere because he didn't see anything to lurk for and he did want to get in a little work on his ostriches, so he begged a ride for his flagging spouse and himself from the MacVicars who were of course happy to oblige. Osbert then got Dittany tucked up in bed with *Anne of Avonlea,* for she wanted the twins to have the benefit of however much culture they might be able to absorb in their prenatal state, and went back downstairs to round up his herd of ostriches.

Arethusa and Clorinda had wearied of the tango and settled down to a hard-fought game of Parcheesi with a plate of cookies and a jug of cocoa to spur them on. All was serene on Applewood Avenue; the only sounds Dittany could hear from her bedroom were the rattle of Osbert's trusty Remington and an occasional wild "Huzza" from Arethusa when she'd made a successful play. How lovely and peaceful it was! Twins did demand a great deal of a mother's energy. She reached the bottom of her page, had she strength enough left to turn another? As Dittany wondered, her eyelids closed. *Anne of Avonlea* slipped from her grasp. She slept.

She waked. What the heck was going on downstairs? The Big Ben on the nightstand read half-past eleven, hardly the time to be raising a ruckus. Were they having a bomb threat? Had Ethel met a skunk? Dittany grabbed hold of the bedpost and hauled herself upright, found her slippers, wrapped the "Rest and Be Thankful" quilt around her, and padded downstairs.

The Parcheesi game had been put away. Clorinda had either gone to bed or been getting ready to do so; she was now arrayed in a peach-colored satin negligee and a pair of Minnie Mouse bedroom slippers with her hair all skew-gee. Osbert must still have been working, as he sometimes did when the fit was upon him. He was still in his sweatshirt and jeans and his cowlick was flopping like a wet rooster's comb. Arethusa was—no, Arethusa wasn't. The hysterical figure in the purple cape was Daughter Matilda.

"Where's Arethusa?"

That must have been the wrong thing for Dittany to ask.

Daughter Matilda's wails rose from loud to fortissimo. "She's gone! They took her!"

"Who did?" Dittany dropped the quilt and hastened to get a clean linen towel and a glass of water. "Here, Daughter Matilda. Drink this. Take this."

"A cup towel? What for?"

"To wipe your face on. You're streaky."

"I'm what? Oh." Daughter Matilda sipped at the water and rubbed her face with the cloth. "I looked so ghostly I put on some makeup before I—she's gone! They took her!"

"So you mentioned. Sit down and tell us about it, why don't you? Have some cocoa, if there's any left."

"There isn't," said Osbert. "Try this brandy, Matilda. Liquor is quicker." He produced a tot he'd poured, for some reason, into a chipped jelly glass.

"Th-thank you," said Daughter Matilda. "I'm sorry. I guess I'm a little upset. They hit me."

"That was extremely rude of them." Clorinda was back. "I couldn't find the smelling salts so I brought some eau-de-cologne to bathe her forehead with."

"I'm not sure this is quite the time to bathe her forehead, Mum," said Dittany. "Why don't you put on the kettle and make us all a nice cup of tea?"

"What a splendid suggestion, dear. Arethusa must be thrilled to pieces."

"About what?"

"Oh, hasn't anyone told you? She's been abducted."

"I'll be gum-swizzled! Where, how, why, when, and by whom?"

"The international spies, I believe. Or the mob."

"You mean those two thugs who—" Dittany glanced nervously at Daughter Matilda, whose wails were fading off into dejected whimpers thanks to the brandy and the moral support.

"It's all right, Dittany," the mincemeat heiress said dully. "Never mind about hurting my feelings. They've gone numb. You mean those men who killed Daddy. It must have been the same two. Who else would it be? Could I have a little more brandy, please?"

"Of course," said Osbert.

"And maybe some animal crackers or a nice tuna-fish sandwich?" Clorinda suggested. "A full tummy makes a stiff upper lip."

"Cookies," said Dittany. "Sugar for the shock."

Daughter Matilda shook her head. "Nothing, thanks. I'd be sick if I ate. They hit me."

"Where did they hit you?" Dittany was determined to get at the facts.

"In the garden. What happened was, my car started making a funny noise after I left here. I got back to Lammergen all right but the noise kept getting funnier. I thought I hadn't better take it out again, so VP Suet and VP Lemon Peel offered to drive me back here. They knew I was planning to sleep at Arethusa's because I'd happened to run into them earlier and—"

"Yes, we know about that. So they did in fact drive you where? Here to the house?"

"No, they let me off at the corner and I walked. I asked them to, I wanted the air. Having to be nice to all those people, with Daddy lying there in the open casket—I'm sorry." She blew her nose in a halfhearted way. "Anyway, that's what I did. And Arethusa was here waiting for me and she said let's aroint, so we did."

"On foot?" said Osbert.

"Oh yes. I still wanted some more air. You have wonderful air over here."

"I offered to drive them," said Clorinda, "but it's really no distance, as I don't have to tell you. And she did want the air. She said so."

"And I offered to give Arethusa back her cloak because I'd brought along my black suede jacket. But she said she'd wear my jacket instead, so she did. We thought it was a giggle, swapping clothes. I needed some fun by then, I can tell you. Poor Mother, I felt mean running out on her, but Cousin Penelope was there. Pen and Mother were always great pals, so I knew it would be all right. And there really wasn't any place left for me to sleep.''

Daughter Matilda dabbed at her nose again. "So anyway, Arethusa and I walked over, and her house looked so romantic by moonlight with all those turrets and gargoyles and everything that I just stood there gawking. Then she asked if I'd like to go around back and see the donjon-keep, so I said sure, and we went.''

"What did she mean, the donjon-keep?" snarled Osbert. "Since when did she have one?"

"I expect Arethusa was referring to that lean-to where she keeps her garbage cans," said Dittany. "Go on, Matilda. So you went around into the garden and—"

"And here came these two men. I suppose they must have been men. I can't imagine any woman acting so unladylike except perhaps VP Cloves. She's a pretty tough cookie when she gets riled up. But I really can't say for sure because they were wearing trench coats with the collars turned up and felt hats with brims turned down. And they had bandanas tied over their faces.''

Chapter 17

"But that's not suitable!" cried Osbert. "My editor would never allow bandanas with trench coats and felt hats. Silk scarves, maybe."

"Or stocking masks?" said Clorinda. "Or—"

Dittany felt a burst of unladylikeness coming on. "Osbert, don't be such a purist. Mum, let her finish. What happened, Matilda?"

"I don't really know. One of them grabbed me. I tried to fight him off but he did something awfully painful to the side of my neck and I must have passed out. While I was struggling, I saw the other one put a white pad, like a folded handkerchief, over Arethusa's mouth and nose. I thought I smelled chloroform although I don't actually know what chloroform smells like. It could have been ether, but it certainly wasn't eau-de-cologne."

"How awful! Then what?"

"Then I woke up lying on the ground with the cloak all wadded up around my head. I pulled it away, sat up, and looked around for Arethusa. But she wasn't there! I thought maybe she'd gone into the house, so I went and knocked and tried to get in but the doors were locked and there were no lights inside. That was when I realized those men must have abducted her. I found her handbag with her keys in it, but I was too scared to go inside the house alone. So I ran over here and—and here I am."

"We'll have to let Sergeant MacVicar know what's happened," said Osbert. "I'll phone the station, for whatever good it may do. You didn't hear a car drive off?"

Daughter Matilda shook her head. "I was really out of it, I can't tell for how long. Do you remember when we left here?"

"It was two minutes past eleven," said Clorinda. "I noticed because my husband hadn't called. If Bert hasn't called by eleven that means he isn't going to, so I decided I might as well go and get ready for bed. It's twenty till twelve now. You've been here maybe six or seven minutes. It doesn't take more than three or four minutes to walk to Arethusa's, so allowing say five minutes to look at the gargoyles and be attacked—how long does it take to chloroform somebody, Osbert?"

"Not long, I shouldn't think. Say another five minutes at the most for the abductors to get Arethusa unconscious and into their car. I'm assuming they must have had some kind of vehicle, I don't see how they'd have managed without. We'll have to ask the neighbors whether they noticed anybody driving off."

"But the only neighbors close enough to have seen are Grandsire Coskoff and his second wife," Dittany pointed out. "They both take off their hearing aids and eyeglasses and go to bed with the birds, so a fat lot of help they'd be. What it boils down to is that Matilda must have been lying there unconscious for as much as ten minutes, maybe even more. By now, Arethusa could be halfway to—heaven knows where."

Her own voice had grown a bit wobbly by now. "Osbert, do call the station. Maybe the Mounties—"

"Yes, darling, I'm calling. Sit down and take a few deep breaths. Look after her, Mum. Hello, Bob? Deputy Monk here. I want to report a probable kidnapping. No, it's my Aunt Arethusa. She appears to have been snatched from her own backyard about twenty minutes ago. We're guessing the kidnappers are the same two who shot Charles McCorquindale, but we have no description except that they were both wearing trench coats and felt hats and had bandanas tied over their faces."

Dittany could hear loud squawks from the telephone clear across the room. "Tell him to shut up and listen," she said crossly.

"Yes, darling. Bob, shut up and listen. Mr. McCorquindale's daughter Matilda was with my aunt. Matilda was knocked unconscious by the kidnappers, and didn't come to until just a few minutes ago. She couldn't get into Arethusa's house so she ran back here. You'd better alert the chief and start canvassing the neighborhood to see if you can get a make on a strange car or van, or even a truck. No, no idea whatsoever. This would have to be a different vehicle than they had before. As far as I know, that car with the bullet holes in it is still over at Scottsbeck."

Osbert hung up and came back to Dittany. "Feeling all right now, pet?"

"I don't know. Are you going out with Bob?"

"No, I'm staying right here with you, and so is Cousin Matilda. You'd better get Matilda to bed, Clorinda. Can she bunk in with you for the night?"

"She may have my bed. I'll sleep down here on the cot."

"Let me sleep on the cot," Matilda protested. "I don't want to put you out of your room."

"I don't want you down here where you'd be easy to get at," Osbert objected. "Not to scare you any worse than you are already, Matilda, but hasn't it occurred to you that Arethusa may not have been the person they meant to kidnap?"

"Well, of course," said Dittany. "Matilda and Arethusa look so much alike, and they were wearing each other's wraps. Who wouldn't have been fooled? So this is the bold stroke."

"The what, dearie?" asked Clorinda.

"What Sergeant MacVicar misdoubted the bad guys would be trying next. Don't you see what this means? They're planning to hold her for ransom, and the ransom's going to be Mother Matilda's mincemeat recipe."

"They can't do that!" cried Daughter Matilda. "Granny's recipe is a sacred trust. Mother would never give it up, not for anything."

"Can you be sure of that?" said Osbert. "Your mother's just lost her husband on account of the recipe. Would she risk losing her daughter, too?"

"But she hasn't lost me. I'm right here."

"Yes, but only by a fluke. And you're going to stay here till we find out what the heck is going on. Furthermore, you're going to lie low and keep out of sight because once those crooks realize they've got hold of the wrong hostage, they'll be out looking for the right one. You don't want to put your mother through another ordeal, do you? Go on upstairs with Clorinda and try to get some sleep."

"But what's going to happen to Cousin Arethusa when they find out she's not me?"

That was what the Monks were trying not to think about. Osbert wet his lips. It was Dittany who found the wits to answer.

"Arethusa's a very rich woman, Daughter Matilda. I expect what the kidnappers will do is simply change their plans and hold her for ransom instead of you. We'll be getting a request for a million dollars in unmarked bills, no doubt, as soon as they've had a chance to get hold of some paste and a newspaper."

She didn't believe what she was saying. She didn't suppose any of the others believed it, either; but this was the one straw they had to cling to, so they clung. "Such a nuisance for them having to hunt out all those menacing words and stick them down one by one," said Clorinda, "but it serves them right for being so nasty. Come along, Matilda. You'll have to wear one of Dittany's maternity nightgowns, I'm afraid. We don't have anything else to fit you."

"That's all right. I can sleep in my slip."

Daughter Matilda had sense enough left to yield to reason, at any rate. Everybody breathed easier as she allowed Clorinda to lead her upstairs.

Osbert sat down on the cot and put his arms around Dittany. "Want to go up now, pardner?"

"Hadn't we better wait for Sergeant MacVicar? Won't he want to grill Cousin Matilda?"

"Why should he? She can't tell him any more than she's already told us. Darn it! Aunt Arethusa's such a pain in the neck, why do I have to be so worried about her?"

"Because you're a darling pussycat, that's why."

"Scratch my whiskers."

"Harr'mph."

"There," Dittany sighed, "I knew he'd be along just as we got comfortable. We should have remembered to lock the door. Sergeant MacVicar, why aren't you out hunting for Arethusa?"

"I did not wish to lose time following up false leads," their unwelcome visitor replied. "If you can bring yourself to let go of young Romeo there, lass, perhaps he and I might hold a wee council of war. Deputy Monk, I infer you do not care to join our search party?"

"Sorry, Chief, but we've got Daughter Matilda bedded down in the spare room and somebody's got to stand by to repel attackers. Since I can't imagine why anybody in his right mind would want to abduct Aunt Arethusa, I'm operating on the premise that those ornery coyotes snatched the wrong hostage. As soon as the chloroform wears off and they realize what happened, they'll probably come galloping back to try their luck again."

Osbert explained in detail what Matilda had told them and why it would have been easy for the kidnappers to make so grave a mistake. "Dittany thinks this is the bold stroke you were expecting and I'm inclined to agree with her."

"Aye," said the chief. "That's the only thing that makes sense."

"Well, maybe not the only thing," Osbert demurred. "I can think of six or seven other plots which might work pretty well in the same circumstances, but that's just my professionalism leaking out. Anyway, I don't dare leave Dittany and her mother alone here with Matilda. Somebody's got to try to get a line on those two sidewinders though, so I guess it's up to you and the guys, Chief. I expect your wife's pretty sore at me for hauling you out of bed, but what else could I have done?"

"Dinna fash yoursel', lad; a policeman's lot is not a happy one. You might as well get on with scratching his whiskers, lass."

But the magic had gone out of the moment. Clorinda was downstairs again with a pink-and-white polka-dot boudoir cap over her curlers and her arms full of assorted bedding, a box of peppermint wafers, and *Anne's House of Dreams*. Osbert helped his mother-in-law make up the cot while Dittany rinsed out the last batch of teacups and saucers. Then he and his beloved left Clorinda in the kitchen with Ethel to guard her from frustrated abductors and whatever other things might conceivably go bump in the night, and made their grateful way upstairs.

At least Daughter Matilda wasn't lying awake bemoaning the vicissitudes of fate. They could hear some fairly brisk vibrations of the soft palate from the spare room.

"Snoring her head off, bless her heart," Dittany whispered. "The poor thing must be plumb tuckered out. Darling, what are we going to do?"

"Hit the hay and grab a few winks ourselves is the best thing I can think of at the moment. We do still have that key to Arethusa's house, don't we?"

"Yes, of course. It's hanging in the pantry."

"Good. I was thinking maybe what we ought to do is send Matilda over there tomorrow. She can sit pounding the typewriter and pretending to be Arethusa so the kidnappers won't catch on to their mistake."

"But they're bound to, darling, as soon as Arethusa comes to and starts threatening to stap their vitals."

"Maybe she won't get the chance."

"Osbert! You don't mean—"

"Precious, of course I don't mean. What I mean is, if her abductors are really VP Lemon Peel and VP Suet or anybody else from the mincemeat factory, they'll have to show up at VP Nutmeg's funeral tomorrow morning. That means they can't be off in some fell den standing guard over Aunt Arethusa. It might be quite a while before they get back to her."

"Then it might also be quite a while before she gets

anything to eat. Maybe they'll forget where they put her and she'll starve!''

"Darling, they won't forget where they put her. Kidnappers aren't that absentminded. Anyway, I believe they always have a deaf old crone on the premises to fetch the prisoner's bread and water, though I suppose it'll be mincemeat tarts in this case. Darn it, that brings up another problem. Mother Matilda's really going to be bent out of shape if Daughter Matilda fails to show up for her father's funeral. We'll have to get her there somehow.''

"But if the kidnappers are there, too, they'll see right away that they've got the wrong hostage,'' Dittany objected. "Then they'll whiz back and kill Arethusa so she won't expose them for the rotters they are. What we'll have to do is send Daughter Matilda to the funeral disguised as Arethusa impersonating Daughter Matilda in order to spare Mother Matilda the pain of learning that her daughter's been kidnapped.''

"You're right," said Osbert. "It's the only sensible thing to do. Since we've got that matter settled, pet, I don't suppose you'd care to consider giving a poor, tired ostrich rustler a little good-night kiss?''

Gradually slumber overtook all the inhabitants of the ancestral Henbit homestead. Came the dawn, even Daughter Matilda woke with her lip considerably stiffened and came downstairs to breakfast looking fairly chipper in a pair of Osbert's pajamas and a frisky robe his mother had brought him from Hawaii although nobody could ever figure out why.

"I thought I might feel a little more up to facing the day if I had a cup of tea into me first," she half-apologized.

"Don't we all?'' said Dittany. "Here you are. Pass her the milk, Mum. Toast or muffins, Matilda, and how do you like your eggs?''

"Toast, please. Muffins seem a bit too self-indulgent at such a solemn time, don't you think? Poor Daddy, I can't help thinking—''

"Of course you can't. How about scrambled?''

"Why not? That's the way I feel. Just one egg, please.

I've been racking my brain about Arethusa. What are we going to do?''

"I'm glad you asked," said Osbert. "Dittany and I have a plan all worked out. It's going to require some clever acting on your part."

"How clever? I'm not much of an actress."

"Nonsense," said Dittany. "You're your father's daughter, aren't you? All you have to do is go to the funeral pretending to be Arethusa pretending to be you."

"Oh. Well, I—how?"

"Easily enough. After breakfast, you'll put on the same clothes you wore last night and go over to Arethusa's house. Mum will go with you, she and Arethusa have been running back and forth ever since she got here. If any of the neighbors see you, they'll just take it for granted you're Arethusa and you've dropped over here for breakfast, as she sometimes does."

"Or came for a midnight snack and just finished eating it," Osbert put in, then looked abashed. "I wish to heck she had!"

"I know, dear, don't we all." Dittany gave him a pat on the cowlick. "Have a muffin, you've got to keep your strength up. Here's your egg, Matilda. It won't be too hard for you to impersonate Arethusa. Just remember to look infathomable and mutter an occasional 'gadzooks' or 'by my halidom' if any of the VPs starts sidling up to you."

"They'll think I've gone nuts. VP Nuts." She laughed a bit jerkily. "That's all right. If I can spare Mother needless grief and agony while not jeopardizing Cousin Arethusa's life any worse than it's jeopardized already, I don't care what they think."

"Noble soul!" cried Clorinda. "You weren't planning to send this poor child to the funeral alone, were you, Osbert?"

"Not on your tintype. Matilda's not going anywhere without a bodyguard. What I have in mind, Matilda, is to ask Sergeant MacVicar's wife—that's your mother's recently discovered Cousin Margaret—to drive you both to the funeral with her. Nobody's going to think it strange for her to pay her respects as a relative. Clorinda, maybe you can be another cousin who takes after the other side of the family. You'll think of something, you always do. I want you handy to help Matilda out if she wobbles in her lines."

"You're not coming to the funeral yourself?" Matilda asked him.

"No, I'm too new an employee. It would look pushy if I showed up. Besides, I have other things to do. Now I've got to get hold of the MacVicars. You two had better scoot over to Arethusa's as soon as you're dressed and find something appropriate for Matilda to wear. And for Pete's sake, Clorinda, don't get carried away."

"Dearie, when did I ever?"

Osbert cast a despairing glance at Dittany. Dittany fixed a glittering eye on Clorinda. "You'll be fine, Mum," she said. "Put on your nice brown suit. Matilda can wear that black Pola Negri dress and coat Arethusa got for the last Hearts and Flowers convention, and the black toque with the spotted veil that goes with the outfit. Only take off the ostrich plumes and that big rhinestone clip."

"But dear, the plumes and the clip are what give it the pizazz."

"Pizazz is inappropriate for a funeral. And nix on the purple eye shadow, in case you were about to ask. Bring Matilda back here after she's dressed so we can drink her in. By the way, Matilda, when you walk over to Arethusa's, be sure to let that purple cloak billow out around you the way she always does. And stay right with Clorinda every minute. Now, not to hurry anybody but you said the funeral's at ten, which doesn't give you a heck of a lot of time to get ready. So move it!"

Chapter 18

Margaret MacVicar had been only too pleased to oblige. She was waiting in the Monks' kitchen when Clorinda came back with a somberly chic Daughter Matilda in tow.

"Do I look all right, Dittany?" she asked with a slight quaver in her voice. "The dress fits pretty well, don't you think? But it's not exactly me, is it?"

"Yes, it fits fine and no, it's not, which is precisely the effect we're trying to convey. You look just exotic enough in an indefinable sort of way to reassure the guilty that you're not really you and to make your relatives think there's something about you they can't quite put their finger on but it's certainly an improvement over a purple gingham wraparound."

"They'll put it down to shock and grief," said Margaret MacVicar, pulling on her own black gloves and picking up the car keys. "We'd better get cracking, then. Don't worry, Osbert, we'll take good care of Matilda. I do hope Donald turns up something on that car today. He's had no luck whatever so far. You *are* going to help him, aren't you?"

"Yup," said Osbert. "I shouldn't be surprised if I help him quite a lot."

"What are you going to do, old pard?" Dittany asked him as they watched the three women drive off to the funeral, Matilda a little too svelte in Arethusa's black ensemble, Margaret trim and sensible in heather tweeds and a gray fedora, Clorinda more or less demure in brown with a little brown-and-beige hat that should have been decorous enough but somehow managed to convey the impression that it was a fried egg.

"When you say 'you,' you mean of course 'we,' " Osbert replied. "Last night I dreamed about a herd of green ostriches that all had their beaks stuck in a big bucket of plaster of paris. Get your glad rags on, gal. I think it's an omen."

"Darling, you do have the most intriguing subconscious mind. I see exactly what you mean. How glad am I supposed to be?"

"Maybe you could wear that pregnant prairie princess outfit with your mother's red hat."

"So I could and so I shall. In fact it's about the only thing I can get into these days. If these kids get any bigger, I'll have to steal Arethusa's cape away from Cousin Matilda. Are we taking Ethel?"

"Why not? She may add just that extra *je ne sais quoi*."

"Oh, she'll do that, all right, but there's no earthly use expecting her to bite the kidnappers, if that's what you had in mind."

"Nope, that's not what I had in mind at all. Shall I put the butter in the fridge?"

"Do. And the bread in the breadbox and the jam pot in the pantry and feel free to carry out any other spot of titivating that strikes your fancy. I'll be down as soon as you've finished the dishes."

True to her word, Dittany reappeared in a short while wearing her blue denim tent with the red-edged ruffles and the red cartwheel hat. Ethel was already out in the wagon, eyes aglow and tail athump at the prospect of blazing new trails. Osbert put on his buckskin vest, his Stetson hat, and his silver concho belt, and they were ready to roll.

Dittany was not at all surprised to see Osbert taking the Lammergen road; green ostriches with their beaks set in plaster could mean only one thing. She was enchanted by the flamingos.

"Darling, they're lovely! You didn't tell me about the flashing red taillights."

"I didn't know," Osbert replied. "Those must have been a fresh inspiration. They do lend a certain cachet, don't they?"

In fact they weren't real taillights but only plastic bicycle reflectors. With the morning sun bouncing off them, however, the effect was all an artist's heart could desire. And here came the artist herself, looking brisk and competent in a pair of bright orange overalls. Ethel bounded out over the tailgate and rushed to make friends. The Monks' pleasure in the flamingos' taillights was as nothing compared to Mrs. Phiffer's rapture at her first sight of Ethel.

"How did you *ever*? What *is* it? Let me guess. You dyed a merino sheep—no, that wouldn't account for the ears. You dressed a bear in a bath mat? Wrong again? Then I give up. You've stumped me."

"Don't let that bother you," said Osbert. "We don't know, either. She just came that way. Her name's Ethel. The one with the hat is Dittany and we've come to visit the prisoner."

"But you're not even supposed to know she's here!"

"Is that what Mr. Wardle told you?"

"Yes. You could have knocked me over with a flamingo feather when he showed up here last night dry as a bone, with a beautiful woman draped over his shoulder. She was making odd noises."

"Did they sound like 'gadzooks'?" Dittany asked her.

"No, more like 'zounds'! Though now that you mention it, I believe she did say 'gadzooks' once or twice."

"Good, then she's sticking to the script. What's she doing now?"

"Sleeping. Is that all right?"

"It depends," said Osbert. "We'll have to check. Has she been awake? That is to say, has she waked up at all since she went to sleep? I assume she was awake when she got here or she wouldn't have been making noises. And Wardle wouldn't have been able to get her up the stairs unless she was more or less ambulatory, would he?''

"I doubt it, she's so magnificently statuesque. Do you suppose she'd let me take a mold? I could make half a dozen life-size plaster casts and use her for caryatids. Can't you just see her holding up a fireplace?''

"Holding up a fork would be more lifelike," Osbert muttered, but Dittany shushed him.

"I hardly think she'd care for being molded. She's awfully ticklish. But she is breathing, isn't she? She's supposed to breathe, it's in the script." Dittany hoped she didn't sound so panicky to Mrs. Phiffer as she did to herself.

Apparently she didn't. Mrs. Phiffer took the question in stride. "Oh yes, she's breathing like anything. One might almost say she was snoring, except that it would be unthinkable for anybody so gorgeous to snore. Does she have a name? Mr. Wardle didn't tell me.''

"That's because he's supposed to be the bad guy," said Osbert. "Did he tell you to feed her only bread and water?''

"He didn't specify. He merely hurled her roughly on the bed and shackled her to the bedpost. I thought it rather rude of him at the time but naturally I realized he had to follow his own sense of what was appropriate. He told me to keep a careful watch on her and under no condition to let her escape, which I must admit I found a bit thick; but he's paid up his rent till the end of next week so there wasn't much I could say about it, was there?''

"Not a great deal," Osbert replied. "But was that all he said? He didn't mean for you to play watchdog the whole time, surely?''

"I don't know. He said he'd be back, but he didn't say when. He says she's to be treated as a relatively harmless lunatic, and that when she wakes up she's going to tell me she's Mother Matilda's daughter who's been kidnapped.

It's a lovely script! I've been thinking she'll probably demand mincemeat tarts, though, and I haven't a speck of mincemeat in the house. You wouldn't care to run to the grocery store for me, I don't suppose? Otherwise I wouldn't have a thing to give her for breakfast except bacon and eggs and fried bread and fried tomatoes and maybe some baked beans on toast and a piece of pineapple custard pie and a few cookies and things.''

"You wouldn't happen to have any mustard pickles with little onions in them?"

Mrs. Phiffer shook her head sadly. "I'm afraid I don't. That is to say, I have the mustard pickles, but I've picked out all the onions and eaten them myself. I always do, that's why my husband left me."

"I don't blame him a bit," Osbert burst out. "My aunt does the same thing. I'd leave her too, if I could. Only you can't desert an aunt. At least I suppose you could, but the gesture would seem rather hollow. Sorry, Mrs. Phiffer, I didn't mean to reopen old wounds. As for the mincemeat tarts, Daughter Matilda could have those any old time. I'm sure she'd much prefer fried bread and tomatoes and all that other great stuff you mentioned. Don't you agree, Dittany?"

"Absolutely, no question. Yours will be just the sort of breakfast she'll like best, Mrs. Phiffer. She can easily get along without the pickled onions for a meal or two. But you're sure Mr. Wardle didn't tell you how long he meant for you to keep her here?"

"He said it would depend. He didn't say on what."

"You didn't ask for further details?"

"Oh no, that would have been totally inappropriate. One simply does not ask another to explain his concept before it's fully developed. I respect Mr. Wardle's artistic integrity as he does mine. At least I think he does, though I must confess I found myself wishing he hadn't shown up here alive at half-past twelve last night with a semi-anesthetized prisoner for me to look after, just when I'd put the finishing touches on his funeral wreath. It's quite lovely, I used gilded bottle corks and a sweet little rubber duckie on a styrofoam life preserver I'd been meaning for ages to do something with. I was planning to float the wreath on Bottomless Mere this afternoon while playing 'Rocked in the Cradle of the Deep' on my comb with a piece of purple tissue paper folded over it. For mourning, you know. Would you care to come and see what I've done?''

"We'd love to," Dittany replied. "Is it all right if Ethel comes along, or should we shut her in the car?"

"Mercy no, just so she doesn't wag her tail too vigorously and disturb the pinwheels. Though it might be rather interesting to see whether she could stir up enough of a breeze to set them all spinning at once."

"Perhaps another time. Let's see how the prisoner's doing first, shall we? We do have to get on with the script. Daughter Matilda will be dreadfully upset if she wakes up shackled to the bedpost and we're not there. You are thinking of her as Daughter Matilda, aren't you, Mrs. Phiffer?"

"I haven't quite grasped the essence yet, but I'm trying like anything. Should I go and start frying bread?"

"In a few minutes. Let's get her free first. I must say I'm pretty miffed at Mr. Wardle for shackling her to the bedpost. That's not how we rehearsed. She was supposed to beguile the time admiring the pinwheels and counting the ducks out back, wasn't she, dear?"

"She certainly was," said Osbert, "and I'm pretty darned steamed at Wardle, too. Maybe he got carried away in the inspiration of the moment, but that's no excuse for padding his part out of all proportion. I hope he at least left you the key to the shackles, Mrs. Phiffer."

"He wasn't going to, but I did put my foot down on that point. Creativity is one thing, Mr. Wardle, I told him, but one can carry the divine afflatus too far, and that's a darn sight farther than I have any intention of carrying a bedpan. So he gave me the key but he said I must be sure and shackle her right up again afterwards.''

"He had to say that," Dittany told her, "because he's the bad guy. But we're the good guys, so we can let her loose whenever we want, and nuts to him. I hope she bops him with a duck as soon as she gets the chance."

"Oh, goody," cried Mrs. Phiffer. "I adore improvisation. You're not planning to write the duck into the script, I hope? Wouldn't you find it more aesthetically satisfying just to leave a duck sitting where she can get at it handily and see what develops?"

"A brilliant suggestion," said Osbert. "You wouldn't happen to have an expendable duck around here, by any chance?"

"Flocks of them. I'll just nip out to the garage and see what's available. You can go straight on up if you want, she's in Mr. Wardle's room. Goodness knows what the neighbors are going to think about that."

"Surely you weren't planning to tell them?" Dittany protested.

"Naturally not, but you know what neighbors are like. Oh, here's the key in my pocket. You'd better take it with you in case she's awake and needs to you-know-what before I get back with the duck."

Mrs. Phiffer darted off, Ethel frolicking gaily at her heels. Dittany watched them out the door.

"You know, darling," she mused, "this could be the start of something beautiful. Arethusa's going to feel perfectly at home with Mrs. Phiffer."

"Maybe she'll want to stay!" For a moment Osbert looked hopeful. Then his face fell. "On the other hand, though, she may invite Mrs. Phiffer over to Lobelia Falls and we'll be stuck with all those flamingos. Come on, we'd better go see how she's doing."

Mrs. Phiffer had made further changes in the decor since Osbert was last here. The stairwell was now hung with dozens of pinwheels on long strings, his own among them. He pointed it out with thinly veiled smugness.

"I made that one."

"Yours is much the nicest," said Dittany. "I must say,

dear, it was awfully clever of Mr. Wardle, whoever he may be, to bring his prisoner here. Mrs. Phiffer's probably the one person in the world who's loopy enough to accept such a scheme without question and sane enough to help him carry it out. But how did you guess she would?''

"It wasn't guesswork, darling. Considering the way Mrs. Phiffer handled that so-called suicide note of Wardle's last weekend, I figured she'd most likely react pretty much the way she has. She didn't even mention the note to Chief Slapp, you know; just left it on the pillow where Wardle had put it, so as not to disturb the artistic integrity of the scene.''

"Do you suppose Wardle used the note as a test case?''

"I'm sure he must have. And he'd lived here three months, so he'd have known Mrs. Phiffer's good-hearted enough to make sure Daughter Matilda was fed and cared for, which meant he wouldn't have to keep hanging around the house or coming back to check.''

"She must not have told him you'd been here, or he wouldn't have dared take the chance.''

"That's a point,'' said Osbert. "Of course she'd been pretty busy hanging the pinwheels and putting those tail-lights on the flamingos. She seems pretty detached about anything she's not personally involved in. Oh my gosh! Why the heck didn't we bring a camera?''

The bed's headboard was of wrought iron with brass knobs, therefore ideal for handcuffing abducted ladies to. Wardle had made the most of its advantages. Arethusa was shackled not with one pair of handcuffs but with two, one to each wrist. She'd evidently just this second waked up—perhaps their voices and their footsteps on the stairs had roused her. And she was not taking her situation philosophically.

"Varlets! Caitiff knaves! If this is your idea of a joke, forsooth—''

"Shush, Arethusa,'' said Dittany. "We've come to rescue you. In case you hadn't noticed, you've been abducted.''

"Gadzooks, so I have! Stap my garters! By whom, prithee? Don't tell me Andrew MacNaster's back in town lusting after my flesh again?"

"No, this was a couple of other fellows, as far as we know, one of them being a fraudulent ex-anchovy buyer who calls himself Quimper Wardle. He thought you were Daughter Matilda."

"Pah! How could he?"

Dittany shrugged. "Aside from the fact that Matilda looks enough like you to be your doppelgänger, is just about your size, had on your familiar and easily recognized purple cape, and was known to be spending the night at your house, I really couldn't say. Except, of course, that it must have been fairly dark out there by the donjon-keep."

"Must it? I don't remember. Nay! By my halidom, I do remember. Some scurvy cur got an armlock on me and clapped a pad sopped in some noxious fluid over my nose and mouth and—and then I don't remember. Where, to employ what I believe is the accepted phraseology in circumstances such as these, am I?"

"You're in the spare bedroom of one Mrs. Phiffer over in Lammergen," Osbert explained. "Mrs. Phiffer is Mr. Wardle's landlady. She's quite a nice woman who has a thing about artificial birds. At the moment, she's out in her garage getting you a plaster duck."

"For what purpose, prithee?"

"Her feeling is that you may want one handy to bop Wardle over the head with when he shows up again to rattle your gyves."

"A kind and considerate hostess i' faith, and a wholly sound idea. But what makes Mrs. Phiffer think I intend to lie here waiting upon the blackguard Wardle's leisure? Unloose me these fetters and I'll be over the hills and far away. You do have a trusty steed parked out by the curb, I trust?"

"We have Ethel and the station wagon. That was the best we could do in the time available. If you want to be unfettered, you'll have to quit squirming so much, Aunt Arethusa. These fiddly little keyholes on the handcuffs are—ah, got it! Now I'll do the other hand. There you are, free as a smee."

"Let me rub your wrists to get the circulation going, Arethusa," said Dittany. "Ugh, they're all chafed and swollen. What a rotten beast that Wardle is! I'd like to wrap a flamingo around his neck, myself."

"You're welcome to remain here and do so when the occasion arises," the ex-captive replied. "As for me, I feel a disinclination to impose on Mrs. Phiffer's hospitality any longer. That is to say, any longer than necessary. Where is the necessary?"

"It's across the hall," said Osbert. "We'll go with you."

"Outrageous churl! You will not."

"I only meant we'd see you safely to the door."

"Oh well, in that case you may give me your arm. My head feels like a pinwheel. Was I drugged?"

"Thoroughly and efficiently, on the face of the evidence. Daughter Matilda is of the opinion that the kidnappers used chloroform to knock you out. You were most likely given some other drug after you were brought here, otherwise you wouldn't have slept so long. You may wish to examine your arms and legs for puncture marks."

"Later, perhaps."

Arethusa had been put to bed fully dressed in the clothes she'd been wearing when she'd left Applewood Avenue with Daughter Matilda, except for her shoes and Matilda's jacket, which were lying on the bedroom floor. That Wardle hadn't tried to undress her was a small boost to her amour propre, but it hadn't done much for her skirt. She did what she could in the bathroom with a damp towel in lieu of a clothes brush, and emerged after a few minutes looking somewhat less unkempt.

"Let me borrow your comb and lipstick, Dittany. Those churls must have taken my handbag."

"Not to worry, we have it at home. Matilda found it lying in the grass."

"Did she, forsooth?" Arethusa mumbled through a mouthful of hairpins. "Why wasn't she rescuing me instead of it?"

"Because she couldn't. The kidnappers knocked her out cold and left her lying in the grass, too. She didn't regain consciousness until some time after you'd been taken away. Oh, and that reminds me. There's still one little glitch to be dealt with. You can't leave."

Chapter 19

The hairpins fell from Arethusa's lips. Her hands froze in the act of twisting her black mane into its customary chignon. "What do you mean I can't leave? I've virtually left already."

"But don't you see?" said Dittany. "If the kidnappers come back and don't find you here, they'll rush off and kidnap Daughter Matilda again. Only this time they'll make sure it is in fact Daughter Matilda they're abducting. Once they've got her, they'll have Mother Matilda in their power."

"Why can't they be satisfied with having got me in their power, egad? I know a demm'd sight more about being abducted than those mincemeat-mashing Matildas do."

"That's my point exactly," Dittany urged. "You're a superb abductee, an absolute pearl among captives. Moreover, you can probably knock the lost work time off your income tax, or charge it up as research. The thing of it is, Arethusa, Osbert and I and Sergeant MacVicar are all convinced that the reason Wardle and his confederate kidnapped Daughter Matilda—or rather didn't kidnap her but think they did—is that they've planned a bold coup to hold her hostage until Mother Matilda forks over her secret mincemeat recipe to them by way of ransom."

"Then there was a method to their machinations," Arethusa said thoughtfully. "And who is this confederate you mention so glibly? Are there two Wardles?"

"We're inclined to think there isn't even one Wardle. That is to say, we believe the name Quimper Wardle to be merely an alias, but we don't know whom it's an alias for. All I can tell you is that the man calling himself Wardle got taken on at the mincemeat factory three months ago using forged references."

"Ah! The plot thickens."

"You don't know the half of it, Auntie," said Osbert. "This past weekend, Wardle staged an apparent suicide by drowning. His motive was supposed to be remorse over some dirty tricks he'd been pulling at the factory in order to steal segments of the mincemeat recipe."

"What dirty tricks, prithee?"

As Osbert began to explain, they wandered back into the bedroom so that Arethusa could put on her shoes and rehabilitate Daughter Matilda's jacket, which had accumulated a good deal of lint and dust from lying on the floor. Arethusa was still picking off debris when Mrs. Phiffer reappeared with a peach-colored plaster duck tucked cozily under her left arm.

"He has a little chip on his beak. I always think of peach-colored ducks as hims and blue ones as hers, I don't quite know why. But I hardly think the chip will matter considering the purpose to which you may put him, Daughter Matilda. You see, I'm becoming quite comfortable with your persona. Did you have a good rest, and should I start frying bread now?"

"For what purpose were you planning to fry this bread, Mrs. Phiffer?" Arethusa inquired warily.

"Why, for your breakfast, Daughter Matilda. I was also planning to fry tomatoes, bacon, and eggs, and to make you a large pot of tea. Or coffee, if you prefer. With this modest but wholesome repast, I could offer a choice of muffins, toast, and/or sticky buns with various jams, jellies, and marmalades including quince, of which I myself am particularly fond."

"You are? Gadzooks, a woman of taste and discrimination! Allow me to relieve you of that duck, Mrs. Phiffer, so that you can get on with the frying, brewing, toast-making, and bun-warming. You were saying, Dittany, that I'm expected to remain under house arrest here until such time as this Wardle shows up again and I bop him with this plaster duck?"

"You're supposed to improvise with the duck," Dittany said with a nervous glance at Mrs. Phiffer. "You don't have to bop Mr. Wardle if you don't want to."

"But what else would one do to a rascally abductor, assuming one had a plaster duck ready to hand? Unless someone would care to nip back to Lobelia Falls and fetch me my dueling sword?"

"You'd better stick with the duck," said Osbert. "Why don't I just nip downstairs instead and help Mrs. Phiffer set the table, Dittany? You can stay here and sort of explain things to—er—Daughter Matilda."

"Don't you think it would be more appropriate if you explained while I set the table?"

"A splendid suggestion," said Arethusa. "Here, varlet, hang onto this duck in case Wardle shows up. Scat, Dittany, and don't forget to put out the quince jelly. By my troth, I do feel peckish. When I mentioned toast and buns a moment ago, Mrs. Phiffer, it was with no intention of omitting the muffins. Muffins will be most acceptable. Along, of course, with the toast, eggs, bacon, tomatoes, fried bread, assorted preserves, et cetera."

"I quite understand, Daughter Matilda. I'm just so mortified that I didn't know you were coming in time to lay in a supply of mincemeat."

"Think nothing of it, Mrs. Phiffer. We all have to make sacrifices when duty calls. Godspeed, and give my kindest regards to your frying pan."

"Such a wonderful personality!" Mrs. Phiffer remarked to Dittany as they picked their careful way downstairs among the pinwheels. "So fresh and unspoiled despite her aristocratic lineage and high position, don't you think?"

"Oh, definitely," Dittany agreed. "You and Daughter Matilda ought to get along just fine. If she seems to be growing a trifle restive, just offer her something to eat. Anything at all, it won't matter a bit.''

"I suppose she's used to a varied diet because mince-meat has so many ingredients in it?''

"Very penetrating of you, Mrs. Phiffer. Yes, growing up in an atmosphere of mincemeat has made her quite ecumenical in her eating habits. Don't bother fixing anything for Osbert or me. We had breakfast just a while ago and we really ought to be getting along.''

"Osbert?'' queried Mrs. Phiffer. "I could have sworn Mr. Monk told me yesterday that his first name is Reginald.''

"Ah, but that was yesterday. Tomorrow he's planning to be Ralph. Perhaps you should simply continue to call him Mr. Monk, it's less confusing. I do like those ducks in the backyard, particularly that third one from the left in the fourteenth row. Daughter Matilda's going to have a lovely time here now that she's got her handcuffs off. It's awfully kind of you to be her jailer.''

"Not at all, I'm savoring every minute. Do you actually have to go?''

"I'm afraid so, but I expect one of us will be back later on today. Bringing groceries,'' Dittany added considerately. "Would you like to give me a list or shall I use my womanly intuition?''

"Just wing it, why don't you? That's always more fun. What I do often as not is walk down the aisle with my eyes shut. As the mood seizes me, I reach out and take something off whichever shelf I happen to be passing. It makes for a fascinatingly varied diet, though one does sometimes wind up with a great deal of floor wax and not much to eat. I did acquire a lovely pink flyswatter that way once. Would you like to see it?''

"I'd love to, but not just now, thank you. The flyswatter will give me something to look forward to on my next visit. I believe I hear Daughter Matilda coming downstairs. She likes her fried bread just nicely browned, in case you were wondering.''

"Oh, thank you for telling me. I'll remember.''

Mrs. Phiffer became engrossed in her cooking, Arethusa

in her eating. Dittany, Osbert, and Ethel were able to slip away almost unnoticed.

"Where to now, Old Paint?" Dittany asked as Osbert started the wagon.

"Home, don't you think? I need to let Sergeant MacVicar know Aunt Arethusa's all right and see what Margaret and Clorinda have to report about the funeral. I'd also like to jot down a few notes about the ostrich rustlers that popped into my mind when I saw those red taillights on the flamingos. All that concentrated creativity around Mrs. Phiffer's place sure does get the old dynamo sparking. Though I suspect I'd short-circuit if I had to hang around her too long. Do you want to stop anywhere along the way?"

"I did promise Mrs. Phiffer I'd send some groceries back," Dittany replied. "You know how Arethusa eats."

"I ought to," snarled Osbert. "I've watched her often enough. Speaking of which, how'd you like me to buy you a mincemeat tart? There's this quaint little café and live bait shop over in West Lammergen."

"Darling, please don't talk about live bait. I'm in a delicate condition, remember?"

"Okay then, let's say we swing over to Scottsbeck for the groceries and have custard pie at the Cozy Corner."

"I liked your first suggestion best. If we go straight home, I can put my feet up and make a grocery list. When Mum comes back from the funeral, we'll send her for the groceries. In the meantime, you'll have got back to your ostriches and they'll all be wearing red taillights."

"Now you're talking. I knew there was some reason why I married you, precious. Aside from the fact that it would have been totally impossible not to, that is. Remember that first night I got up nerve enough to kiss you in the pantry?"

"And we were engaged by the time you got your breath back, and Arethusa caught us and said we were out of our minds because we'd only known each other for about four days."

"And I told her to stuff it," said Osbert, "and she's

been stuffing it every since. But I don't care, even if I do wax a tad wroth about the pickled onions now and then. If I hadn't been visiting Aunt Arethusa, I might never have met you. I'd have become just another dried-up tumble-weed rolling around on the barren sands of time.''

''Never, darling! We'd have met somehow or other. Fate would have ordained it.''

''I don't know, pet. Fate can be pretty screwed up sometimes.''

''Well, fate's not going to screw us up,'' Dittany insisted, ''because we're kind to aunts and animals. I do hope Ethel isn't going to be jealous of the twins. She got into a real snit that time we baby-sat the Coskoffs' pet hamster while they went to Vancouver for the fair.''

''Well, I didn't think much of that hamster myself, if you want the truth,'' Osbert confessed. ''I thought it was somewhat wanting in the intellect. Which brings us back to Aunt Arethusa. Do you suppose she'll stay the course without raising a howl?''

''Oh yes, I expect so, as long as the food holds out. Have you any plan afoot to trap Wardle and his accomplice?''

''All I have is an idea, and you know how it is about ideas.''

''Yes, dear. You mustn't talk about them or you scare them away. So who's going to handle the stakeout at Mrs. Phiffer's? Fridwell Slapp doesn't sound capable of staking out anything livelier than a plate of mashed potatoes, and Sergeant MacVicar has no jurisdiction in Lammergen. Does that mean you're planning to go yourself, or shouldn't I ask?''

''Ask as much as you like, pet. Don't expect a coherent answer, though. As of now I'm just pinning my faith on Aunt Arethusa and that plaster duck. I have a hunch nothing's going to happen for a while yet.''

''How long a while?'' asked Dittany.

''I don't know, dear.''

''It's hard to get a decent hunch these days, isn't it?'' she sympathized. ''Though I expect Mrs. Phiffer has a few spare ones in her attic that she's planning to do something with one of these days.''

Thus chatting, they reached home. Ethel had gone for a stroll and Osbert and Dittany were sharing a companionable sandwich lunch when Clorinda and Margaret returned.

"No, we don't want anything, thank you," said Margaret. "We had coffee and mincemeat tarts at the McCorquindales' after the funeral, but we didn't think we ought to stay there too long. It wouldn't have looked right.''

"Besides," said Clorinda, "Daughter Matilda didn't need us a bit. She was managing just fine, dropping the odd 'forsooth' every now and then, and bursting into tears if anybody got too nosy. Some people seem to think she's slightly unhinged by grief and shock while others are wondering whether she may not in fact be the person she seems to be, which is precisely the effect we wanted to create. So now all we have to worry about is finding Arethusa.''

"Not to worry, Mum," Dittany chirped. "Osbert went straight to her like a homing pigeon. We left her enjoying a comfortable repast whose menu I shan't recite to you just now because it makes me queasy to think about. Would you believe that ornery coyote Wardle had the nerve to park her on his landlady?''

"The one with the flamingos?" Margaret MacVicar could not but smile. "How remarkably astute! Your Mrs. Phiffer sounds like exactly the sort who'd take a hostage in stride. She's been given to understand Arethusa's abduction is merely some kind of jolly jape, I suppose?''

"Precisely," said Osbert, "and it's our job to keep her thinking so until further notice. That's why I have to talk to the chief. Is he around?''

"I couldn't say. I haven't been home yet. Why don't you phone the station?''

"I'll drop by on my way. I have to go to Scottsbeck to pick up some groceries for Mrs. Phiffer. Or somebody does," Osbert added with a meaningful glance at his mother-in-law. "You know how Aunt Arethusa eats.''

"Eats!" exclaimed Clorinda. "I'd entirely forgotten.

Arethusa's supposed to be having dinner at the inn with Miss Jane and the twins. The Yarnspinners' League are sponsoring a cribbage tournament there tonight. Miss Jane's a charter member, of course, and she signed herself and the twins up. They needed a fourth, so they drafted Arethusa. If she doesn't appear, people are going to wonder.''

"Rats!" said Osbert. "Now what are we going to do? We can't expect Daughter Matilda to impersonate Aunt Arethusa at the cribbage tournament right after her own father's funeral. Matilda did say she was planning to come back here tonight though, I hope?"

"Oh yes," said Margaret. "We made sure of that. The relatives are staying another night so she still has no place to sleep at home. She's supposed to phone you when she sees her way clear to leave her mother. Then whichever one of us is available will nip over and pick her up. Donald didn't think Matilda ought to be driving herself even if her car was ready in time, and I quite agree. Don't you?"

"Absolutely. But dad-rat it, this does pose a problem. How come you weren't invited to play, Clorinda?"

"Five's a crowd, dear. Besides, to tell you the truth, I'm growing just a wee bit fatigued with Glanville and Ranville. Furthermore, I'm not sure it's quite the thing for a married woman to keep running around with a pair of attractive bachelor gentlemen joined at the spine. I have to admit that the more I see of the twins, the more I miss Bert. You wouldn't mind too awfully, dears, if I were to skip off next week for a few days? Bert's coming to Ottawa, and he's asked me to join him there."

"Oh no, Mum, we wouldn't mind a bit," cried Dittany. "Not a smidgin. Would we, Osbert?"

"Absolutely not. Stay as long as you like, Clorinda. We'll manage. There's nothing left here for you to knit except maybe some awnings for the kitchen windows."

"He's joking, Mum," Dittany put in hastily lest her mother dash out and start measuring the windows. "But you know I have scads of friends to call on if I need them, and there's always Mrs. Poppy."

In fact, there was seldom Mrs. Poppy, since the lady who was engaged to clean the house twice a week managed in fact to show up about three times a month; but that was a detail they all chose to ignore.

"True enough," said Clorinda. "And even if I did swallow my scruples and go to the tournament in Arethusa's place, that would be almost worse than nothing because it would emphasize the fact that she hadn't come. Then everybody would want to know why, since Arethusa never misses a cribbage tournament as well you know."

"And seldom fails to beat the pants off everybody except Grandsire Coskoff," Osbert added. "Dang-blang it, I never thought to see the day I'd have to admit Aunt Arethusa is indispensable. She's got to make an appearance at the tournament. But how can she?"

"Quite simply, dear," said Dittany. "All we need is to get hold of an experienced actress who's a mistress of disguise, knows all Arethusa's mannerisms, imitates her voice to perfection, and can also do a plausible imitation of Daughter Matilda if need arises."

"In a word," said Clorinda, "me."

"You?" snorted Osbert. "You're not even tall enough."

"A bagatelle. I'll just put on my high-heeled green snakeskin wedgies with the two-inch platform soles, the ones Aunt Daisy fell off in 1949 and twisted her knee, which is how I happened to inherit them. Aunt Daisy never liked me much. She thought I was a little smarty-pants."

Osbert was too much of a gentleman to say he thought so too, but the snakeskin wedgies had clearly failed to convince him that Clorinda was right for the role. "You don't have long, black hair."

"I do so, unless somebody's borrowed it and not brought it back. Where's that long, black wig I wore in the Addams Family skit, Dittany?"

"On your closet shelf in one of those old hatboxes, I forget which. Try the red with the gray stripes."

"And where's the key to Arethusa's house?"

"Hanging in the pantry next to the dog food."

"Thank you, dear. I've found it. Margaret, would you

mind going to Arethusa's house with me for just a few minutes? I'd as soon not go in alone, and I need to pick up her floppy-legged blue satin lounging pajamas.''

"But you can't play a cribbage tournament in green snakeskin wedgies, blue satin lounging pajamas, and a Halloween wig," Osbert protested.

"Of course I can't, dear," Clorinda replied sweetly. "But I can be playing Arethusa over at Mrs. Phiffer's while Arethusa plays cribbage at the inn."

"Lumbering longhorns! So you can. Come on, I'll take you over to get the pajamas myself."

Chapter 20

Having to transform herself into another surrogate Daughter Matilda meant that Clorinda wouldn't have time to shop for Mrs. Phiffer's groceries, but Osbert didn't mind. Before going to Scottsbeck, he spent some time in earnest confabulation with Sergeant MacVicar. By the time Osbert was ready to leave the station, the sergeant was rubbing his chin and looking even more than usually Caledonian.

" 'Tis a long shot, Deputy Monk. A long, long shot."

"But you think it's worth trying?"

"Oh aye. Aye, lad, it's worth trying. Half-past ten, you say?"

"That should be about right. You don't have to come along with me, you know."

"Lad, lad! Were our positions reversed, would you hang back?"

"Heck, no. Wild mustangs wouldn't keep me away. Right then, Chief. Half-past ten on the button. Now I've got to shop for Auntie's supper. Or not, as the case may be."

Osbert bought quite a lot of food, including a jar of pickled pigs' feet and a couple of curly cabbages that he thought might tickle Mrs. Phiffer's fancy. While he was in the market, he picked up several jars of baby food. The twins wouldn't be ready for strained applesauce till about March, he didn't suppose, but one did want to be prepared.

What with one thing and another, Osbert didn't get back to Lobelia Falls till almost three o'clock. It was time to think about driving Clorinda over to Lammergen, not that he had any great expectations about the efficacy of her disguise. He was, therefore, astonished to enter the kitchen and see Arethusa at the table drinking tea.

But wait! This could not be Arethusa. All the woman had in front of her was a cup and saucer; no cookies, no scone, not so much as a piece of cinnamon toast.

"Pretty good, Clorinda," he applauded, "only shouldn't you be eating something?"

"Touché," his mother-in-law replied merrily. "Of course I should, I'll remember next time. How do I look?"

"It's uncanny."

It really was. Clorinda and Arethusa didn't look a bit alike. Somehow or other, though, the ex-Traveling Thespian had contrived with her black wig and stage makeup not so much a duplication as an effect of Arethusa. When Clorinda stood up, the floppy legs of the 1930s style pajamas fell almost to the floor, their unbroken line creating an illusion of even greater height than the extra four or five inches which the clunky green wedgies added to her small stature. The long jacket, loosely caught around the hips by a wide sash whose ends dangled down to where her knees ought to be but probably weren't, had Joan Crawford-style shoulder pads that made her look wider than she was. But most convincing of all was the atmosphere of Arethusa-ness which Clorinda managed somehow to project.

"The real secret," she explained, "is to *think* I'm Arethusa. To *feel* I'm Arethusa. To *be* Arethusa."

Osbert was awed. "In short, to immolate your own personality on the altar of your art. Gosh, little did I know the sacrifices you were prepared to make. What if you can't get back to being Clorinda?"

"Not to worry, dear boy. Once I kick off these wedgies and remove my hair, I'll be plain old me again."

"And I'll be plumb glad to see you," Osbert replied gallantly. "Now let's put this show on the road, time's getting short. You did remember the purple cape?"

"Dahling, I'm a trouper! How could you doubt? Bye-bye, daughter dear, I'll see you after the final curtain."

"Break a leg, Mum." Dittany had done enough trouping herself to know the actor's blessing, but thought she'd better tack on a qualification, since one never quite knew with Clorinda. "Figuratively speaking, you understand. In those clodhoppers, you might all too easily trip over a frog or a duck."

"And muck up my act, ecod? Zounds, child, don't you know me better than that?"

Perfectly imitating Arethusa's walk notwithstanding the clodhoppers, Clorinda sashayed out to the entry, plucked the purple cloak off the peg on which Arethusa always parked it when she happened to remember, and swirled it over her lounging pajamas. "Shake a leg, you whey-faced churl!"

"By George, she's got it!" cried Osbert. "You're going to lay those flamingos in the aisles, temporary Auntie dear. This way to the coach and four."

Osbert's mother-in-law insisted on sitting alone in the back seat to practice her hauteur and think herself into her role. Now that she'd got Arethusa down pat, Clorinda still had to work on being Arethusa pretending to be Daughter Matilda. That was fine with Osbert as he himself had plenty to think about. One detail that didn't much concern him was whether Mrs. Phiffer would accept yet another substitute Daughter Matilda; and indeed there was no reason why he ought to have worried. Mrs. Phiffer was absolutely delighted, and said so quite a number of times.

"I love you! Love you! Love you! Not that the real Daughter Matilda isn't perfectly right for the part, you understand; but you're so ineffably, subtly, kitschily *wrong*! I can't quite put my finger on the difference, but I feel it *here*."

She thumped herself on the bib of her orange overalls, probably inflicting some discomfort since for some reason known, Osbert supposed, to herself, Mrs. Phiffer was now carrying another from her apparently inexhaustible supply of plaster ducks.

"But you will think of me as the real Daughter Matilda?" Clorinda pleaded. "Your willingness to be deceived is essential to the thrust of the plot. We're working up to the dénouement, you see. Everything depends on our remaining in character: you as the innocently trusting landlady, I as the loyal friend who has bravely and selflessly volunteered herself as a substitute for the beleaguered kidnappee. Think of me as a female Sydney Carton, Mrs. Phiffer. Try to bear in mind this is a far, far better thing I do."

"Never fear, substitute Daughter Matilda. I shan't forget for a second, cross my heart and hope the cat spits in my eye. Nor shall I forget you, true Daughter Matilda," the landlady added, turning to the true Arethusa. "You are the veritable epitome of sad affliction nobly borne and I do wish I could offer you a little snack before you leave, but I'm afraid there's not a crumb left in the house."

Arethusa cast a wistful eye at the groceries Osbert had brought with him, but stiffened her upper lip enough to reply that it didn't matter since they'd only just finished their tea, and she'd look forward to visiting Mrs. Phiffer again in the near future. She then shook hands with her hostess, kissed Clorinda very carefully on the cheek so as not to roil her complexion, thanked her in moving terms for the far, far better act she was about to perform, and sailed out to Osbert's wagon wearing the real Daughter Matilda's now quite lint-free black jacket.

"A heart of gold," she remarked once they'd got headed back toward Lobelia Falls. "But a mediocre cook. Were you perchance intending to stop for ice cream?"

"Sorry," Osbert told her. "I'm planning to get you back to your house as fast as I can so you'll have time to ease back into your own persona, if you can remember who you were, and hike yourself over to the inn. Perchance it's slipped your mind that you have a date with

Ranville, Glanville, and Miss Fuzzywuzzy for the Yarn-busters' cribbage tournament.''

"Yarnslingers, I believe. Gadzooks, you're right! That chloroform must have fuddled my memory. I don't generally forget cribbage tournaments.''

"Much less dinner engagements,'' Osbert added to make her feel more like her real self again. "I'll stand guard while you change and run you back to our house when you're ready. We can all three go to the inn together.''

"To what three do you refer? Dittany's not up to the vicious thrust and parry of a cribbage tournament, surely?''

"No, but she's up to eating a meal out instead of having to cook. Don't worry, we're not going to horn in on your tête-à-tête with Ranville and Glanville, as the case may be.''

"Is that a reason or a threat? *Entre nous,* nephew, I'm beginning to wish you'd think of some urgent reason to fetch Archie up here for a few days. It would be an agreeable change to spend an evening in the company of a man who doesn't come with a carbon copy attached. Surely not all twins are so relentlessly identical? I believe Chang and Eng, the original Siamese twins from whom the name is derived, were totally distinct personalities.''

Osbert said he believed so too, and they finished their ride in unwonted amity. After checking to make sure no kidnappers were lurking about the premises, Osbert left his aunt to gird herself for the coming affray and went downstairs to telephone his wife.

"Mission accomplished, darling. Do you feel up to dining at the inn and if so, could you be ready in fifteen minutes? We're at Arethusa's now and will be over to pick you up as soon as she's finished changing her clothes and polishing her forsooth.''

Dittany said she'd love to go and would be ready. She met them at the door, wearing an elegant golden-brown maternity dress with a deep lace collar and cuffs. Osbert was enchanted.

"You look like a butterscotch sundae, dear. Where did you get that fancy gown?''

"You've seen this dress before, silly. It's the one Mum brought from Montreal. I've decided I might as well get my use out of it now because I don't intend to have twins again in a hurry. Arethusa, we're glad to have you back. How was your visit?"

"Different. Mrs. Phiffer let me blow on her pinwheels to make them spin, and showed me how to paint a duck. I acquitted myself creditably, if I do say so."

"I was the one who taught her how to make pinwheels," Osbert couldn't help bragging.

Arethusa gave him a look. "Methinks a little learning is a dangerous thing. Now may we cease the rodomontade, addlepate? I have to think myself into the tournament."

"By all means do," said Osbert. "You are therefore planning, I trust, to banish all recollection of what's happened since last night when you were struck behind the ear and found yourself some time later lying on the grass in your own backyard, at which time you staggered to your feet, picked up your handbag, and fled to us for succor and a midnight snack."

"Did I, forsooth? What did you give me?"

"Whatever your palpitating heart desired, though you're not too clear about the menu since at the time you were still dazed from the stunning blow which had been dealt you. You naturally will refrain from bringing any of this up in conversation tonight unless somebody asks you specifically for details, which in fact nobody ought to do because Sergeant MacVicar has decided we should all keep quiet about the whole affair. This is customary procedure in the case of abductions, where silence may become a vital factor in safeguarding the abducted from violence."

"Dost think me a numbskull, forsooth? I've abducted more heroines than you've rustled coyotes."

"Indeed you have, and I'd be the first to say so, Auntie. Then you know that on the entire subject of Daughter Matilda you remain resolutely mumchance. If anybody should mention having seen Daughter Matilda at her father's funeral and being surprised at how much she reminded them of you, you will naturally cling to your mumness but permit yourself a sly and enigmatic smile. Got it?''

"Got it. Now shut up and let me concentrate. Oh, has Mother Matilda received her ransom note yet?''

"She hadn't as of half-past five when I last checked with Sergeant MacVicar, who'd just talked with Daughter Matilda. The note may come any time now, but we can't hang around to find out. I understand, by the way, that your cribbage tournament should be over by eleven or so.''

"Half-past ten is the posted closing, but it's usually eleven by the time all the players have pegged out. They never run any later out of consideration for Grandsire Coskoff. The playoffs will probably have to be held over until next week, I can hardly wait. Glanville and Ranville, I add in parenthesis, will have left town by then.''

"That so? They've definitely made their plans?''

"So they aver, and who am I to doubt, pardie? Osbert, is there no way short of a garotte to turn you off?''

But Arethusa herself couldn't stop talking. "Where do I sleep tonight?''

"In your own bed, God willing. I don't know whether you'll have company or not. Daughter Matilda will be coming back to Lobelia Falls because there's no place for her in Lammergen; but we'll have to decide where to put her, depending on how things work out.''

They'd reached the inn by now. Osbert let his passengers out at the front door and took the car around to the parking lot. The place would be jumping tonight, cribbage ranked next to archery as a form of gladiatorial combat in Lobelia Falls. Since Dittany had had the forethought to ring up for reservations, she and Osbert did get a table, though it wasn't very well situated.

Miss Jane and the twins had booked earlier and were the cynosure of all eyes, sitting back to back in the middle of the room. Arethusa had now joined them, even more a cynosure in a crimson velvet dinner gown and several yards of false pearls which she wore, it was whispered by some of Grandsire Coskoff's more fervid rooters, as a means of distracting her opponents.

Grandsire Coskoff himself had a habit of thrusting his false teeth halfway out of his mouth during moments of tense play and then snapping them back with a click that could be heard halfway across the room, so Arethusa's fans didn't see where his crowd got off making cracks about the pearls, even if maybe their champion did have this little nervous habit of rattling them together or swinging them around like a lariat while waiting for her vis-à-vis to settle the tormenting question of which two cards he must sacrifice to her crib.

As far as Dittany and Osbert could see, Ranville and Glanville were doing most of the talking, which didn't surprise them a bit. Miss Jane was responding with eager smiles and nods, managing to get a few words in now and then. Arethusa barely opened her mouth except to insert food. Although that did mean her mouth was open a good deal of the time, it didn't exactly make her the life of the party. Finally Ranville and Glanville must have said something about her lack of sociability for she shrugged and made a two-word rejoinder that looked to Dittany, who was in the more favorable position to lip-read, like "I'm concentrating."

"So she's holding the line," Osbert murmured. "Good old Auntie! I hope she licks the pants off those two smarmy sidewinders."

"Darling, I have the impression you don't much like Ranville and Glanville," said his wife.

"I've been getting the impression that nobody's all that crazy about Ranville and Glanville," he replied. "Clorinda mentioned a while ago that she found them wearing a bit thin, as you may recall, and Arethusa said much the same to me on the way back from her house. She wants me to invite Archie up for a few days."

"Fine," said Dittany, "just so he doesn't bring his bagpipes this time. Though if Mum goes off with Bert, we might find things a trifle quiet around the house."

"May we never have a worse misfortune! You won't

mind riding herd on Daughter Matilda by yourself for a while later this evening, will you, dear? Or you could get Margaret to come and stay with you."

"Does that mean you and the sergeant have something on?"

Osbert merely cocked an eyebrow and applied himself to his baked potato. By now the dining room was full and the noise level high enough to make conversation difficult unless a person wanted to scream, which neither of the Monks did. They finished their meal in relative silence, then looked in for a few minutes at the tournament room where players were settling themselves at the cribbage boards with tightened lips and resolute looks. Roger Munson, as head proctor, was handing out new decks of cards still in their transparent wrappers; Arethusa was eyeing hers with an avidity she usually reserved for pickled onions. Dittany decided she'd better go home and put her feet up. A battlefield was no place for a woman in her condition.

Chapter 21

"You didn't have any trouble with the manager?"

Osbert spoke in the softest possible whisper. He wasn't used to being in rooms engaged by people who'd have been exceedingly irritated to catch him poking through their belongings, and couldn't help feeling a trifle uneasy even though this had been his idea in the first place. Sergeant MacVicar, who wasn't turning a hair, shook his head.

"Yon manager knows better than to give me trouble. Did you find anything, lad?"

"I think so." Osbert held up a garment taken out of a suitcase whose lock he'd just jimmied.

"Aye."

There were two double beds in the room. With no further exchange of words, Sergeant MacVicar slid under one of them and his perspicacious deputy under the other. Fortunately, the inn went in for elegant decor; heavy dust ruffles around the box springs hid the men completely. Osbert gave the housekeeper a high mark for keeping the carpet underneath well-vacuumed; he and the chief would probably be able to keep from sneezing and giving themselves away. His biggest problem would be to see what was going on up above. He achieved a partial solution by finding a corner where the panels weren't stitched together and nudging them aside the merest slit. He assumed Sergeant MacVicar was doing the same; naturally he didn't ask.

The hideout was a trifle stuffy although comfortable enough thanks to the carpet. Osbert only hoped he wouldn't drop off to sleep if the wait was a long one. However, he needn't have worried. Glanville and Ranville must have got creamed in the tournament, though they were both in high spirits as they entered their room.

"Am I glad that's over!" he heard one exclaim. "Hurry up with your side of the harness. If I don't get to scratch my back pretty soon, I'll go nuts."

"You and me both," said the other. "What I'm itching for is the scratch we'll get when we hand over that mincemeat recipe to our contact at Redundant Relishes. I only wish I could have seen Mother Matilda's face when she opened that ransom note."

In the dark under the bed, Osbert smiled. Little did these two jolly rogues know that Daughter Matilda had managed to intercept the special delivery envelope when it came to her mother's house, and had brought it with her to the Monks' well over an hour ago. Right now she was most likely sitting with Dittany, waiting for Arethusa to return triumphant from the tournament. Osbert was enjoying a silent chuckle when something landed with a thump only a few inches from his nose. Through his slit, he viewed the object with interest. So this was how they managed. Just as he'd suspected.

"Get that harness out of sight fast!" snapped one twin.

Osbert drew back lest any ray from the bedside lamp reflect a gleam from his all-too-interested eyeball as the other twin picked up what looked like two halves of a surgical corset sewn together. The twin was stowing it under the mattress, he could feel the bed jiggling. Now coat hangers were being rattled and a suitcase opened.

"Why can't you be Wardle tonight?" the first twin was saying fretfully. "I did him last night."

"But you're a better Wardle than I am," the other replied. "Besides, I did most of the dirty work. All you had to do was give Daughter Matilda the chloroform and shove her off on Mrs. Phiffer. Though I have to say it was a real pleasure slugging our dear friend Arethusa. I thought she'd be out of commission tonight from that whack on the neck I gave her, but she's right in there at her cribbage board, mopping up all comers. That old bird must be tougher than a boardinghouse steak.''

The twins' Oxford accent had deteriorated considerably; they were beginning to sound like a couple of characters from an old George Raft movie. Clorinda might have been right about the mob at that, Osbert thought. Or else Ranville and Glanville had grown up near a cinema that showed a lot of outdated American gangster films.

"I'd like to take her for the same kind of ride we gave Charlie McCorquindale," snarled Twin Two. "I still can't figure out how he twigged on."

"That's because you never think anybody but yourself has a brain, Ran. McCorquindale was smart, that's all. And gutsy. That's the worst of these sneaky Canadians. You think they're pushovers, then the next thing you know they're all over you like ants at a picnic. But we'll give them what-for. Hand me the Wardle suit, since you're scared to tackle Mrs. Phiffer yourself."

"I'm not scared, just cautious. There's nothing more dangerous than a scatty broad, you know that. Are you sure we didn't make a mistake stashing Daughter Matilda with her?"

"Listen, what else could we do? We had to stay right out front the whole time where everybody could watch the cute little freaks doing their song-and-dance routine, didn't we?"

"I know, I know. We've got the perfect alibi, but I'll be one glad Siamese twin when we don't have to be nice to jolly old thirty-second cousin Fuzzywuzzy any longer. Sometimes I wish we'd stayed with the carnival."

"Like fun you do. This is the best racket we've hit yet. Go ahead, blow up George and get into bed. I'll just nip down the back way and pinch the innkeeper's car long enough to make sure everything's ticketty-boo at Phiffer's, and leave the darling daughter's amputated finger with Mother Matilda to show her we mean business. Want anything from the live bait shop?''

"Yeah, fetch me back a strawberry milkshake, will you? Ta, Ran. See you later.''

Osbert heard the door close, then sounds of puffing. Then he felt the bed joggling again. That rotter Glanville hadn't even bothered to brush his teeth, he thought disapprovingly. He waited till the twin overhead was comfortably settled and had begun to snore, then poked his head out from under the dust ruffle. Sergeant MacVicar's head poked out, too. They exchanged nods. Then, noiseless and lithe as two sidewinders, they slithered out from their respective hiding places.

Sergeant MacVicar stayed on one side of the bed, Osbert crept silently around to the other. Together they confronted the two prone figures, one a bona fide half of a Siamese Twin act and one a blown-up rubber dummy that might perhaps have deceived a chambermaid glancing in to see if it was all right to make up the bed but that certainly would never have fooled Sergeant MacVicar or Deputy Monk. In dire and fateful tone, the sergeant gave utterance.

"Glanville Bleinkinsop, if that is in fact your name, I arrest you in the name of the law.''

"Huh? Who? What?''

"He means you're pinched,'' said Deputy Monk. "Bring your friend there along to the station if you're uncomfortable without a backup.''

Osbert picked up the phone. "Room service? You can send Officer Ray up now. Don't worry, Mr. Bleinkinsop, we're not going to break up the act. I'm on my way now to collect your brother. Too bad about that strawberry milkshake.''

Officer Ray dashed in, burning to be of use, so Sergeant MacVicar let him carry the ingenious corset which the brothers had used for their act and which was now being impounded as evidence. Osbert didn't wait to see this done; he was already out of the inn and into his trusty wagon.

It was as well that Sergeant MacVicar had been forced by protocol to keep off Chief Slapp's territory. He was much too intrinsically law-abiding to have borne with equanimity the rate at which his deputy covered the road to Lammergen. Osbert had every confidence that Ranville had meant precisely what he'd said about delivering Daughter Matilda's amputated finger to her mother.

But it wouldn't be Matilda's finger, it would be Clorinda's! He stomped the accelerator clear down to the floor, roared into Lammergen like an avenging angel and managed to slow down enough not to flatten any late revelers who might be going home from the live bait shop before he drove the wagon into the field across from Mrs. Phiffer's house so that Ranville wouldn't see it and be warned away.

Osbert could spy no car in Mrs. Phiffer's driveway and none parked out front, but he wasn't taking any chances. Ranville too might have stashed his purloined vehicle somewhere out of sight. It wouldn't be a good idea to risk the doorbell, either. The door was locked, but Osbert had a knack with locks. Careful not to trip over any frogs, he let himself into the house and tiptoed down the hallway.

A light showed through from the kitchen. From the sound of merry voices, both female to his extreme relief, Osbert judged that Ranville must have decided to go for the milkshake before he came for the finger. He further deduced from hearing Mrs. Phiffer declaim, "Fifteen for two, fifteen for four, and a run of three, so there!" that a cribbage game was in progress. Clearing his throat loudly, he stepped into the room.

"Evening, ladies. I'm sorry to interrupt your game, but I think you ought to know that the ransom note's been delivered and Quimper Wardle's on his way here to cut off Daughter Matilda's finger."

"But why?" gasped Clorinda.

"If Daughter Matilda loses a finger, she'll never be able to play 'The Flight of the Bumblebee' again," said Mrs. Phiffer severely. "Has Mr. Wardle considered that?"

"I don't suppose he has." Actually Osbert hadn't considered it himself, but this was not the time to say so. "You're plumb right, ma'am, and we can't let it happen. Have you two got your plaster ducks ready?"

"Oh yes, right here," Clorinda assured him. "We haven't been without them for a minute. Have we time to peg out?"

"I could make some cocoa," Mrs. Phiffer offered.

"Sorry," said Osbert, "there's no time for cocoa. We've got to batten down the hatches and stand by to repel boarders."

"Then I'll get you a duck. Here, you can hold mine while I run out to the garage!"

"No, Mrs. Phiffer! Stay here with us. I don't want Wardle to catch you alone out there in the dark. His improvisations are getting too gol-darned grisly. What I want both of you to do right this second is take your ducks upstairs to the room where he handcuffed the other Daughter Matilda to the bed. We'll leave the front door unlocked to make Wardle think he's really got you fooled, and I'll lurk among the pinwheels to nab him as he comes up the stairs. If he gets past me, you two bop him with your ducks as hard as you can."

"But what if we hurt him?" Mrs. Phiffer asked.

"Then I'll make you another pinwheel. If you knock him out, I'll make you two."

"*Wunderbar!* But suppose Daughter Matilda and I both miss Mr. Wardle and knock out each other instead?"

"Then you forfeit your duck and don't get any pinwheels."

"And I get my finger cut off," said Clorinda. "Don't fret, Osbert, we won't miss. Hark! Isn't that a car stopping out front?"

"Upstairs, quick!" hissed Osbert. "Clorinda, lie down on the bed and make believe you're handcuffed to the headboard. Mrs. Phiffer, lurk behind the doorway with your duck at the ready."

Osbert realized bitterly that he'd counted too much on that strawberry milkshake. Ranville must have found the bait shop closed. And he himself was still weaponless! Hastily he snatched up one of the oversized plastic frogs and herded the two women up the stairs and into the room for which the self-styled Quimper Wardle and his equally wicked counterpart were still paying rent.

He'd barely managed to conceal himself in the shadows where the pinwheels hung thickest before the front door was flung roughly open and Ranville burst in. There was enough light in the hallway for Osbert to notice that the fiendish twin was wearing a green jersey and gray flannel slacks identical to the garments which the elderly person had attempted to impound on the banks of Bottomless Mere. More importantly, Ranville carried in his hand a mean-looking switchblade knife, and the expression on his formerly bland face was even meaner than the glint of that menacing blade.

The plastic frog, evidently designed to plant marigolds in, was hollow and had a hole the size of a dinner plate in its back. As Ranville slunk up the stairs with the knife thrust out in front of him as villains in old movies were ever wont to do, Osbert upended the frog and bated his breath until the would-be amputator came within arm's reach. Then, with a swiftness none of Lex Laramie's heroes could have bettered, he kicked the knife from Ranville's hand and slammed the frog down over the miscreant's head. As the now frog-faced Ranville lunged blindly toward his assailant, Mrs. Phiffer cracked him smartly across the shin with her duck.

"Oh, well ducked, Mrs. Phiffer!" cried Clorinda from the bed. "Jolly good show, Osbert! Chase him over this way so I can get a whack at him, too."

But Ranville had no fight left in him. He didn't even try to struggle while Osbert was securing his formerly murderous hands with the selfsame handcuffs he'd used to chain Arethusa to the bed. He just kept whimpering for somebody to please, please take off that frog. As it now transpired, this perfidious tool of the rival mincemeat magnates, this cold-blooded killer, this vicious kidnapper and sneaky impersonator was afraid of the dark!

Sergeant MacVicar had got in touch with Fridwell Slapp by telephone and been cordially invited to come over and assist with the formalities once Slapp had been assured that both Ranville and his somewhat less bloodthirsty but by no means less evil brother were safely under control. All in all, it was quite a party. By the time formal charges had been laid, statements taken, and both twins, whose name turned out to be not Bleinkinsop but plain Blenk, had been carted away to the county jail, the night was far spent and so were the participants.

And Mrs. Phiffer still hadn't got her pinwheels. Osbert promised faithfully to come back in the afternoon of what was by now already the next day, accompanied by Dittany, Clorinda, Arethusa, and the real Daughter Matilda, whom so far Mrs. Phiffer still hadn't got to meet. They'd all make pinwheels together and drink a nice cup of cocoa. And no, Osbert didn't believe Mrs. Phiffer was under any obligation whatsoever to refund the balance of the alleged Mr. Wardle's room rent considering the extra work she'd been put to in taking care of his prisoner, not to mention the fact that one of her frogs and two of her ducks had been damaged in the recent affray. Which, as Mrs. Phiffer herself remarked, entering into the spirit of Osbert's argument, was all Mr. Wardle's fault in the first place.

Chapter 22

It need hardly be said that the pinwheel party wound up taking place not in Lammergen but at Dittany and Osbert's. Punctually at three o'clock, a plaid 1952 DeSoto with a sporran on its radiator pulled up to their driveway and Mrs. Phiffer burbled in, her arms full of peach-colored plaster ducks wearing cupcakes on their heads. Dittany was charmed.

"How sweet of you, Mrs. Phiffer! No, Ethel, these cupcakes aren't for you. Or are they?"

"Well, perhaps they shouldn't be for anybody," Mrs. Phiffer replied. "I did put quite a lot of plaster of paris in the batter. But don't you think they look rather fetching on the ducks?"

"Delightful! Let's line them up on the windowsill so that everybody can see them. Osbert, see what Mrs. Phiffer brought us."

"Just what we needed," he said dutifully.

"Well, one never knows when a plaster duck will come in handy," the donor replied modestly. "Oh, and you've made my pinwheels. How perfectly lovely."

Osbert permitted himself a gentle smirk. "I thought those midget plastic frogs in the middle would add a certain *je ne sais quoi*."

"Oh, they do! They do! I think I may get really serious

209

about frogs now that I have the flamingos pretty well finished. Daughter Matilda the First, how delightful to see you again!"

"Actually I believe I'd have been only the second Matilda the fourth, but as it happens I'm really Arethusa Monk the only. Ah, I see you've brought cupcakes."

"Don't eat them," Dittany warned. "They're plaster."

Arethusa took the news bravely. "Zounds, one never knows, does one? Then I trust you have a few genuine cates and dainties at the ready? Plaster cupcakes notwithstanding, it's good to see you, Phyllis."

"What a euphonious name," said Dittany, "Phyllis Phiffer."

"In point of fact, I'm Agnes, but we don't have to be stuffy about technicalities, do we?"

"Not at all," Dittany's mother assured her. "While we're on the subject, I'm Clorinda Pusey, and here comes the genuine Daughter Matilda now. Osbert, could that be Mother Matilda with her?"

It could be, and in fact it was. Margaret MacVicar and the sergeant were right behind them. Dittany signaled to Osbert to trot out the cookies they'd been hiding in the pantry so Arethusa wouldn't eat them all up before the company came. Amid the greetings and introductions and exclamations over Mrs. Phiffer's ducks, Clorinda raced to scald out the teapot and urge the kettle to greater efforts.

The two Matildas gave Dittany a jar of mincemeat they'd brought and said they weren't hungry because they'd just been sampling Cousin Margaret's cullen skink with an eye to future mass production. They ate some of Dittany's cookies anyway and found them excellent, though probably not adaptable to commercial distribution. As they all sat around sipping and munching, it became clear that nobody was really much interested in making pinwheels today. What they basically wanted to do was rehash the details of recent events.

"What I can't figure out, Cousin Osbert, as I expect we might as well call you considering the striking resemblance between my daughter and your aunt and bearing in mind that my mother's maiden name was Monk,'' said Mother Matilda, ''is how you ever happened to think of suspecting those Siamese twins in the first place.''

"That's a good question," said Osbert. "I guess I'd have to say it wasn't so much one big thing as a bunch of little ones. To begin with, there seemed to have been what you might call a stagey air about that shootout: Aunt Arethusa talking about international spies and Clorinda saying it was mobsters, and all that stuff about felt hats and trench coats. Daughter Matilda told me her father wore his because he was an actor and got a kick out of dressing up; so I suppose it gradually seeped in that the others might have been actors, too. Then there was something about the way Glanville and Ranville moved and talked and managed to hug the limelight wherever they went. I had no way of knowing whether that was a natural way for Siamese twins to act since I'd never met any before, but it did strike me after a while as being awfully slick and professional.''

"I know just what you mean, darling," Dittany put in. "Remember that cross talk they got off at lunch the first day, with all the outdated gangster slang?"

"That's right, pet. There was also the fact that they'd come from England, though maybe a lot sooner than they said they had, and Wardle was supposed to be English, too. He'd told Mrs. Phiffer he had a brother over there, which maybe doesn't mean much but it was another little drop in the bucket.''

"Oh, definitely," said Mrs. Phiffer. "You do have the most fascinating subconscious, Ralph. You are Ralph today, as I recall.''

"I wish I were Ralph every day," Osbert replied with a baleful glare at his aunt.

Arethusa got set to snarl back, but Daughter Matilda tactfully changed the subject. "What about that note Daddy was supposed to have written and didn't?"

"The fake Wardle would have had plenty of chances to pinch a piece of your father's paper and forge his handwriting, though not very successfully," Osbert replied, "and it would have been a cinch for the twins to plant the note in Miss Jane's doll when they visited the shop after they'd ditched the cars and got into their Siamese twins suit. As for those two asinine robberies, they'd have had to be the work of somebody who either knew Lobelia Falls pretty well or else knew a couple of friendly ladies who could be coaxed into telling them where they might find a jeweled dagger, or a reasonable facsimile of one, and a ream of plain white paper."

Osbert politely refrained from catching Clorinda's or Arethusa's eye. "But I think the real thing that steered me on to the twins must have been that I'm writing about ostriches. You see, ostriches don't bury their heads in the sand."

"Egad," yelped Arethusa, "is that what you call a thought process?"

"I believe what he means is that ostriches are smarter than people," said Agnes, as they now knew Mrs. Phiffer to be. "I've suspected it for quite some time."

"To tell you the truth, ostriches are no great brains by and large," Osbert confessed. "All I meant was that people have been led to believe that ostriches bury their heads in the sand when they want to hide, but naturally it doesn't work because here's this great big body sticking out. So they never think of ostriches as being anything but visible, when the truth is that ostriches can hide easily enough by lying down on the ground and stretching their necks out flat on the ground. Or getting behind a gnu. They hang out with gnus and zebras a lot."

"I didn't know that," exclaimed Agnes.

"And I didn't want to," Arethusa added sourly. "Get to the nub, jackanapes."

"What I'm driving at is that everybody also knows Siamese twins are joined together, so they don't stop to wonder whether in fact they might be able to come apart. Once you're convinced that two people have to function as one, like Dr. Doolittle's Pushmi-Pullyu, you automatically write off any possibility that they could turn into two separate men in trench coats holding a running shootout with a vice president of a mincemeat factory. Or one twin hauling another vice president's pants down in his own office, if you'll excuse the vulgarity."

"What is there to excuse?" said Daughter Matilda. "That's what they did, isn't it? One of them, anyway. Which twin was Quimper Wardle?"

"Ranville appears to have been the more proficient Wardle of the two, though Sergeant MacVicar and I gathered from what we heard in their room at the inn that he and Glanville had been taking turns. As a matter of fact, I shouldn't be surprised if there were often two Wardles in the factory, so that one could be establishing an alibi while the other was manhandling a VP with felonious intent. Don't you agree, Chief?"

"Aye," said Sergeant MacVicar, "so the evidence would indicate. As you know, ladies, the clothing purporting to have belonged to the alleged Quimper Wardle was left in Mrs. Phiffer's spare room at the time of the so-called suicide, but Deputy Monk and I found duplicate garments hidden in a suitcase at the inn. Along, I should say, with two trench coats and two felt hats with the brims turned down."

"That doesn't mean the twins were both in the factory at the same time," Mother Matilda argued. "How could they be? Gerald the security guard keeps careful tabs on who goes in each morning."

"And does he check them off as they leave?" Osbert asked her.

"Why should he? It stands to reason the same ones have to go out as went in."

"Not necessarily. What if somebody hid inside till everybody else had left and the factory was locked up for the night?"

"Then the night watchman would catch him and throw him out."

"How many night watchmen do you have?"

"One," Mother Matilda replied with some asperity. "That's all we've ever needed."

Daughter Matilda was swifter to grasp Osbert's point.

"One's all we've ever thought we needed, Mama, but it's a big building. However dutifully he makes his rounds, a single watchman can't be everywhere at once. And we certainly can't expect him to check out every closet in the offices or every box and bag in the warehouse, can we? A master of disguise like those Wardle twins or whatever their name is could easily pose as a sack of raisins or a crate of apples, wouldn't you think, Cousin Donald?''

"Oh aye," said Sergeant MacVicar. "They're a wily pair, no doot about that. Once one twin had gained entry in the accepted way, he could stay overnight by some ruse or guile. The second twin would arrive the following morning with nobody the wiser, and there'd be the two of them inside, you see. The first could leave at closing time and so it could go, for as long as they chose."

"Then how would the extra twin get out?" demanded Mother Matilda.

"Easily enough," said Osbert. "He could slide out a window on a rope, or just walk out at quitting time like the other one, if the first twin left right on the button and got out of sight fast, and the other one hung around and mixed in with the last bunch of employees to leave. They wouldn't both need to be in the factory very often, only when they were planning to steal another piece of the mincemeat recipe.''

"Got an answer for everything, haven't you?" Mother Matilda sounded a bit cross, and who could blame her? "One thing sure, this awful business has taught me a terrible lesson. Eternal vigilance is the price of mincemeat. I don't suppose you'd want to consider becoming our permanent Director of In-House Security, Osbert?''

"I'm sorry, Mother Matilda, I just can't. I've got this herd of ostriches to rescue from the ostrich rustlers, my stepfather-in-law's clamoring for Clorinda to go back on the road with him, and my wife has me booked to be VP Diapers.''

"We were afraid you'd say that," said Daughter Matilda. "I have to tell you that VP Citron's going to take your defection pretty hard, Osbert. I do see, though, that it could never have been.''

''I'll say it couldn't,'' said Dittany. ''Well, maybe some day her prince will come. And yours too, Daughter Matilda.''

''Oh, mine's already on the premises. VP Cinnamon has finally got up the nerve to declare himself.'' Daughter Matilda smiled fondly. ''I've known for ages that Cin was my VP Right, but he had all these high-flown notions about not wanting to be called a fortune hunter for marrying the boss's daughter. Last night after the funeral he dropped by the house, caught me having myself another quiet bawl over dear Daddy, and—and overcame his scruples. It'll have to be a quiet wedding, of course. Just family. Cousin Donald, you'll have to give me away.''

''It couldn't be a more suitable match,'' said Mother Matilda. ''Cin's the man Charles always hoped would step into his shoes as VP Nutmeg when the time came. And he's connected with the McCorquindales on his mother's side and with Monks on his father's. Well, we must run along now. I've got to make some decisions about personnel changes and call up that rotter Throckmorton at Redundant Relishes and let him know what's going to happen if he sics any more of his thugs on me. And then I'm going to sit down in front of Charles's and my wedding picture and have myself a good bawl. Monday we'll get the factory back to humming. And then, Cousin Margaret, you and I will tackle the question of Granny's cullen skink. Fun's fun, but work's better. All right, Osbert, if you won't come to work for us, you may as well go round up those ostriches.''